Capacity for Murder

Books by Bernadette Pajer

The Professor Bradshaw Mysteries
A Spark of Death
Fatal Induction
Capacity for Murder

Capacity
for Murder

A Professor Bradshaw Mystery

Bernadette Pajer

Poisoned Pen Press

*Poisoned
Pen
Press*

Copyright © 2013 by Bernadette Pajer

First Edition 2013

10 9 8 7 6 5 4 3 2 1

Library of Congress Catalog Card Number: 2012952569

ISBN: 9781464201264   Hardcover
       9781464201288   Trade Paperback

Poisoned Pen Press
6962 E. First Ave., Ste. 103
Scottsdale, AZ 85251
www.poisonedpenpress.com
info@poisonedpenpress.com

Printed in the United States of America

To my sisters, Becky & Beverlee.
I'm so glad we are the three little B's.

Note

A note on spelling: Sanitarium verses Sanatorium. In 1903, the former spelling was commonly used to indicate several types of healing centers: health resorts (such as Kellogg's famous one in Battle Creek), facilities that treated tuberculosis (TB), asylums for the insane or "feeble-minded," and hospitals for recovering alcoholics and addicts. Eventually, "sanatorium" was officially chosen for TB hospitals, but "sanitarium" continued to have many meanings. In this book, "sanitarium" is used to indicate a health resort.

Chapter One

It all began with a freckle-faced youth delivering a telegram.

WESTERN UNION

To: Professor Benjamin Bradshaw, Electrical Forensic Investigator, c/o the State University, Seattle, Wash.

Message:

Your expertise urgently needed. Accident of electrical nature. Normal routine suspended until resolved. Please come at once.

> (signed) Dr. Arnold Hornsby, owner and chief
> physician, Healing Sands Sanitarium.
> Ocean Springs, Wash., August 17, 1903.
> c/o Hoquiam Western Union Office

To which Bradshaw replied:

To: Dr. Arnold Hornsby

Message:

I regret my obligation to teach prevents travel. Please send particulars. Will examine.

> (signed), Benjamin Bradshaw

And Dr. Hornsby replied:

To: Professor Benjamin Bradshaw

Message:

Impossible. Your presence required. I beg you!
Bring students. Abundant education at Sanitarium.
Nature, science, ocean. All expenses paid. PLEASE
COME AT ONCE!

(signed) Dr. Arnold Hornsby

Such urgency, blended with the generous cordial invitation, gave Professor Benjamin Bradshaw the impression that Dr. Hornsby was fond of hyperbole. Bradshaw had never been to a sanitarium and couldn't see the appeal. The very idea of being subjected to a rigorous diet, exercise, and questionable treatments in a social setting made him cringe. However, electrotherapeutic equipment was likely involved in the "accident of an electrical nature," and this intrigued him. He'd once built a portable electrotherapy outfit for Arnold Loomis, a medical supply sales-man, and he knew their construction and safety issues well. He glanced at the location. Ocean Springs. That was on the remote coast. He'd read in the paper about the new Northern Pacific line under construction in that area, but it hadn't yet reached the coast, which meant the area was unlikely to have telephone or electricity. So was battery power involved in this summons? What sort of accident would prevent the resumption of normal routine and yet allow the invitation of so many? He ought to simply say no. His first duty was to his students, and he couldn't drag them to the remote coast.

Could he? As Doctor Hornsby said, there was an abundance of education to be had at the coast. And there was the lure of the ocean itself. The endless vistas, the crashing waves, the sheer power of nature. It was tempting.

This was happening more frequently to Bradshaw, this tug between teaching and investigating. His career as a teacher he'd chosen, studied for, pursued. His career as an investigator had been dropped in his lap. Two years ago, he'd been the prime suspect in the electrocution death of a colleague and was forced to investigate to clear his name and find the true killer. Afterward, the Seattle Police began seeking his help in cases involving electricity. Word spread, and soon he was consulted by insurance companies, manufacturers, power companies, even private individuals. Those investigations had often led him far beyond electrical forensics, and so he and his investigative partner Henry Pratt, who boarded in Bradshaw's home, were both now licensed private detectives.

What surprised him most was how much he enjoyed the investigations. But since he also found great satisfaction in teaching at the university, he had moments of being torn between the two. As he was at this moment.

He lifted a critical eye to his students. Five young men, a diverse collection of personalities, they had in common their love of learning. They sat perched on stools at the lab tables with magnets, copper wire, aluminum pipes, Leyden jars, vacuum tubes, and other bits and pieces, playfully yet diligently connecting and assembling components and noting the results. The class was called Experimental Physics. Each summer, Bradshaw invited five students from across the entire engineering department to take this hands-on exploration of physics, and he was rewarded by observing their discoveries, those "aha" moments of seeing and truly understanding the forces at work.

While they undoubtedly enjoyed the class, all week he'd seen their covetous glances out the basement windows at the blue sky and beckoning sun. Summer had come at last to Seattle, and they were missing it in pursuit of higher learning.

He hesitated, thinking of other faculty members qualified to assume his class, but none of them were currently free. Perhaps he *could* take his students to the coast. The university encouraged field trips.

"Sir, do you want to send a reply?"

The telegram boy stood so quietly Bradshaw had nearly forgotten he was there. Beads of sweat glistened on the boy's freckles and darkened the brim of his cap. He'd cycled three times round trip from the telegraph office in the hot sun.

Bradshaw smiled at the boy, then said to his students, "May I have your attention?"

All eyes turned in his direction. The telegram boy, who was no more than twelve, squared his shoulders importantly under their gaze. Bradshaw said, "I don't suppose you would all like to relocate for the remainder of classes to the ocean? To study the physics of sand, the generating capabilities of the wind, and the potential in tidal movement?"

They stared at Bradshaw, then they stared at one another. Then Knut Peterson, the clown of the group, whooped, and the others joined in, and they dissolved from disciplined young adults to jubilant children.

A crooked grin lit the face of the telegram boy. "I think that's a yes, sir."

Bradshaw tore a clean page from his lab tablet and wrote out a reply to be wired to Dr. Hornsby. Before handing it to the messenger boy, he quickly tore out another page and wrote a separate message. He asked quietly, "Do you know the florist on Second Avenue?"

"Of course, sir."

"Please give this note to the clerk."

The boy accepted the request without question, his eyes widening when Bradshaw added a generous tip. When he'd gone, Bradshaw told his students to settle down, conclude their experiments, then go home and pack their bags. They were all of an age that required no parental approval, but he instructed them to inform their families, and he would inform the dean. They would be departing first thing in the morning for Washington's North Beach on the Pacific Ocean.

Chapter Two

The sight of a large body of water was nothing new to anyone who called Seattle home, Besides Puget Sound, there were Lake Washington, Lake Union, and Greenlake, and flowing into them all were numerous rivers, streams, and creeks. Water surrounded Seattle, fell often from the sky, and topped the ring of mountains in glorious white.

But the ocean was different. The difference was reflected on the face of Bradshaw's ten-year-old son. The boy stood barefoot in warm, soft sand, his mouth agape at the never-ending expanse of steely water cresting in a series of waves that thundered and crashed, then withdrew with a hiss. Bradshaw's heart tightened. Why had he not brought Justin to the ocean before now? What sort of father was he that he let the first decade of his son's life go by without showing him the ocean?

A final, grateful wire from Dr. Hornsby had provided directions to Healing Sands. It had been a journey of more than one hundred miles and nine hours, to the southwest coast of the state. The train had brought them as far as Hoquiam, and from there they'd taken a steamer across Gray's Harbor to a trading post called Oyehut, and finally, they'd traveled by horse-drawn wagon up the North Beach. The tide was low and the sun was quickly dropping to the horizon, bathing the beach in a golden glow.

Everyone had wanted to come along. He'd brought his assistant Henry, of course, and his five students, as well as Justin, and

Justin's best friend, Paul, and his housekeeper Mrs. Prouty, and Missouri Fremont, Henry's twenty-four-year-old niece.

Missouri's inclusion both pleased and distracted Bradshaw. She'd been visiting Henry when he arrived home with the news that they'd been invited to the ocean, and she'd asked if she could go, too. A slender young woman with unfashionably short mahogany hair and a regal nose, her penetrating amber eyes seemed able to read his very thoughts.

How could he refuse her? What excuse could he give? Certainly not the truth. He couldn't say, no, you can't go because you'll distract me. Or, no, because the thought of you barefoot on the beach is more than I can stand. Or, no because for the past two years, I've managed to avoid seeing if the look in your eyes matches the desire in my heart, and at a place as romantic as the ocean I might just make a fool of myself.

Impossible. Not being able to come up with any other plausible excuse, he'd avoided her eyes and said yes. And now here she was, barefoot in the hot glittering sand, as distracting as he'd feared.

All but Bradshaw had stripped off their shoes the minute they'd climbed down from the wagons and were now prancing about in the soft sand, and dashing down to the harder-packed damp stretches where white foam rushed at them, licking their toes.

Bradshaw, his feet shod, hat in hand to keep the brisk wind from taking it away, kept his gaze upon his son, preferring the guilt of fatherhood to the sight of Missouri's bare feet and slender calves.

"Professor Bradshaw?"

Bradshaw turned his back to the ocean to see a young man approaching. He had a round, clean-shaven face and was dressed in a drab summer suit with the star badge of the Chehalis County Sheriff's department on his lapel. Why was a lawman here?

The young man extended his hand. "I'm Deputy Mitchell. Thanks for coming." He had none of the manner of a lawman; his posture was relaxed and his expression open. "Sheriff Graham is up in Taholah, but he'll return in the morning."

The muscles of Bradshaw's spine tightened. "I was told there was an accident of an electrical nature. How serious was it?"

Deputy Mitchell's boyish features looked apologetic, as if he hated being the one to break bad news. "About as serious as an accident gets, Professor. The handyman is dead."

Bradshaw glanced quickly over his shoulder at his romping entourage. Mrs. Prouty, his stern and stout housekeeper, was giggling and dancing a jig in the edges of the surf, holding her skirts nearly to her knees. Henry was elbow-deep in a dune with Justin and Paul, lifting handfuls of glittering sand and watching the wind whisk it away. Four of his students were near the water's edge, poking with sticks at the tiny jets of water squirting up from the wet sand. His fifth student, Colin Ingersoll, a lanky and intelligent young man who was the natural leader of the student group, was now leading Missouri up the beach.

For a second, Bradshaw's thoughts went blank. He forced himself to look away, shifting his gaze.

He shifted his gaze to the three-story main house of the sanitarium, sitting beyond a driftwood boundary. Its shape was boxy, ordinary, yet fitting, as it appeared to have been built nearly entirely of sun-bleached drift logs. The windows and doors were trimmed in crisp white, matching the white wrap-around porch that reflected the dying rays of the sun. Beside the double front doors, a porch light glowed. An electric porch light.

This was unexpected. He ran his eye over the roof and eves and spied the incoming power line that ran to a barn-like struc-ture at the base of the cliff. A generator? No smoke rose from the structure, so it wasn't coal or wood-fired. It was difficult to be sure at this distance, but it looked as if a pipe ran up the cliff, at the top of which stood gnarled and stunted Sitka spruce, their branches reaching inland, deformed by the constant attack of salty wind. A penstock supplying flowing water to a waterwheel? Another pipe ran from the barn to the creek their wagon had just waded across.

"Dr. Hornsby is waiting," the deputy said.

Bradshaw called out to his group. Knut whistled to get the attention of Colin and Missouri, who heeded the sound and turned back without breaking from their conversation. She looked up at the young man and laughed. He looked down at her, entranced.

A development as unforeseen as the electric light. And more disturbing.

They all gathered their shoes and socks and picked their way across the sand and drift logs to the porch of Healing Sands.

Dr. Hornsby was a short, stocky gentleman of fifty plus years, with a white goatee and small mustache. He wore a pale linen suit with a white shirt and tie, his feet in felt house slippers. His dark eyes were puffy and red-rimmed, and when they met Bradshaw's directly, they flashed with a desperate emotion before shuttering. He shook Bradshaw's hand almost painfully, and greeted them all with a resonant bass voice. Bradshaw resisted the impulse to chastise the doctor for leaving out of his invitation the vital detail of a man's death.

Mrs. Hornsby added her gentler greeting to the doctor's. Her smile, like her husband's, was a welcoming mask that didn't touch her eyes. She was slightly taller than the doctor, and plump featured but not fat, with straw-colored hair pulled tight into a bun. Her dress and apron were white and simply cut, and she, too, wore felt house slippers.

"Now, I know you are not here as patients but visitors; still, this is a place of healing, and we have certain rules that apply to everyone staying here. You will find signs posted in every room, and we ask you to please read and respect them. I see most of you have already removed your shoes, and we ask that you remove them every time you enter Healing House and the cabins. Place them in a cubby here on the side porch. Choose a pair of new felt house slippers from the chest. The slippers are yours to wear during your stay and to take home with you. Write your name in them if you wish. If you misplace them, simply take another pair."

As they all began to obey this unusual requirement, Dr. Hornsby went on to explain in powerful tones that somehow lacked conviction, his reasoning for the slippers, his practiced sermon ending with, "This ritual prepares you to approach your visit to Healing Sands with a sense of respect, belonging, and active participation in your own well-being."

Once slippered, they were ushered inside to the dining room at the back of the house, where they found long tables laid with herbal tea and fresh blackberries, which they served themselves. They were then sorted into various sleeping quarters. Bradshaw's five students chose to bunk together in Hahnnemann House, one of the large cabins that flanked the main house. Justin and Paul wanted a cabin adventure, too, and Mrs. Prouty was a good sport and agreed to bunk with them in Paracelsus Cottage, once she was assured the cabin was furnished with real beds and she'd have her own room. Henry and Missouri both took rooms on the second floor of Healing House, the main building they were now in, and Bradshaw, on a whim, chose to bunk on his own in Camp Franklin, one of the small cabins.

"It's named for another inventive Benjamin, Professor," Dr. Hornsby said, a brief smile lighting his eyes. The fourth and final cabin, Hippocrates Hut, he explained, was occupied.

Fighting yawns, his group dispersed to their beds, saying general good-nights. Only Colin Ingersoll singled out one of them to wish a good night's rest. Missouri was pleasant in her "you, too" reply, but not effusive, nor did her eye linger for any length of time on Colin's obviously smitten face, but that gave Bradshaw small comfort. He would have to keep that young man busy.

Annoyance had its advantages, and one was its ability to revitalize strength. Bradshaw was wide awake and ready to begin his investigation as he climbed the stairs. He found Dr. Hornsby in his second floor office, collapsed in the desk chair, and Deputy Mitchell standing at the window, staring out into the night. He closed the office door and sat across from Hornsby.

The muted roar of the ocean was the only sound in the room until Bradshaw asked, "Who was the handyman, and why was I not informed of the seriousness of the accident?"

Hornsby struggled to sit up, his movements sluggish. Bradshaw thought the doctor might be inebriated until he saw the anguish on his face and realized he was struggling from collapsing into tears. "I-I'm sorry, Professor. I was afraid you wouldn't come if you knew. I couldn't risk—I need your help. I can't—" Hornsby closed his eyes, his face contorted with emotion. "The handyman was David Hollister. My son-in-law. I killed him."

Chapter Three

For all his grief and desperate need for answers, it was obvious Dr. Hornsby dreaded entering the room where his son-in-law had died. Bradshaw didn't press him. He offered to send his students and family home, but Hornsby insisted having them at the sanitarium would help restore a normal routine to his family.

"We've had to cancel all of our reservations for a fortnight because I can't practice medicine until this is resolved. It's been dreadful having the place so empty."

Bradshaw was no stranger to the echoing melancholy of an empty house or the comfort of routine.

"Can you tell me what happened?"

"David Hollister," the doctor said, struggling to control his emotions, "was a good man. Solid, dependable. He could fix or build nearly anything. We called him the handyman, but he was much more than that. You noticed our electric lights?"

"I did. And a penstock down the cliff? To a water-driven generator?"

"Yes, you're right. He built a water motor and installed all the lighting in the buildings. The washhouse was his pride and joy. He was always chipper about his work. A good man. My wife and I," he paused, shaking his head, swallowing hard, "we couldn't have asked for a better man for our daughter." He reached out for a framed photograph propped on his desk and handed it to Bradshaw.

A bride in white lace and a groom in black tails smiled at him from the porch of Healing Sands.

"That's Martha, my eldest daughter, and David."

Martha resembled her mother, fair and plump featured. David had been tall and dark, with an open face and broad smile. They looked happy, but didn't most couples look happy in their wedding portraits? Hadn't he and Rachel?

Bradshaw asked, "Was he ill?"

"Oh, no. He was healthy in all regards but one. He couldn't father children. Mumps in his youth had left internal scar tissue. That's what we were attempting to heal with electrotherapy. No one knew about the treatments, not Martha, not my wife. We didn't want anyone to get their hopes up, you see."

"I do see." He returned the photo to the desk. "Doctor, I know this won't be easy for you, but I need to ask very specific questions about the accident. Would you prefer to wait until morning?"

Hornsby drew a breath. "No, no. I appreciate your consideration. But tomorrow won't be any easier. What do you need to ask?"

"How was the electrotherapy administered to Mr. Hollister?"

"If you'd be so kind, please refer to him as David. It's what he preferred, and how we know him. *Mr. Hollister* puts him at an uncomfortable distance. He's David. Our David."

"I understand. Please tell me about David's treatment."

Hornsby wiped his eyes and blew his nose. "I was using the autocondensation method. That's the technique utilizing the medical chair pad as one plate of the condensers, and the patient as the other. There are several connection methods using the hand holds or the foot plates, but I prefer a felt pad electrode to maximize heat in the vital organs." Dr. Hornsby indicated with his hands a region stretching from the lower sternum to the lower abdominals. "Earlier this summer, we'd completed a round of diathermy directly applied through specialized probes to the scarred area, and we believe we achieved a small measure of success in clearing a passage. We had only recently moved on to autocondensation. It's a more general application and has been shown to increase blood flow and nervous system circulation as well as to speed the elimination of toxins and promote healing. I was, if not hopeful, at least optimistic. The body can accomplish much self-healing if given the right conditions and encouragement. That final session…" Dr. Hornsby dropped his head into his hands.

Bradshaw gave him a moment, then asked, "What is your experience with electrotherapy?"

Hornsby lifted his chin, his forehead creased. "I'm no newcomer. I've been studying electrotherapeutics for well over a decade. You'll find dozens of books in the library on the subject and all the latest medical journals and you're welcome to read them, but I daresay you know all about it. The field is maturing, the quack devices being separated from those with legitimate medical uses. The machines that allow the physician the greatest flexibility have proved to be the most beneficial."

"And your equipment?"

"It's the very latest. State-of-the-art. I wish to heaven I'd never bought it." He shook his head and blinked rapidly again, unable to prevent a tear from running down his cheek. "It makes no sense!" Hornsby got to his feet. "Come on, I can't put it off any longer. You must see and tell me what happened."

The deputy moved to a side door, pulling a bronze ward key from his pocket. Bradshaw stopped him from inserting the key. This was not a simple accident investigation. A man had died, and any time Bradshaw was called to a scene involving death, he took nothing for granted.

He examined the cut-glass doorknob and the ornate bronze plate, noticing a faint but distinct sharp odor. "Vinegar?"

Hornsby said, "Oh, yes. The knobs are cleaned daily."

The key hole showed no sign of tampering, but it likely wouldn't even if unlocked by an unauthorized hand. The trouble with ward locks is their ease of access. Nearly any skeleton key will open it.

Hornsby asked, "What are you looking for, Professor?"

"Has this door been locked since the incident?"

"Yes, it's my habit to always keep the room locked."

"Where is the key normally kept?"

"In my desk drawer."

"Who has entered the electrotherapy room since the incident?"

"Who?" Hornsby's eyes crinkled with thought. "Why, I don't know for certain. Is it important?"

"It would be helpful if you could recall."

Hornsby scratched his beard. "My wife and Martha came in, I'm certain of that. Mr. Thompson might have entered, I'm not sure. He offered assistance, but he was too ill to help. We carried David to his bed." He scratched his beard again. "I'm fairly sure no one entered after that. I locked the door before I went into Hoquiam for the sheriff. That's when I wired you. I unlocked the door for the sheriff that evening. He didn't enter the room; he just stood in the doorway and looked about and said he wanted nothing touched until you arrived. This is the first time the door's been unlocked since."

"May I?" He held out his palm and the deputy handed over the key. Bradshaw inserted it in the lock and listened as the wards hit their slots and slid back the bolt. Removing the key, he placed his fingertips on the ridges of the cut glass knob and turned. The door swung open into darkness.

Hornsby said, "Oh—I hadn't thought. We have no light. The machine is plugged into one of the light sockets and the switch is off. It was daylight when...I'll get some oil lamps." He hurried off, sniffing and fumbling into his pocket for his handkerchief.

Bradshaw pressed the door fully open and hunkered down in the doorway to allow the office light to penetrate more deeply into the room. The equipment stood out against the white plaster walls that reflected the meager light, an electrotherapy chair, a glass-paneled cupboard of instruments, and atop a storage cabinet, a portable electrotherapeutic machine. The sight of it sent a chill through him.

It looked very much like the outfit he'd designed a few years ago for Arnold Loomis. But they'd been beaten to the market and the design never sold to a manufacturer.

"What is it, Professor?"

"I'm just thinking, Deputy." He began to stand, then noticed a faint scratch on the otherwise perfectly smooth, polished hemlock floor. He bent lower to inspect the scratch, turning his head sideways to better view the surface. He spied a speck. From his pocket, he retrieved his small leather tool pouch and removed the tweezers. These he used to pinch the speck and discovered it to be a grain of sand. Sand in a house on the beach was expected—but in this house, with the felt-slipper policy, and on the second floor, was perhaps not very common.

Hornsby arrived with three lit oil lamps, pausing at the doorway when he saw Bradshaw holding the tweezers.

"Doctor, have you a small jar or dish I might borrow?"

"What did you find?"

"A grain of sand."

"Is it important?"

"I don't yet know."

Hornsby lifted his brow, glanced at the deputy, who only shrugged. He pushed the office door closed with his foot and set the lamps on his desk.

"How about a vial?" Hornsby pulled a small glass vial from a porcelain basin and gave it few shakes to expel water droplets.

Bradshaw took the vial and dropped in the grain of sand. It clung to a bead of moisture. He capped the vial with a small cork, then dropped it into his pocket. He lifted a glowing lamp. It was fueled with good-quality kerosene and put out a bright light.

"I'd like to go first and move slowly into the room."

Dr. Hornsby stared at him. His face, already somber with grief, transitioned to alarm. He looked from Bradshaw to the deputy and he began to sway. Bradshaw grabbed a chair and slid it under the doctor as he sank.

"I—you—" Hornsby looked about the room, his eyes unfocused. "You will think me a fool, gentlemen. I just now realized what is happening here. You believe this may have been intentional. You are looking for evidence of—of murder? You think

I killed him on purpose. You think I killed David intentionally. I did not. I swear to you I did not! His death was an accident!"

Deputy Mitchell hurried to calm Hornsby. He shook his head. "No, no, Doctor Hornsby. This being an unusual sort of death, Sheriff Graham just wanted the matter thoroughly looked at. No one's accusing you of anything."

Bradshaw had never seen a lawman in such a rush to relieve a probable suspect. In his experience, the police hardened themselves to such displays of emotion, knowing truth or confessions often spilled from them.

"You've done nothing wrong," the deputy went on. "We only want to help."

Hornsby said, "I don't know why I didn't understand before. The shock, I suppose. But I should have realized when the sheriff refused to let us leave. The door—I thought you hoped it had been locked so the evidence of my stupidity would still be present." He stared at Bradshaw with wide, fearful eyes. "But you're looking for more than just an accident."

"I am simply gathering facts, Dr. Hornsby. It's how I approach all of my investigations. Most often, the accident proves to be just that, an unfortunate accident. But in the beginning, I gather every bit of data I find and save it until I know its value, or lack thereof."

Dr. Hornsby looked unconvinced. The young deputy chewed his lip, and Bradshaw resisted the urge to tell him to buck up.

He moved to the doorway and held up his lamp. Under this greater illumination, the electrotherapy machine so much resembled Bradshaw's he nearly swore aloud. But he wouldn't let his curiosity drive him too quickly across the room. He dropped down again to floor level. The surface of the polished hemlock floor was smooth and free from grit, sand, or dust. He inched forward and found another faint scratch. He continued to move, following the direction of the scratch, until near the foot of the cabinet he found a circular gouge the size of a large pinhead. Three inches under the cabinet, he found several grains of sand clumped together. Careful not to touch the cabinet, he used the flat edge of the knife from his pocket toolkit to scoop the clump into the glass vial.

A search of the rest of the floor turned up nothing. Bradshaw retrieved the other two oil lamps and held them before the electrotherapy machine, stifling a curse. This was not the outfit that had beaten his to market. This was *his* outfit. The very one he'd built. The prototype for Arnold Loomis. The pattern of the grain in the mahogany case was as familiar to him as the face of an old friend. Without looking further, he knew beyond doubt it was his when he saw the unmatched hinges on the access panel, one brass, the other nickel. He'd used spare parts he'd had on hand in his basement workshop.

What was his outfit doing here? Arnold Loomis had sold it, yes, but to a doctor in Seattle, for a price that just barely covered the cost of building it. Yet here it was, more than a hundred miles away, involved in a man's death.

Aware that he had stood staring for too long, unsure what this meant for him or the investigation, he said nothing as he moved around the cabinet.

Withholding information was now standard procedure for him in the early stages of an investigation. His first half-dozen cases had taught him that his explanations could alter what he was later told. Witnesses would, mostly unintentionally, change their stories to bring them in line with the new facts. But he'd never withheld anything that potentially incriminated himself.

He forced his thoughts to the insulated braided cord that extended from the outfit case up to the electric light socket, which appeared in fine condition. He tapped the cord with his knuckles. Receiving no shock, he unscrewed the cord from the socket and tucked the end into his jacket pocket for safekeeping. It was perhaps an unnecessary precaution. He didn't imagine Dr. Hornsby or the deputy would attempt to reconnect the cord while his back was turned. It was an action born of habit and one that had kept him quite safe in all his electrical endeavors.

He applied his knuckles to the access panel as well before opening the latches, then bent to examine the working components in the narrow space. He found the c-shaped discharger where he'd mounted it four years ago, on the inside of the panel, and holding it by the ebonite handle, he touched the balled ends to the Leyden jar capacitors to release any remaining charge. His touch was met with silence, and now he felt safe examining the familiar components more closely. His heart tightened.

All was as he last saw it, his patented coil with its distinctive bell shape, the metal-wrapped glass Leyden jars, the assorted wires and binding posts necessary to change the settings for various applications. Everything appeared in order.

He examined the outside of the outfit, finding nothing to alert him. Indeed, other than a few superficial scratches, only one thing had been altered since he last laid eyes on it. The engraved brass plate affixed to the front no longer bore his name but read, The Loomis Long-Life Luminator.

Loomis. Arnold Loomis.

"May I enter, Professor?"

"Yes, Doctor."

Two sets of footsteps told him both Hornsby and the deputy had entered and now stood behind him.

The doctor asked, "Ever seen anything like it?"

"Yes, I have."

"Do you see anything wrong?" Hornsby's voice trembled. "Anything that could explain what happened?"

"No, but I will need to do a more thorough exam and testing tomorrow. You say you've had it just a few weeks?"

"Yes. It's supposed to be the best, and the safest, on the market. It has all the latest capabilities, you can see, with a superior style of coil. It's proved to be very easy to operate; much thought was obviously put into the design." He leaned down to peer inside at the internal workings. "Is there *nothing* to show how it malfunctioned?"

"Nothing immediately obvious."

Hornsby straightened and exhaled deeply. "You'll want to talk to the representative, Mr. Loomis. I could get him now, if you like."

Bradshaw removed the plug from his pocket and draped the cord over the machine. "Loomis is here?"

"Yes, we were all detained, my staff, which is just my family, and the few patients present at the time."

"What does Mr. Loomis have to say about the incident?"

"He's flabbergasted and appalled, of course. But the sheriff wouldn't let him near the machine, not until you got here."

"He's a patient?"

"Oh, well, no, not strictly speaking. A guest, you might say. He delivered the unit and has been here ever since."

Bradshaw closed the access panel. He moved to the patient chair that sat upon a short insulating platform and brought the light close. It was a dark wooden chair, square in shape, the back and seat covered with a rubber pad sewn over metal sheeting. Curved metal grips were mounted on the ends of the arms. Box-mounted metal footplates sat before the chair. A typical setup.

He moved through the rest of the room, shining the light fully on Dr. Hornsby's cupboard of instruments. The glass electrodes in various shapes to suit specific needs were neatly labeled, nasal, throat, rectal, and so on. There were small stacks of pristine white probe covers, metal clamps, rubber insulated handles, and an assortment of rubber-coated copper cords. Next to the cupboard sat a commode with wash basin stocked with soap, sanitizer, salt, and white towels.

He took out his small notebook and pencil, made a few notes, and sketched the layout of the room and the configuration of the electric outfit while Hornsby and the deputy waited.

"That's all until morning," he said at last, tucking away his notebook and leather toolkit. "The door should remain locked until my investigation is complete, and please take care not to touch the inside knobs."

Hornsby's brow furrowed for a moment, but grief and exhaustion quickly extinguished any questions he may have had. He nodded silently.

"Just let me know when you want back in." The deputy locked the door behind them.

Chapter Four

Outside, in the glow of the electric porch lamp speckled with flitting bugs, Bradshaw changed into his shoes, then carrying a lantern, tromped around the drift logs and through the sand to his cabin. There was no moon, but the sky shone with the light of countless stars and gave a dusky glow to the surging ocean swells. The cool, slight wind carried the scent of salt and kelp and the smoky pine residue of a bonfire.

The large cabins south of the main house were dark, but the murmur of deep voices told him some of his students were yet awake.

A little spark of anticipation met Bradshaw on the covered porch of Camp Franklin. How long had it been since he'd truly been alone at night, without someone else in the house with him, even his son? More than a decade? He found a pair of the required felt slippers in a covered box on the front porch, and when he stepped inside the one-room cabin, he was immediately transported to his childhood by a nostalgic scent. It was the musty scent of space long exposed to damp sea air, the scent of the modest hotel in Seattle, then still a frontier town, where he'd spent a week with his parents while on the cross-country holiday that had sown his love of the Pacific Northwest.

The cabin was spotlessly clean, the white linens and navy blue spread on the two narrow beds freshly laundered, and the glass in the windows so clean they were perfect black mirrors.

He closed the navy blue curtains and felt snug in his temporary home. There was a small woodstove, a simple table with a lamp and two chairs, a wash basin and fresh pitcher of water, and as foretold, a framed sign hung like a painting listing the rules. Written politely, the rules essentially said no shoes, no smoking indoors, tidy your own room.

Other signs with health-related quotes from Benjamin Franklin drew his eye. Some he knew. "Early to bed, early to rise" and "God helps those who help themselves." Some were new to him. Given his experience with patent medicines, he particularly liked, "He's the best physician that knows the worthlessness of most medicines."

He unpacked his clothing, hanging his spare suit in the wardrobe. Cradled in his pajamas was a white ceramic urn. Where to put it? The windowsill was too narrow, the table too prominent. He rested his hand on the cool lid, and his mood dimmed. He was suddenly bone weary. With a sigh that became a yawn, he set the urn on the floor in the corner. A few minutes later he was tucked in bed in the crisp white sheets, breathing the nostalgic cabin air, eyes closed. He tried not to think, but his mind was such a jumble he knew he must sort his thoughts before sleep would come.

He lined up details logically, dealing first with the concrete facts of David Hollister's death, the presence of his own invention, and Arnold Loomis, who had chosen not to come forward this evening. When he could see the logical progression of known facts, and the gaps he had yet to fill, he allowed his mind to meander to other concerns. He recalled the look of wonder on his son's face at the sight of the ocean, and he vowed to begin traveling more with him, to take time away from teaching and investigating, on a regular basis, and spend it with his son. He'd take him camping, fishing, and across the country to Boston to meet his grandparents. He'd been an infant when they'd moved to Seattle after his mother's death. An infant. And now the boy was ten. Where did the time go?

Time was so elusive, so malleable. Missouri probably had a theory about time. She had a theory about everything. Her theories often didn't conform to his traditional beliefs, but they made sense. They made him think, and question, and doubt. And he was not a man who liked to doubt. He marveled at her imagination. With a sigh, he thought of her bare feet in the sparkling sand. With a grunt, he thought of her wandering down the beach with Colin Ingersoll.

Oh, he was never going to sleep.

But he underestimated his exhaustion and the healing of the fresh, salty air. He listened to the regular rhythm of the roaring ocean, reaching and retreating, until he slipped into a deep sleep.

Toward dawn, the cold woke him. He climbed from bed and fumbled in the dark for the linen closet where his hand found a thick wool blanket. On the way back to bed, he bumped into the table. He heard a sound like "plink" and for an instant, a bluish light flashed on the floor.

He bent and skimmed his fingertips along the floor and found the little glass vial, thankfully unbroken, and gave it a vigorous shake. The grains flashed blue, then darkened. He shook it again, and this time the flash was dim. A third shake triggered only the faintest flash.

Still clutching the vial, he climbed back into bed. He'd not noticed the sand's luminescence when he'd dropped the grains into the vial. Either the brightness of the lanterns had prevented his noticing, or more likely, the grains hadn't been jarred enough by the action of placing them into the vial to produce the glow.

He shook the vial again. It remained as dark as the rest of the night. He was soon warmed by the blanket, but sleep was now impossible.

Chapter Five

Bradshaw watched the morning lighten from his porch. Birds of great variety and abundance swooped down and glided across the surface of the water, dipping and diving for their breakfast, then alighting on the wet sand. Several types of grey and white gulls, brightly feathered ducks, and species whose names he didn't know. In a few wind-tattered treetops, bald eagles gathered, occasionally spreading their expanse of wings and announcing their domain with piercing cries. In the distance, the smokestack of a steamship puffed steadily, and nearer shore, a native paddled in a cedar longboat.

The sun had just begun to warm the sand when Justin and Paul came running out of their cabin in their blue-and-white striped flannel suits. Mrs. Prouty followed at a more decorous pace, wearing a decade-old ballooning sunbathing costume. He waved to them, and Justin made a detour to say good morning.

"What's on your agenda today, son?"

"We're going to rebuild the castle and have the moat lead to a holding pool that we'll fill with crabs so they'll be able to crawl over and attack it. Will you come see it when it's done?"

"I'll try. I'll be working today."

"You've got until high tide, that'll be after lunch sometime."

Justin ran off, and Bradshaw made his habitual pat-down before leaving the cabin, checking that his pockets contained his notebook, pencil, tool pouch, and the vial of sand grains. He put on his hat and picked up his investigation kit, a second-hand leather doctor's bag with a hard bottom and inner compartments that held his instruments snugly.

He found Deputy Mitchell on the porch with a mug of herbal tea that he took as an omen of the absence of coffee. He asked anyway, but was resigned when his fear was confirmed.

"Doc Hornsby isn't keen on stimulating beverages. Or intoxicating ones. The tea is quite good, though."

Bradshaw said he'd pass for now. "I'd like to talk to you about your observations. Can you give me a tour of the house?"

"Sure, I'll show you around."

Both of them changed into slippers, and after disposing of his kit upstairs in Hornsby's office, they returned to the foyer to begin the tour.

From the entry, a hallway split the house in two. The first room on the left held an impressive library, walled with shelves, leather-bound books, a selection of dime novels, and stacks of medical journals. Wingback chairs and polished tables invited readers and writers. All was picture-perfect. Even the hearth in the stone fireplace had been laid with care, the crisscrossed twigs sprinkled with matchstick-sized kindling, ready to light should the weather turn cool.

Next came Dr. Hornsby's Osteopathic Room, a bright airy space with white plaster walls, a gleaming hemlock floor, a manipulation table, pulleys, hanging bars, several contraptions designed for self-realignment, and a device best described as a medieval torture rack.

"That one," said the deputy, pointing to the rack, "takes out all the kinks. You just strap yourself in and lay back and it pulls you in four directions at once." He shrugged his shoulders and wiggled his neck as if to demonstrate the flexibility of his joints.

They came next to a bathing room that had been divided into three private baths with claw-footed tubs and overhead shower faucets and shelves of white towels.

"Are these showers for guests to use? Or part of a therapy?"

"Both. Oh, you're in for a treat, Professor. First you soak in a hot mineral bath, then shower in pure creek water. You do that right before bed, you'll sleep like a baby. I followed that routine last night, and I can't recall ever having a better night's sleep. Here, feel this."

The deputy plucked a towel from the pile and pressed it to Bradshaw's cheek.

"Ever feel anything so soft?"

Unsure of the proper reaction to a deputy stroking his cheek with a towel, he said, "No."

"Wait until it's wrapped around you. And they don't mind how many towels you use, because of that laundry house, you know."

The deputy continued to wax poetic over the relaxing bathing experience, and Bradshaw wondered how much the man had missed since his arrival while making use of the facilities.

At the back of the house were the kitchen, pantry, and larder. Bradshaw had seen the kitchen and the adjacent dining room on the south side of the hall the previous evening, but now he took more time looking around.

"What are you looking for, Professor?"

"Nothing. Everything."

The deputy snorted. "I get you. Just getting the lay of the land."

"Indeed." While in the kitchen, he stepped into the larder, looking for meat. A slab of beef, a chicken breast, a pork roast. Anything with a good bit of moist flesh. But there was not a scrap of meat. Only stores of fruits, grains, vegetables, and large crocks of things fermenting. He settled for a round patty pan squash the size of his palm, slipping it into his pocket when the deputy wasn't looking.

He was led next to a large airy room with polished floors, outfitted solely with the latest Victor Talking Machine sprouting a gleaming black horn beside a collection of Victor and Columbia disc records.

"Dr. Hornsby calls this the Dance Therapy room. It's for foul weather, mostly. He says the next best thing to walking outdoors is to dance indoors."

"What sort of dancing?"

The deputy turned pink. He cleared his throat and said, "He calls it Free Movement. You just do whatever you feel like doing. Sway, waltz, twirl."

"Good God."

"It's really very liberating, once you get over being self-conscious." The deputy whistled a lively version of "Beautiful Dreamer" and began to bounce.

"I get the idea. It seems you spent a great deal of time yesterday making use of the facilities, Deputy."

"Oh, Doc Hornsby said I was free to try it all out. He has several Stephen Foster's in his collection, and some of the latest songs, 'Bill Bailey', and 'In the Good Old Summertime', and the like. You'd have thought he would only have classical, but he's a modern man, our Hornsby."

"Shall we move on?"

The deputy shrugged, reluctantly abandoning his bouncing rhythms and the lure of Free Movement.

"There's just one more room on this floor."

They entered the room for which the entire sanitarium was named, Healing Sands. This room featured green potted ferns, much sunlight filtering through French doors, and several sand beds tucked discreetly behind white cloth screens.

"And how do you find the sand therapy, Deputy?"

"Cured my hip, I kid you not. I've had this pain on and off for years. Doc Hornsby said it was sciatica and that I was out of alignment. I didn't want to bother him about it, because of the circumstances, but he said there was never a bad time to help someone heal. Nice fellow. He did something he called an osteopathic adjustment to get my bones lined up proper, then buried me in the warm sand. I'm a new man, I tell you."

Bradshaw cocked his head. "How long have you been with the sheriff's department, Deputy Mitchell?"

"Two months. I didn't much care for it until I got this assignment."

"Aah. Upstairs?"

"Upstairs? Oh, yes. The tour continues." He grinned happily.

The next floor consisted mostly of bedrooms. He wasn't shown those that were occupied, although he told the deputy he might later need to see them.

"Is that allowed? I'll have to ask the sheriff. I mean, don't you need some sort of warrant to poke around in someone's private room?"

"I don't yet know what I'm looking for. Don't worry. I'm certain everyone will give me permission if my investigation leads beyond the electrotherapy room."

"But it was an accident. All that stuff Hornsby was saying last night, he was just upset."

Bradshaw studied Deputy Mitchell's earnest, trusting face, and predicted a short career for him in law enforcement.

Mr. and Mrs. Thompson had separate rooms; it was apparently part of the healing regime that spouses sleep apart.

The deputy gave Bradshaw a knowing grin. "I dare say it makes for some late night visits down the hall. Reminds me of a joke about this feller—"

Bradshaw raised an eyebrow, and the deputy cleared his throat. "That room there is Arnold Loomis, then your friend Mr. Pratt, and his niece next to him." Both doors were firmly shut. Henry was a late sleeper. Missouri, he knew from the brief months she'd lived in his home when she first moved to Seattle, had likely been awake for hours, and was either writing in her journal or already out on the beach. Was Colin?

"And here are the Hornsbys' private rooms, the doctor's office, and electrotherapy room. We can return to those; do you want to see the third floor?"

They climbed the stairs to the topmost floor, empty of guests and staff.

"Hornsby says these rooms fill up a few times a year, but they weren't being used when the accident happened."

Bradshaw opened a door to an empty room on the front of the house and crossed to the window. He saw his son and Paul digging, Mrs. Prouty reading under an umbrella, and his students launching a kite into the air. Missouri was not with them.

They returned to Hornsby's office where they found the doctor in his white suit, looking as if he'd not slept much.

Sensing the doctor would appreciate a businesslike approach to keep his emotions at bay, Bradshaw launched directly into his investigation. He asked the deputy for the door key, and after opening it as he had the night before with his fingertips, he pulled his magnifying glass from his pocket to inspect the glass knobs on both sides of the door. The pristine flat planes of the cut glass on the outer knob sparkled with reflected light. He detected a faint whiff of vinegar.

"How often are the doorknobs cleaned, Dr. Hornsby?"

"Daily. Every morning by seven, when we have guests. Abigail was here cleaning this morning, but she only cleaned that outer knob."

Bradshaw aimed his magnifying glass at the inner knob with slightly more hope. Smudges dulled the reflection of several flat surfaces. He'd need more light to see if distinct fingerprints were visible.

"Abigail hasn't cleaned that knob since Monday."

Monday. The morning of David's death. He asked for more light, and Hornsby produced one of the lanterns from the previous evening. The light shining up through the glass revealed two muddled prints, one on top, likely a thumb, the other on a lower right facet, likely an index finger. But they were layered, one print on top of another, and impossible to separate. The prints told him only that since Abigail had cleaned the knob Monday morning prior to seven, only right-handed visitors had turned the knob. He vividly recalled that Arnold Loomis was left-handed.

He took the light to his electrotherapy outfit.

"Before David's session on Monday morning, when had the machine last been used?"

"I don't give treatments on Sundays, so it would have been the day before that, Saturday, on Mr. Thompson, the only other guest undergoing electrotherapy."

"What time Saturday?"

"Ten in the morning. We finished at half-past the hour."

"Between half-past ten on Saturday, and David's session on Monday at—?"

"At about a quarter of ten, it was supposed to be earlier, but Martha sent him up to the garden for blueberries, so he was delayed."

"For those intervening hours, was this room used? Did anyone other than you or David enter?"

"Mrs. Thompson came to speak to me Monday morning, before David arrived. She didn't enter, though. She stood in the open doorway."

"On Sunday evening, Doctor, did you observe the phenomenon of the glowing sand?"

"Glowing sand? Oh, yes. I'd nearly forgotten. Seems a lifetime ago."

"Did you go out and walk in the sand?"

"Certainly, we all did. All the staff and patients. It's very rare to see that phosphorescent glow. I'd only seen it once before myself. It actually sparked when you kicked it. We were like children out there playing. David had us all laughing…."

"Pardon me? Glowing sand?" The deputy leaned forward.

Dr. Hornsby said, "It's a marine phenomenon, rare this far north. The crest of waves glow with bluish light, and the wet sand emits a blue glow when you walk on it."

"I'll be damned. I'd like to have seen that. I was in Aberdeen on Monday night. What makes it glow?"

Hornsby said, "Some sort of phosphor in the water, I believe. Is that right, Professor?"

"That's what's commonly believed," he said, sticking to his habit of not muddying an investigation by adding previously unknown facts. The truth was more complicated than simple phosphor. The glow was created by ocean plankton. Always present, when the conditions were right, they experienced enormous blooms. The action of the waves and the impact upon the sand triggered the tiny creatures to glow in a process known as bioluminescence.

Hornsby's brow suddenly furrowed, and then he gasped with a sharp intake. "The glowing sand, Professor, it didn't affect the apparatus here, did it? Is there some electrical aspect to it? It sparked!" Panic filled his voice. "Should I have not have performed an electrotherapy treatment so close to such an event?"

"No, Doctor Hornsby. The glowing sand did not alter your equipment."

Even so, tears rolled silently down Hornsby's cheeks and welled in his mustache.

"We will discover the truth of what happened here, but it will be difficult for you."

Hornsby nodded. "That doesn't matter. Whatever you need, I'll do."

"First, tell me. Was David in here alone at any time?"

"The sheriff asked me that, too. He was alone for a few minutes that morning. As I said, Mrs. Thompson had come to speak to me. Freddie, her husband, had a severe bilious attack during the night and was still feeling poorly. I went to see him, and determined his usual treatment might improve his condition, so I escorted him back to my office and got him settled there. By then, David was here waiting for me. During that time, I suppose it's possible he tampered with the settings, but probable? No! Why would he? And you said you saw nothing wrong."

"But David was killed, and so we know something went terribly wrong."

"But I can't believe he'd do anything so foolish, and I couldn't live with myself if I falsely blamed David for his own death. He was a good man, devoted to my daughter. I loved him like he was my own son."

"I understand. But I still must ask you what David knew of electrical matters."

"Quite a bit, although he wasn't a trained electrician. His knowledge was all practical. He was very clever. You'll see for yourself when you visit the powerhouse and laundry. He knew enough to never have done anything to harm himself or others."

"Can you say with complete certainty that nothing had been altered on the machine when you entered the room?"

"No! If only I could, this tragedy would never have occurred. If I'd seen it had been touched, I would not have continued with the procedure! I looked at the machine, as I always do, and I saw nothing unexpected. I didn't examine the entire outfit, you understand, or open the panel. Why would I? I've kept up on the maintenance, and I knew the Leyden jars had adequate saline solution. I looked at it in the usual way with my mind on the procedure and saw that the settings were as they should be for administering autocondensation. My eye met nothing unusual and yet I can't say for certain now what I saw."

Bradshaw spent the next half hour running standard tests on the individual components and found all in perfect working order. He asked Dr. Hornsby and the deputy to stand back at a safe distance, then he threw the knife switch, energizing the machine. At once it began to thrum, and a tiny spark buzzed across the narrow gap of the spark interrupter. The glass electrode wand that Bradshaw had attached by cord to the diathermy post glowed purple. He touched the tip of it with his knuckles, feeling a slight stinging buzz, then he picked it up, shook back his cuff to expose his wrist, and applied the end to his skin. He felt a pricking heat, and smelled the sharpness of ozone. He glanced at Hornsby and saw him shaking his head, his eyes wide.

"I understand you weren't using diathermy on David, I'm simply checking the output."

"It's not that, Professor. It's the sound. The sound is different. It was different."

"The sound emitted by the spark interrupter you mean? How so?"

"Now it sounds as it usually does. Crackling, and with that small bright arc. But with David that morning, it was different, more like a hiss. And the arc flamed."

Hornsby's confused expression showed his lack of understanding, but Bradshaw's chest tightened. He knew what that change in sound indicated. He unplugged the machine, discharged the Leyden jars, then examined the interior closely. Using a magnifying glass he examined the insulating space between the primary and secondary coils, then he went over every inch of the Leyden jars, spotting two inconclusive darkish smudges on the outer foil and the connecting posts of the caps.

He straightened, leaving the machine open.

"Doctor, would you step into your office, please? Leave the door ajar. Have a seat, and when I tell you to, please listen carefully."

Hornsby did as asked without question, for which Bradshaw was grateful. He was about to attempt to replicate what had happened to David Hollister and it was unnecessary for Hornsby to put himself through it. It would be enough that from the adjoining room he would be able to hear the sound of the spark gap.

Deputy Mitchell rubbed his chin, looking uncomfortable. "Where do you want me, Professor?"

"In the doorway is fine if you want to observe."

The deputy took up a position in the door where he could see both Bradshaw and Hornsby.

From his electric kit, Bradshaw found a length of copper wire, and he stood for a moment considering it. He glanced around the room at Hornsby's electrotherapeutic supplies, searching for something of the right size and conductivity. The electrodes and knives all possessed insulated handles. A small spool of copper or a roll of sheet block tin would suit his need, and many physicians who worked on their own machines and fashioned their own instruments possessed them. He stepped to the doorway and asked Hornsby about them.

Hornsby shook his head. "I don't keep wire or tin in here. David has those in the washhouse. If I ever needed anything, I'd simply ask him."

"I see. Thank you."

He returned to the open cabinet of the outfit and positioned the copper wire across the Leyden jars in a manner that shorted the path of the current passing through them. With a glance to the doorway to see that the deputy wasn't paying attention, he pulled the patty pan squash from his pocket, and inserted a small electrode into the flesh to ensure a current path. He turned the machine's dials to the autocondensation settings, soaked the felt pad in salt water and placed it over the squash on the therapy chair, which he also attached to the machine. His last step was to wire an ammeter into the circuit to measure the current. When all was in readiness, he screwed the plug into the light socket and threw the knife switch. The spark gap produced a glowing, hissing flame, distinctly different from the earlier crackling spark. He heard a gasp from the other room. The ammeter registered a lethal amperage. The felt pad steamed.

David Hollister would have been dead almost instantly. With a small tremor, and perhaps a silent gasp. Or an attempt to gasp. His heart would have stopped, irrevocably damaged.

Bradshaw cut the knife switch and slipped the warm patty pan into his pocket before asking Dr. Hornsby to return. The deputy stepped aside to allow Hornsby, pale and trembling, to enter.

Bradshaw asked, "Did you recognize the sound?"

"Yes, that was it exactly. What did you do?"

In short-circuiting the capacitor, he'd sent a fatal current from the coil directly to the electrodes, but he hesitated explaining this to Hornsby. He unattached the ammeter, weighing the disclosing of information against the gathering of further testimony. It was Hornsby's devastated eyes that decided him. He had no evidence, but he didn't believe Dr. Hornsby was to blame.

He could perhaps lessen some of the doctor's overwhelming feeling of guilt by revealing this fact with a partial disclosure. "I altered the configuration, increasing the current to the electrodes."

"I don't understand. How could it have made that sound when I ran it? Can it do that all by itself, spontaneously?"

Not if the machine was in good working order, which it was. He said simply, "No."

Hornsby began to tremble. "I thought—I noticed the sound— but I thought it was simply operating efficiently. It sounded so smooth. I didn't know it might mean—"

Hornsby sat heavily, dropping his head into his hands. For several minutes, throat painfully tight with emotion, Bradshaw pondered the implication of the change in the spark interrupter's sound emission, while Dr. Hornsby was swept by grief and Deputy Mitchell stared out the window at the ocean.

When Hornsby's sobs quieted, he whispered in horror, "But who? Why?"

Bradshaw said, "It could not have been David. The evidence has been removed."

The deputy's head snapped around.

Bradshaw said, "It would be best to keep this to ourselves for now. The sheriff must be told, of course, but no one else." The deputy nodded his understanding, but Hornsby was too stunned to respond.

"Dr. Hornsby, I must ask you to mention this to no one, not even your wife."

"Not Miriam?"

"Not yet. I'll let you know when it's safe to tell her."

"Safe? Oh, yes, of course. I'll keep her safe. Not a word."

"Good. Now, tell me. What happened next. After the incident?"

Hornsby took a deep breath. "I went into my office. Mr. Thompson was still there, waiting for his session. He asked me what was wrong. I frightened him, I think. I must have been a sight. I told him there'd been a terrible accident and to go get Mrs. Hornsby. He did so. And Martha came…after awhile, after I administered a sedative to Martha, and my wife got her to bed, I locked the door. I left to report what had happened. The tide was high, so I walked to Copalis. By the time I arrived, the tide had dropped, and I got a ride the rest of the way, with the mail.

I wired you from Hoquiam after I talked to the coroner. The sheriff and deputy and coroner returned with me."

"Before you returned, did anyone leave the sanitarium?"

"No, everyone is still here. We aren't many. Just four guests and minimal staff. We were between sessions. Sheriff Graham said we were to go nowhere, but where would we go? We wouldn't abandon our home. We wouldn't abandon David."

Chapter Six

The color of old paste, the oat groats sat in a congealed lump in Bradshaw's porcelain bowl with blackberries bleeding rivulets into the crevices. He lifted a spoonful and sniffed. Earthy, sour. Like a barn floor.

Henry was giving his bowl the same inspection. "They ain't been cooked, I'd bet a hundred bucks."

"Mrs. Hornsby called them fermented."

"Only thing I like fermented comes in a bottle."

At another table, Justin and Paul were devouring their bowls while Mrs. Prouty took more skeptical bites. Bradshaw braved a taste. Mostly sour, with a tinge of sweet, as it smelled, oaty with a hint of vinegar. Foreign to his tongue, not awful, but he found he could eat very little before a sort of revulsion took hold.

Henry ladled more blackberries into his bowl, shrugged, and dove in.

They'd had to serve themselves, following the posted rules, filing through the kitchen past a butcher block table stacked with bowls, plates, a cast iron kettle of lukewarm groats, and cut loaves of a dense, dark bread speckled through with seeds. Cutlery and crisp white napkins had been claimed at a sideboard, and each table set with bowls of fresh, slightly mashed blackberries, small pots of creamy butter, and pitchers of a fishy-smelling milk substance Bradshaw hadn't the courage to taste.

The dining room buzzed with conversation. Four of his students found much amusement in attempting to eat the unconventional breakfast. Knut clowned as usual, swallowing with exaggerated difficulty, while Daniel, clever and bespectacled, and Miles, small and precise, gave sporting commentary. Oren, who was rugged and square, happily dumped two bowls of berries into his own and ate with gusto.

Under this noisy cover, Bradshaw quietly told Henry of David Hollister's death and of his morning's investigation. Henry reacted with raised brows and an increased rate of chewing.

At the table nearest them, Colin sat with Missouri. They ate their fermented meal without much attention as they swapped childhood histories and life ambitions. Bradshaw tried not to listen, but snatches of their conversation came to him anyway. He'd known Colin was fascinated with mechanical vehicles, automobiles, and the latest advances in flight, but he hadn't known Missouri had decided to quit the university in order to study homeopathy. He wasn't sure what to make of it. A moment later, their conversation had veered toward the financial when Colin suggested she marry a man with plenty of money in order to support her many goals. She declared she'd never marry a man for his money, and Colin said it was a shame because he planned to be rich.

Missouri said, "Oh, I didn't say I would never marry a man *with* money. You must pay attention to my prepositions."

"I will, if you pay attention to my propositions."

A grunt alerted Bradshaw that Henry, too, was listening.

Henry growled, "We ever that nauseating?"

"Yes, which is why I avoid such discussions altogether."

"Yeah, well, I'm usually smart enough to have a few drinks under my belt before I make the attempt."

Bradshaw turned his attention back to his buttered bread, which was chewy but didn't cause a revolt at the back of his tongue. He felt Henry watching him, heard him clear his throat like he had more to say on the subject. Then he did.

"I reckon if you can sit there calmly listening to that drivel then…I mean, it's been two years…."

Bradshaw knew exactly what Henry was getting at and he had no intention of discussing his former or current feelings for Missouri Fremont.

"Henry, why don't you go swap stories with that miner." Bradshaw nodded toward the only person in the dining room not of their group, a man sitting by himself in the corner. Hornsby said there were just four guests at the hotel. He must be one of them.

Henry listed away from the table to get a better look. "How you know he's a miner? Looks like an undertaker to me."

The man wore a somber, expensive-looking black suit, custom sewn for his stocky frame. He was clean shaven, hawk-nosed, with deep-set dark eyes and fat lips.

"What clues am I missing, Sherlock?"

Henry had recently become an avid reader of Sir Conan Doyle's detective novels and fancied himself a superior Watson. He was, but Henry's ego was large enough without Bradshaw's encouragement.

"He's uncomfortable in the suit, although it fits him perfectly, which tells me he's new to wearing it and has therefore only recently come into money. He has a scar on his hand that extends up his sleeve, severe enough that I can see it from here. Combined with his strong build, erect posture, and lack of reading material in his solitary state, tells me he's a man with little education, used to hard physical labor. The tip of his nose has suffered frostbite from which he's mostly recovered; you see the white patch of skin? But it's the button on his lapel that's most telling."

Henry squinted, then gave a grunt, showing he recognized the gold-nugget button. He had one himself as a souvenir of his time up north.

"He'd probably enjoy telling you all about it."

"What am I, one of them masochists? Why would I want to hear how he struck? Poke a stick in my eye, Ben, it'd hurt less."

"His success hasn't made him happy."

Henry listed again. "No, he don't seem to appreciate his good fortune. Looks downright morbid about it. Huh." Henry pushed back his chair and crossed the room to the miner. He introduced himself with a hearty handshake and took a seat without invitation.

While Henry worked his verbal art, Bradshaw studied his silver spoon. It could just span the distance between the Leyden jars in the electrotherapy outfit, but getting it to stay in place would be difficult. If the cabinet were even slightly bumped, it would fall. Knives and forks posed the same problem. His thoughts moved to the kitchen, to the various knives, stirring spoons, graters, and mashers of various metals and coatings from silver to tin to nickel. From the kitchen, his mind roved to other rooms and other conductive items, from gold pens, to gold and silver necklaces, hairbrushes, safety pins strung together, key chains, and watch chains. When his thoughts moved outdoors, his mental pile of conductive items grew to a mountain. All of them could possibly short the machine, but few of them were probable or practical. Only wire, tin foil, or a chain fit the bill. Before Bradshaw finished his bread and grassy tea, the miner left the dining room and Henry returned to his chair, grabbing a slice of bread and slathering it with butter.

"Anything?"

"Name's Zebediah Moss, fifty, never married, brought home a million in dust and nuggets last year. Lives in Seattle. You know that monstrosity up on First Hill? Three-story mansion with the pillars and turrets? That's home-sweet-home."

"So why is he miserable?"

Bradshaw had every confidence in Henry's ability to extract details from the unwitting. Highly intelligent, Harvard-educated though not graduated, Henry had the brains of a scholar and the mouth of a day-laborer. He worked like a laborer, too, although ever since he'd injured his back on his last unsuccessful gold-seeking trip, his labors were of the temporary desk and sales variety, except when working for Bradshaw.

"I think he's pining over some woman but I couldn't drag it out of him. Says he came for a rest cure. He didn't get any electric treatments. Mostly, he got packed up in hot sand and soaked his feet in the surf."

"Is he here alone?"

"Yep."

"What else did he tell you?"

"How he made his fortune. Lucky son-of-a-bitch fell off a cliff and struck gold with his grappling hook trying to climb back up."

"What's he been doing with his money?"

"Not much of anything. Says he can't figure out what to do with it. Says life is empty and has no meaning. I told him to give me the money and I'd find meaning for him. He declined."

As Henry spoke, Bradshaw became increasingly aware that someone had arrived at Healing Sands. He'd heard the whinny of a horse, the clomp of boot heels up the porch steps. The boots didn't pause on the porch long enough to transition to felt slippers, but continued into the house, and down the hall.

By now, everyone in the dining room was aware of the approach of ringing boots steps and looked expectantly at the open doorway. A few strides later, he was there, a man built like a logger with a broad chest and a gleaming five-pointed star on his lapel. Sheriff Graham had arrived.

Chapter Seven

The sheriff's sharp gaze panned the room, pausing long enough to give a polite nod to Missouri, the only female present. His eyes lit on Bradshaw.

"May I see you upstairs, Professor?" Without waiting for a reply, he turned and headed down the hall.

Henry flashed Bradshaw a conspiratorial look. "The game's afoot."

"This isn't a game, Henry."

"That's where you're wrong, Ben. Life is the best game of all. Go solve the puzzle."

◇◇◇

Bradshaw reached the bottom of the stairs as the sheriff reached the top, and he saw that the soles of his boots were clean. In Hornsby's office, after shaking hands, the sheriff seated himself in the doctor's chair, placing his hat on the desk. Bradshaw sat across from him. This was often the most difficult part of an investigation, the first meeting with those officially in charge. Deputy Mitchell hadn't presented any sort of challenge, but Sheriff Graham, from the wearing of his boots to his taking of Doctor Hornsby's chair, was telling Bradshaw he was the one in control. Bradshaw accepted this without relinquishing his own authority.

"My deputy tells me you've figured how David Hollister met his death."

The opening gambit, a challenge thrown to Bradshaw. He never played the game; he simply answered questions in a forthright manner until the official relaxed, confident of his position.

"I know the electrotherapy machine was made temporarily fatal, but I don't yet know how it was achieved." Bradshaw explained what he'd discovered this morning. "The conductive material that was used has been removed, and the likelihood of finding it are slim to none."

"Why do you say that?"

"Because it could have been one of hundreds of items here at Healing Sands. It could be in plain sight and there'd be no way of knowing or proving it had been used."

The sheriff lifted a skeptical brow. "You're telling me that the only evidence for foul play is a change in the sound emitted from the machine, a sound heard only by Dr. Hornsby, and which was triggered by some everyday household item that's impossible to positively identify?"

"Yes."

"You're just full of good news. How do you know Dr. Hornsby didn't short-circuit the damned thing himself and then hide the evidence out of sight?"

"Every action he's taken since his son-in-law's death tells me he is bewildered by what happened. He's not covering up for a foolish mistake or an intentional act."

"So you say, but unless proof of Hornsby's innocence is found, Professor Bradshaw, he'll be held fully responsible for the safety of his equipment and criminally responsible for his patient's death."

"Whatever happened to a man being innocent until proven guilty?"

"Doesn't apply here. The doctor has admitted he administered a fatal dose of electricity to his patient. We know he's guilty, we just don't know why it happened."

"Dr. Hornsby wants the truth as much as we do. He needn't have summoned anyone. He could have said David died of natural causes, or that he had an unusual reaction to the treatment, and who would know differently in this remote location? Would you have questioned David's death if Dr. Hornsby hadn't notified you and given you the full details? He could have easily blamed his son-in-law, said he altered the machine because he was suicidal, or reckless. He has chosen instead to seek the truth despite putting his own life and liberty in jeopardy."

"He'd never have gotten away with saying David Hollister was depressed. Everyone here has stated he wasn't."

"What was the coroner's conclusion?"

"Electrocution was the cause, no doubt. The coroner can give you the gruesome particulars if you want them." A small smile, not of humor but discomfort over those particulars, revealed the sheriff was beginning to relax.

"Not necessary, Sheriff. But I would like to know why you are detaining everyone here if you believe Dr. Hornsby to be responsible for Mr. Hollister's death."

"What do my actions tell you, Professor?" The sheriff sat back, folding his hands across his stomach. It was another challenge, but a friendly one.

"You don't believe David's death was a simple accident."

The sheriff sucked his teeth and seemed to ponder how to reply. "The minute Hornsby mentioned electricity I thought of you. Your reputation has spread even down to our little neck of the woods. And I know a friend of yours, Detective O'Brien? I told Hornsby that you could find answers so he would summon you."

"Why didn't you summon me yourself?"

"I want the cooperation of everyone here. If they all believe you're working for Dr. Hornsby, they'll be more willing to talk to you."

"Are you saying you want me to work for you?"

"I've heard you work for the truth. Does it matter who's paying you?"

"No one's paying me."

"Maybe not directly, but how many guests did you bring with you? Their stay couldn't be cheap."

"Except for the cost of my accommodations for the duration of my investigation, I intend to reimburse Dr. Hornsby for all else."

"Mighty noble of you. I must admit, I respect your integrity."

"And I respect yours."

The sheriff grinned. "Based on what?"

"You wiped your boots."

"You noticed that, did you? Felt slippers undermine the authority of the badge, but I didn't want to be a complete ass."

Bradshaw decided he liked Sheriff Graham.

"The truth is Professor, I'm damned short-handed. Deputy Mitchell has no experience, and I've got five other places I ought to be right now. I'd appreciate it if you'd continue investigating the case. I could deputize you, but how about if we just call you a contractor? That way we can keep the illusion you're working for Hornsby."

"How about I continue working for Hornsby and report my findings to you?"

"O'Brien warned me you were a stickler for the high road. That'll do."

"Doctor Hornsby's having difficulty believing someone here at Healing Sands deliberately sabotaged the machine."

"He's an intelligent man but one who's never experienced evil, Professor. I knew that much the minute I met him."

"What alerted you this was more than an accident?"

"Hornsby himself. His shock, his self-blame, his bewilderment, his reputation for competence. When he came to me and told me what happened, I knew I needed an electrical expert."

"Who are our suspects?"

"That's the trouble, there are damned few of them. Who've you met?"

"Only Doctor and Mrs. Hornsby. My assistant spoke with Mr. Moss, but I haven't yet."

"The staff consists of Hornsby's own family, and there were only four patients here at the time. Besides Moss, there's a married couple, the Thompsons, and Arnold Loomis, representative of the Loomis Long Life Machine that killed David, though he tells me he didn't design or manufacture it."

"No, he did not. Do you have any theories, Sheriff?"

"Not a one. But you've got evidence of either involuntary manslaughter or murder, or so you tell me. The difference between a buzz and a hiss hardly seems like concrete evidence."

"If you knew electricity as I do, Sheriff, you'd feel differently. Can you tell the difference in sound between the firing of a cannon and a pistol?"

"That obvious?"

"To me, yes."

"Point taken. That sound means somebody is going to jail. I don't want to arrest Dr. Hornsby, but I will have to if no other person can be found responsible for that machine killing David."

"Why didn't you allow Loomis to examine the machine?"

"Seemed prudent to get an outside opinion. From someone less involved." The Sheriff smiled.

Bradshaw cleared his throat. The opportune moment to reveal his involvement was at hand, but he let it slip away with a small pang of guilt. "Did Loomis have a motive to kill David Hollister?"

"Maybe you'll tell me. Was that machine tampered with to kill? Or to frighten? Or to improve results? I once was called to the scene of a woman's death in a bathtub. She'd filled it with a face wash that claimed to beautify the complexion, but she didn't bother reading the label to see the active ingredient was arsenic. There's no accounting for stupidity. I don't know what happened in that electrotherapy room, that's why you're here. Loomis' machine has been involved in a death, and as far as I'm concerned, that means Loomis is implicated. If he's peddling a machine that's improperly designed, I want it off the market, the inventor prosecuted, and Loomis duly punished." The sheriff got to his booted feet.

Bradshaw rose more slowly, weighing his duty to disclose fully to this man of authority. He knew he would eventually have to explain that he'd built the machine. But he wanted to know more, first. He wanted to confront Loomis.

He asked the sheriff, "Do any of the others here, besides Mr. Loomis, know anything about electricity?"

"No one has claimed any knowledge. I suppose that limits your suspects?"

"Possibly." But he never limited his investigations with assumptions. "Are you at all concerned that the guilty party might flee the sanitarium? Your deputy has little experience."

The sheriff grunted. "He's got none, that's why I could spare him to stay here. But if someone attempts to flee, we'll know our culprit, won't we? And Healing Sands isn't so easy to escape from. The only road's the beach. The forest? Even I wouldn't like that hike, and I don't think anyone here could paddle a canoe up the coast." The sheriff got to his feet. "It's time to see our suspects. I told the doc to round them up."

Bradshaw's heart skipped a beat. He'd be facing Loomis for the first time in the sheriff's presence, and he would likely undo the camaraderie they'd just established.

◇◇◇

The sheriff's boots announced their approach like a drum roll, and Bradshaw sensed all eyes upon them as they entered the library. Dr. and Mrs. Hornsby sat in the middle of the room with two young women dressed in simple white attire and a young woman dressed in black. A man and woman, whom Bradshaw took to be the married couple, sat in the upholstered chairs by the cold hearth. Zebediah Moss stood by a window, feet braced, arms crossed. And Mr. Arnold Loomis looked just as Bradshaw remembered him only slightly paunchier, his hair a bit more receded. Otherwise, he had the same apparently open and honest face with unfortunate crooked buck teeth. He lounged comfortably in a back corner, his expression innocent, his eyes focused with studious attention on Sheriff Graham.

"I've called you all in here to meet Professor Benjamin Bradshaw of the University of Washington in Seattle. He's also a professional investigator of electrical incidents, and I've allowed

Dr. Hornsby to bring him here so there will be no doubt as to what happened that brought about Mr. David Hollister's death. I'm giving him a few days to complete his investigation. You will all cooperate with him. The sooner we have answers, the sooner you may leave. Am I making myself completely understood?"

Dr. Hornsby said, "Yes, yes," but otherwise, the question was met with silence. The roar of the ocean and the cry of a few seagulls drifted in through an open window, and Bradshaw was struck with the incongruity of examining a death in such a peaceful place.

"Professor, you've met Dr. Hornsby and his wife, Miriam. Dolley and Abigail, their daughters, are housemaids." The young women nodded gravely.

"Their daughter Martha Hollister is the cook and the deceased's widow."

Bradshaw dipped his head. "My sincere condolences."

Martha gave him a tight smile that trembled into a grimace. She looked away, a hand over her mouth.

Sheriff Graham nodded toward the married couple. "The Thompsons, Frederick and Ingrid."

Frederick Thompson said, "How do," in a weak voice. He was thin to the point of emaciation, his mustache too bold for his skeletal, jaundiced face.

Ingrid Thompson didn't speak. She tilted her head, lifted her chin, and studied Bradshaw. Her dark hair was swept up in the latest fashion, with one long tail of hair falling over her shoulder. Her features were too square to be delicate, yet she exuded a feminine charm. Something about her registered in Bradshaw as deeply familiar. It took him no time to understand it was her eyes. Heavy lidded. Sultry. Like his late wife's. With practiced efficiency, he locked away his emotional response.

"Mr. Zebediah Moss over there by the window is another guest—" Moss' expression and stance remained firmly fixed, "— and that leaves Mr. Arnold Loomis, the peddler of the machine you just examined."

If Mr. Loomis was offended by being labeled a mere "peddler" he didn't show it. He had dressed for the occasion in a fine linen suit, but the required felt slippers had a way of humbling even the proudest attire. His gaze had remained on the sheriff, and even now that he was being introduced and he looked in Bradshaw's direction, his eyes were focused somewhere near Bradshaw's ear. "A pleasure, Professor Bradshaw."

It was the lie of those words that decided him. "Is it? Under the circumstances, I'd have thought you'd find my presence anything but pleasurable."

Loomis shrugged, lifting his palms. "On the contrary. You are the electrical expert, and I humbly bow to your authority."

He certainly had nerve. And he looked as harmless as a mouse. Exposing him now meant breaking his rule and risking an alteration in testimony from the others. His gut told him to do it anyway.

"Why is your name on the outfit upstairs?"

"Why? I'm the proud representative of that therapeutic device."

"But you are not the inventor."

"That is true, sir, and I never claimed to be."

"Who is?"

Loomis finally looked directly at Bradshaw, his eyes questioning, searching for complicity. Everyone was watching them now, turning from one to the other.

"Many men of science, including yourself. That machine reflects the brilliance of Michael Faraday and Nikola Tesla."

"When the machine left my basement, four years ago, it bore my name, not yours, and it was destined for a Seattle physician's office."

Someone gasped, Bradshaw didn't know who. Heads turned again. It was beginning to look like a tennis match.

Loomis shrugged, giving a smiling nod. "Indeed it was, and you and I had parted amicably, both of us better for the collaboration and satisfied with the compensation for time and materials."

Doctor Hornsby got to his feet but then seemed unable to phrase a question or accusation and dropped down again, as if his strength had given out. His wife gripped his arm. Beside her, Martha Hollister sat pale and rigid, staring at Loomis.

Bradshaw knew Loomis' debate skills would lead them nowhere constructive, so although he sensed everyone was on tenterhooks wanting to hear more, he put an end to it. "We have much to discuss later, Mr. Loomis." He turned away from him dismissively, sensing everyone's disappointment. He said, "I would like to speak to each of you individually, beginning later this afternoon. Mrs. Hornsby, might I see you after lunch, here in the library?"

"Yes, Professor."

He looked to Doctor Hornsby. "Are there no others on staff?"

Hornsby's expression was blank a moment, and when he replied his voice was distant. "No others. We operate as a health resort, not a hospital. Our guests do much for themselves. It's part of our therapy. We sometimes hire extra hands from families along the beach or from Hoquiam. But not now. Not now." His voice trailed off, and Mrs. Hornsby gripped him more tightly.

Freddie Thompson, slumped in his chair, asked, "On what grounds are you detaining us further, Sheriff? You can't keep us here without charging us with something."

"I could pack up the lot of you and haul you into Aberdeen, where I can guarantee the accommodations won't be nearly as genteel and the time you'd be detained far longer."

"No, no. Just get on with it."

"If you change your mind and get tired of hanging around here, I'm sure I can find you a cell."

Freddie shook his head weakly and closed his eyes, slumping further into the chair.

Sheriff Graham said, "Professor, I need to see you privately."

Bradshaw followed the sheriff out of the library and down the hall to the vacant foyer. There, Graham stood before him nearly toe to toe, hands on his hips, which pushed back his jacket and revealed his holstered revolver.

"You built that contraption upstairs? That should have been the first thing out of your mouth."

"When I'm investigating, Sheriff, I disclose information when and to whom I see fit."

"I'm not sure I ought to leave you on the case. You might be to blame for that thing malfunctioning."

"It did not malfunction. It's not possible for a fatal current to be temporarily allowed to flow through the capacitor without human intervention. It goes against the laws of physics."

"Maybe you're just trying to cover your own hide."

"You could consult a hundred engineers, they would tell you the same."

"Maybe I will."

"Am I staying or going?"

Sheriff Graham studied him hard. "Staying. But don't forget who you're working for."

"You had me right earlier. I work for myself. I work for the truth."

"Blasted philosopher." The sheriff spun on his booted heel, marring the pristine floor, and marched out.

Chapter Eight

After an hour of close inspection and repetitive testing of the "Loomis Luminator" Bradshaw verified his original diagnosis. A conductive material had been placed across the Leyden jars prior to David Hollister's death and removed afterward. Who, what, and why remained impossible yet to answer. A foolish mistake or intentional alteration? Involuntary manslaughter or murder? Who here understood electricity enough to have done it? Who knew what materials were conductive and which weren't?

None of the questions made Bradshaw feel any better about the fact that his son and nine other innocent people were here at his invitation. Logic told him they weren't in danger. Emotion said, beware. The battle between them waged in his gut.

He found his entire troupe on the beach, gathered around a quietly hissing bright red two-seater Stanley Steamer with dandelion yellow wooden wheels. Justin and Paul sat proudly on the bench seat, pretending to steer with the tiller.

Colin crawled out from under the carriage, where he no doubt had been inspecting the construction. "Professor, ain't she a beauty!"

"Yes. Why is she here?"

"To drive!" he said, brushing sand from his backside. "A fellow who lives down the beach a ways rents it by the week. We passed him on our way up, so Knut and I hiked down this morning."

On their journey here, they had passed a small cluster of buildings at Copalis, a modest clapboard hotel and post office, and a few shacks. Bradshaw hadn't noticed an automobile for rent, but then, his eyes had mostly been on the ocean and the look of wonder on his son's face.

Colin continued, "We're going to explore, after our studies are completed for the day, of course. Today, we thought we'd head up to Moclips, maybe further up to the Indian reservation."

"There's not room for you all. Which of you is going?"

"We'll take turns. Today, it'll be Knut and me, and Miss Fremont." Colin smiled at Missouri, and she smiled back. The battle in Bradshaw's gut intensified. She then lifted an eyebrow at Bradshaw, as if challenging him to argue with her inclusion in the adventure.

He said to Colin. "You do realize there are no roads to drive, only the beach."

"The beach is an officially designated highway, the man said, and the sand's flat and safe all the way up, as long as we watch the tides."

Bradshaw glanced at Henry, hoping he would protest his niece's taking part in this extracurricular automobile adventure, but Henry had jumped into the auto, squashing the boys aside on the seat so that he could grip the tiller.

"I see room for two," Bradshaw said, "where is the third to sit? Or is Knut to run alongside?"

"Never!" Knut perched himself onto the back, doing his best to imitate a piece of luggage.

Bradshaw cut short their excitement. "Your free time is your own, but I have news that might limit your explorations." He put a hand on Justin's shoulder. "The accident I was summoned to investigate proved fatal."

He had their full attention. He told them about David Hollister, about the Loomis Luminator being his own invention, and how he would be busy over the next few days trying to find an answer as to why the tragedy occurred. His students looked sick. He could see in their eyes that the thought had never occurred to them that as engineers, the things they designed and built might one day be instruments in someone's death.

He gave them no reason to believe David Hollister's death had been anything more than an accident, even though this left them to conclude he, as the machine's inventor, might be responsible. He could think of no way yet to say he wasn't responsible without telling them more than he wanted them to know. He cautioned them to stay away from the main house as much as possible out of respect for the family.

"They have assured me your presence here is a comfort, and adding a much needed purpose to their daily tasks. But we'll not burden them unnecessarily. Understood?" He looked directly at Justin and Paul as he asked this, and they both nodded solemnly. It occurred to him that ten was one of the best ages for a boy. Old enough to have a measure of independence, young enough to still delight in make believe. He pulled Justin aside and bent down to look him in the eye. Justin was more sensitive than most children his age. Not in a way that made him weak, but in a way that allowed him to put himself in others' shoes, to understand their suffering even if it didn't personally touch his own life.

He said quietly, "The Hornsbys are grieving but they have each other to lean on."

"And you'll help them get everything sorted out?"

"I'll do my best. What would help heal their hearts would be to see children at play. So don't feel bad about enjoying yourself."

Justin nodded his understanding.

Bradshaw stood and called Paul over. He ruffled both their heads to assure them all was well, and they both relaxed, trusting him. He told them to get back to their sand castle, and they ran off. After giving him an unprecedented affectionate pat on the arm, Mrs. Prouty followed the boys. Henry tipped his straw hat and tromped off to investigate. Bradshaw was left facing his students, and Missouri, who all looked as if they were aching to ask him questions.

"Sand," he said, "has properties of both a liquid and a solid. Who can demonstrate those properties for me?"

◇◇◇

At half-past noon, Bradshaw was the last to file through the kitchen with his plate, his hopes for a hearty meal fading with each faded entrée. Depleted greens. Reds so weary they bled gray. He never thought he'd long for Mrs. Prouty's limp peas or mushy broad beans, but he wished for them now. When he emerged with a plate bearing only bread and berries, he found Henry had saved a place for him at his table with Missouri and Colin.

Bradshaw's small appetite shriveled to a painful knot. Missouri had joined his students for the sand lesson, and he'd spent the past hour impressed with her grasp of physics and unimpressed with Colin's admiration of her. The last thing he wanted to do was attempt to share a meal with them, but all the other chairs were taken, and it appeared Henry enjoyed the fact.

As he sat, he leaned toward Henry and repeated the words his friend had shot at him this morning, "Poke a stick in my eye, it would be less painful."

Henry said, "Touché, my friend. But it might also prove informative."

"For who?"

"Me. I want to keep track of developments."

Colin and Missouri, absorbed in a friendly debate about the future of medicine, allopathic versus homeopathic, paid them no attention.

Mrs. Prouty sat with the boys. They were refusing to eat the slimy green piles on their plates, but willing to swallow the mud reds and seedy bread and mounds of berries. Zeb Moss sat with Loomis, neither speaking, both eating dutifully as the only alternative to starvation.

Ingrid Thompson was seated near the window, and Freddie, looking only slightly more alive than he had this morning, brought two plates to their table. She didn't say thank you to her husband but began to eat heartily. Freddie sat, picked up his fork, and stared forlornly at his plate. Without taking a bite, he set his fork down again. Ingrid made no comment. She glanced at the window, which, because of the angle of the sun was behaving like a transparent mirror. She turned her head, smoothing her neck as if self-conscious of a few premature lines.

Bradshaw was struck again at her resemblance to his late wife. A more careful inspection of her features revealed it was only the heavy-lidded eyes they had in common. Yet the resemblance was striking. It was in the way she held her head, her aloofness, her self-preoccupation. Dr. Hornsby had said she'd voiced concern over her husband's health and state-of-mind, but she was showing no concern now.

"What, Ben?"

He looked at Henry. Had he said something aloud? Missouri and Colin watched him. He'd gotten himself into trouble more than once for unknowingly voicing his thoughts. It was a habit formed from too many hours in his basement, alone, talking himself through invention and crime. He was becoming a cliché, an absent-minded professor.

Colin whispered, "Professor, do you suspect the Thompsons? You think they killed the handyman?"

He shook his head. "You musn't mind me when I'm lost in thought. I won't deny I am investigating something more complicated than an accident, Colin, but I have no evidence yet of intentional harm. I don't want to involve you boys in my work. I hope I can trust you not to alarm the others."

"Sir, you have my word, but honestly, *you boys*? The others are boys, yes, but I'm the old man of the group. Were you a boy at twenty-six?"

Henry said, "He was never a boy. Born a creaking grandpa and still waiting for time to make him look the part."

"No offense intended," Bradshaw said to Colin, giving Henry a none-too-gentle kick under the table. Colin nodded, and he and Missouri took their dishes into the kitchen.

Henry tossed his napkin on the table. "OK, spill. What'd you find this morning?"

Keeping his voice low under the chatter of his students, he gave Henry a synopsis of his morning, and Henry whispered, "It doesn't look good for Hornsby."

"No, it doesn't. But he's innocent." Hornsby's tormented eyes flashed before him. For the rest of his life, Hornsby would be aware of having killed his daughter's husband. Killed a man he loved and respected. He wasn't a man seeking to avoid punishment, but praying for a reason to forgive himself.

"Oh? It's not like you to make a judgment without all the facts."

"Sometimes you just know. Find anything of interest this morning?"

"That washhouse is something, wait'll you see. I tromped around the beach and up on the cliff. You hit wilderness pretty quick. Saw an old Indian up there, but he vamoosed into the woods before I could catch him up."

As he listened to Henry, Bradshaw had been watching Ingrid Thompson finish her tea, then send Freddie Thompson for more. "What's your impression of Mrs. Thompson?"

Henry snorted. "I've been watching her. Reminds me of your late witch, the way she preens. There's something else about her, but I can't put my finger on it."

"The eyes."

"By gum, that's it. They're, oh what's the word—"

"Sultry."

Henry snorted again. "Too bad for that square chin. She's no beauty. Not like Rachel."

"Rachel wasn't beautiful."

"Ah, come on, Ben. She was demented, but you got to agree she was beautiful."

"Beauty's in the eye of the beholder. Inner ugliness overshadows physical appearance."

"Inner beauty, too, and hell, ain't I glad of that? If I weren't such a damn sweetheart, no woman could stand to look at my ugly mug."

Bradshaw had thought Rachel beautiful, once. Justin had inherited her coloring, fair hair, blue eyes, skin that freckled. Luckily, he had inherited none of her selfishness or craving for attention. She'd been born willful, her parents had explained after her death. They'd found it easier to give her what she demanded, rather than deal with her rages. Bradshaw wished they'd been as forthcoming before his marriage. But they'd given him no warning. They'd chosen not to tell him of the extreme measures she took to frighten them into getting her way. And yet he could never bring himself to wish he'd never married her because that would wish his son out of existence. He'd as soon wish all air to vanish.

As he sat not eating, his heart made heavy by such thoughts, Missouri came out of the kitchen, alone. She crossed to Justin's table, and the boy's face lit up when she asked about his sand castle. Bradshaw tried to see her objectively. Short mahogany hair plainly cut, large nose, wide mouth, skinny figure. Nope, he couldn't do it. He couldn't be objective. She was the most attractive girl he'd ever seen. Feminine, ethereal, strong. There was something regal about her, although she wasn't the least bit proud.

Henry kicked him under the table. "I don't get you, Ben. I thought that was all over with, and don't pretend you don't know what I'm talking about."

"A man can admire, can't he?"

"Missouri's the image of her mother, and she was no queen of the May."

"You told me your sister was beautiful."

"Because I loved her, that's how I saw her. Eye of the beholder."

"Can we get back to the case, please?"

"In a minute. Who is it you were seeing on the sly?"

Bradshaw shoved his plate away.

Henry persisted. "Every other week, you were giving those classes up in Everett. You could have caught the last steamer home, but you didn't."

He should have guessed Henry had suspected something. Bradshaw was a man of strict routine, a man of economy, a man who avoided society and relationships. He'd surprised himself in accepting Ann Darlyrope's advances. Their private affair had been brief, lasting a few months and ending pleasantly. They'd remained friends. But the classes he'd used as an excuse to meet her had proved popular, so he'd continued them. And Ann? She'd recently landed the starring role with a major company and was going on tour to the Midwest. It was to Ann he'd sent flowers the day Hornsby's summons had arrived, to say bon voyage.

Henry said, "You got a right to your privacy, and teaching at the college, I know you got to be discreet. But when that started up, I figured you'd got over your feelings for Missouri. Am I wrong?"

"I've gotten over the belief that anything could, or should, come of my feelings for her." He'd never said it aloud. His battered stomach gave a clutch of protest, and he thought he now knew what an ulcer felt like. He shouldn't care. He didn't want to care.

"Only because you decided that's how it's gonna be."

"I need you to go Hoquiam. Wire Squirrel and tell him it's urgent."

"Ben—"

"Not now, Henry."

"You see what's happening, don't you? You'd better be sure that's what you want."

"What I want is for you to wire Squirrel."

"All right, I give. You don't want to talk about it. As per usual. Wire Squirrel."

Squirrel was the nickname of Pete Carter, a professional fact-finder, coveted by Seattle attorneys for his skill at digging up deeply buried facts in government records, newspaper archives, trade journals, every bit of printed matter. Squirrel was so popular, he had the luxury of choice and would refuse a job if he didn't like the particulars. A year ago, an attorney turned down by Squirrel exacted his revenge by framing him for the murder his client had committed. Fortunately for Squirrel, the death had been by electrocution—a rigged light bulb in the victim's house—so Bradshaw had been called to investigate. Bradshaw had been Squirrel's favorite client ever since.

"I want everything he can find on everyone here, the Hornsbys, Hollister, Moss, Loomis, and the Thompsons. I especially need to know if any of them have ever had anything to do with electrical matters." He pressed his pocket notebook and pencil at Henry. "Tell him time is of the essence, I'll pay for his speed. Send a wire to Tom—Professor Hill. Tell him to send everything he can find on Arnold Loomis and the Loomis Long Life Luminator, and have him go to the house and find my file on my electrotherapy outfit. Tell him he'll find it in my files in the basement."

Henry nodded, scribbling away.

"And I want information on the coming railroad, news on speculators. Who's buying land? Bringing in businesses? And what about those gas rigs we saw offshore near Copalis? What resources are there here to exploit, and where has the name Arnold Loomis cropped up in connection?"

Henry looked up. "More than one con?"

"He's not here for his health. It'll be a few hours before the tide's low again. Head out soon as it's safe. Be sure to tell Deputy Mitchell you're leaving, but he doesn't need any details. Have Colin drive you in the steamer. I'll repay his rental costs. And you'll have to hire a boat to Hoquiam, the regular steamer only runs three times a week."

Henry shook his head. "Killing two birds, eh?"

"Fastest way to get what I need."

"Like I said, killing two birds. It's not fair to her, Ben. Can't set her free and lock her up, both."

Bradshaw had no answer to that. He carried his plate into the kitchen, feeling guilty for dumping his uneaten bread and berries into the compost bucket and wondering if he should ask Dr. Hornsby for some sort of digestive.

Chapter Nine

Mrs. Hornsby was best described as bosomy. The sort of woman small children loved to be embraced by and that made men miss their mothers. As requested, she was waiting for him in the library. The day had grown warm, and all the windows were open for cross-ventilation. The white sheers danced in the confines of their tiebacks. Bradshaw unbuttoned his jacket as he sat, and found Mrs. Hornsby shaking her head at his dark suit.

"You don't need to be so formal with us, Professor."

"It's my uniform while I'm working." Like Sheriff Graham, he knew a man's attire inspired respect.

"Well, as long as you know we wouldn't think less of you if you dressed more comfortably. Most of our male guests wear linen this time of year. Did you bring beach clothes?"

"I did, thank you." He'd not brought swimming attire, but he did have a lighter weight suit with him. "You've created a unique place, Mrs. Hornsby."

"We hear that all the time. My husband is a very wise man. He just doesn't live life. He analyzes it. He thinks deeply about what makes people happy and healthy. Most people believe that they'd be happy if only they had enough money to be idle all the time, or they'd be healthy if only they could find a miracle cure. When really, health and happiness are lost when we fight our natures and gained when we honor them."

It was obviously a speech she made often, but she spoke with sincerity.

"I'm sorry for the loss of your son-in-law."

"Oh, Professor. We miss him so. It's been awful. Simply awful. I wish to God that Mr. Loomis had never come here, bringing that awful machine. Oh—I didn't mean—you had us all so shocked when you said you'd built it. Did you really build it?"

"I did, years ago. I was shocked to find it here. How did it come to be?"

"I think it started with a letter from Mr. Loomis to my husband. They corresponded a bit, and my husband became interested in the machine. He invited Loomis here a few weeks ago, and the sale was made. Mr. Loomis has been here ever since. Not a paying guest either, mind you." She shook her head. "I'm not quite sure how that happened. He wasn't expected to pay while he was training my husband on the machine, of course, but that took no more than a day. When he stayed on, we kept trying to bring up the subject of payment, but he would say how thankful he was for our generous hospitality and that he'd be sure to spread the word about Healing Sands when he left. But he never left. I used to think out here we'd never be bothered with men like him. But those types find you, don't they? And with the railroad coming, people will be able to get here much more easily."

"You're not happy about the train coming?"

"No, I'm not. We moved here because it was isolated. We came for the peace and seclusion and nature's beauty. It won't be the same, once the railroad comes."

"How close will the nearest station be?"

"Just up the beach, at Joe's Creek. They've renamed the area Pacific Beach and have already begun to plat a town. And I hear Moclips is getting a great big grand hotel, with hundreds of rooms! It'll be another year or two yet until the road is done. They've reached Copalis Crossing, that's a few miles inland, but it's slow going because of the terrain, and the lumbermen have so much timber to clear."

"You might be far enough away from a depot to stay isolated."

"Not the way Mr. Loomis tells it. He says we must expand or risk losing business to someone else."

"And has he proposed a way of helping you expand?"

"Every chance he gets. I wanted him to leave, but my husband—well, my husband can be too kind. It sounds mean to say so, I know, but there are those who would try to take advantage, and Mr. Loomis is certainly one. If you'll forgive me, Professor, I don't completely understand what was said this morning. Did Mr. Loomis steal the Luminator from you?"

"I'm not sure, at least not in the legal sense. I was not fully informed of how and where the machine I built was to be used."

She frowned at him. "You made it sound as if he stole from you, Professor."

"I won't know if a law has been broken until I speak to my patent attorney, Mrs. Hornsby. There are legal crimes, and moral crimes. They don't always coincide."

She worried the hem of her apron, picking at a loose thread, then gave a little huff. "He's a confidence man, isn't he?" She looked at him for confirmation.

"Possibly so. I am still gathering information. I can state only my experience with Mr. Arnold Loomis. He certainly gained my confidence, then took advantage of my faith in him."

"If you'll forgive my asking, what did happen? How did he take your machine from you? And why did it kill our David?"

He was prepared for these questions and had decided in advance how much to reveal when asked them. "Mr. Loomis approached me as a medical salesman with an idea for an electric outfit. I had the knowledge to build it, he the knowledge to market it. Since nothing on it would be newly patentable, it wasn't something I would have undertaken on my own. I don't enjoy marketing. It's much easier to simply collect royalties on patent contracts. When I'd done my work and the outfit was completed, Loomis claimed another similar cabinet had beat us to the market. It's a common enough outcome these days, so I didn't question it. Loomis told me he sold the prototype to a Seattle doctor and paid me for my time and materials. That was in '99."

"What? Mr. Loomis told us the machine was the latest and greatest. We're used to being behind the times out here on the coast, but four years is old even to us."

"Where the machine has been since the time it left my basement and appeared here at Healing Sands is a question I can't yet answer. And how it caused David's death, I don't yet know."

"Was the machine damaged on the way here? Did some internal part break? Mr. Loomis swore to us it was perfectly safe."

"It is perfectly safe, and your husband used it properly. That's all I know for certain."

Her mouth opened and she stared at him. "Are you saying my husband is not responsible?"

"I'm saying your husband followed proper procedures and could not have predicted David's death."

Mrs. Hornsby released her breath. "Oh, Professor, you don't know how grateful I am to hear you say that. Have you told my husband this, he is so distraught."

"He knows this, yes."

She attempted a brave smile and looked at him with motherly concern. "This can't be easy for you, Professor. I do hope you're at least finding our accommodations to your liking. I've noticed that you've barely touched our milk and cultured dishes."

"Milk has never agreed with me," he said, for the first time in his life glad that milk tended to make his belly rumble warnings.

"Oh, that's true of most of our guests when they first arrive. Only young children can readily digest milk, and then it's only the milk of our own species that makes us thrive. We are not cows, are we, Professor?"

"Ah, no."

"In order to make the milk of other animals digestible, it must be cultured, fermented, or soured, and then all those nutrients can be taken up by our systems. Our cow and goat milk come from our own animals. The grazing soil is fertilized with salmon scraps and seaweed. That's why it's that lovely yellow color. Absolutely the most nourishing milk available. You see how my daughters' skin glows."

"I've always been fine with butter," he amended. The butter served had been sweet and nearly white, and if he didn't mention his ability to digest it now, he'd be committing himself to dry bread for the duration. "You've managed to get my son to enjoy washing dishes. I may try to use some of your methods at home. Do you get any resistance?"

"Very little, really. Some of our wealthiest clients have said they found great satisfaction in helping with their own meals and tidying their own rooms."

"Do you ever make exceptions?"

"To the housekeeping rules? Only when someone is physically impaired and unable. We had a lame gentleman here last spring, but even he managed most of the chores from his chair. At the risk of sounding like a gossip, we do now have one guest who resents our rules. Mrs. Thompson. Ever since she arrived, she's been finding ways out of the simple tasks we ask of all our guests."

"She refused to do them?"

"Not exactly. The first day, she complied. She looked stunned when we told her what was expected." A touch of amusement lightened Mrs. Hornsby's expression. "But she must have been up half the night concocting excuses to avoid any work. She'd say she'd left something in her room so her husband would dish up her meal and have it on the table when she returned. She'd say she couldn't manage the knot on her shoe to get her husband to kneel at her feet and put on her slippers. Now she doesn't even make excuses. Although, he's been feeling so poorly of late, she's been forced to do a few things for herself."

"Has she been troublesome in other ways?"

"Oh, no. And I really shouldn't blame her. Her father was a wealthy businessman and she grew up with servants waiting on her all the time. Not a healthy way to raise a child."

"What can you tell me about Mr. Thompson, and the other guests, Mr. Loomis and Mr. Moss?"

"I've had no trouble with them in regards to our household rules. Mr. Moss is in Hippocrates Hut, and he keeps it tidy. I've found bachelors of limited means make excellent guests since they're used to caring for themselves. Oh, I know Mr. Moss is rich now, but he still has his old habits that serve him well."

"What do the patients do while here, other than receive medical care?"

"Oh, they explore the beach, of course. Some venture up to the forest, but they never go far. The Thompsons went on a day excursion up toward Moclips. Up with the morning low tide, and back on the evening."

"Do the guests socialize much?"

"A few times in the evenings they have gathered in the library or conservatory."

"What do they discuss?"

"Mr. Loomis lectures on various topics. He's a very knowledgeable man. Or, I thought he was. I don't know what to think anymore."

"Did you see any of them with your son-in-law?"

"Mr. Loomis spent a lot of time with David. He seemed impressed with all he'd done around here. That made Martha quite proud, that a successful businessman was impressed with her David." Mrs. Hornsby began worrying her apron again, as if she were applying her newly formed doubts of Loomis to past experience with him, something Bradshaw hoped to minimize.

"Can you recall anything specific about what Mr. Loomis and David discussed?"

"Mr. Loomis said David had real potential."

"Potential for what?"

"I never was clear on that. Martha knows more. It had something to do with the washhouse. Have you seen it yet? Oh, you must see it. David designed it himself, and built the water motor, too."

"Did he very much want children?"

"I believe he did, but what he wanted more than anything was to give Martha a child. I didn't realize until after—when my husband told me about the sessions and David's secret hope. Martha knew when she married David that they'd likely never have children, but she loved him and made the sacrifice.

She never once complained, but I'd see her face when friends announced they were in the family way. David was a good, attentive husband. He must have known."

"Tell me, please, all you recall about the day of the tragedy. Where were you when it happened?"

"I was in the kitchen with Martha when my husband came in. I'll never forget the look on his face. He said something had gone terribly wrong with the electrotherapy machine. We were as confused as we were stunned because he said it was David he was talking about, not Mr. Thompson. Martha and I both ran upstairs." She put a hand over her face for a moment, fighting off tears. At last she swallowed hard. "Later, my husband went to Hoquiam to report the death to the coroner."

"Was that necessary?"

"It's what must be done when there's an accidental death in an establishment like this. We've never had it happen before, but we knew proper procedure. Even though David is family, he died under my husband's care. We followed procedure and he brought the sheriff and coroner here. I wish now he hadn't, but I suppose that wouldn't have given us any peace either. My husband would drive himself mad with not knowing what had gone wrong. As it is, he may never recover. No, we must have answers."

Chapter Ten

The zigzagged path up the cliff, although well-carved and laid with sand and stepping stones, had no railing. Bradshaw kept his eyes cast down, his fingertips skimming the tips of dried grass rooted in the cliff wall as he climbed. Recitation always made a fair distraction, but the poem by Shelley that sprang to mind, recalled by the setting no doubt, and learned long ago, was perhaps too distracting.

> *The fountains mingle with the river,*
> *And the rivers with the ocean;*
> *The winds of heaven mix forever*
> *With a sweet emotion;*
> *Nothing in the world is single;*
> *All things by a law divine*
> *In another's being mingle—*
> *Why not I with thine?*

> *See, the mountains kiss high heaven,*
> *And the waves clasp one another;*
> *No sister flower could be forgiven*
> *If it disdained its brother;*
> *And the sunlight clasps the earth,*
> *And the moonbeams kiss the sea;—*
> *What are all these kissings worth,*
> *If thou kiss not me?*

He arrived at the top having avoided vertigo, yet plunged deep in something far more disturbing. The sun's warmth was keener up here. He loosened his collar and removed his jacket, scanning the shore until he saw Missouri in the distance, a slender figure, skirt billowing in the wind. He knew he had no right to wallow in self-pity when his loneliness was his own doing, but it was tiresome always owning up to the responsibility of his life.

And what if she refused him? What if he were to take that terrifyingly bold step and he discovered it was all him? That what he saw in her eyes was only the reflection of his own feelings for her. He'd put the question to Ann, his former lover. She'd said that in her experience, it was worth the risk, even if the answer wasn't the one wanted. She'd confronted the man she loved and learned he felt the same. And that he would never leave his wife.

The path dipped to a garden sheltered from the ocean wind. A full half acre in size, it was enclosed by a deer fence of woven branches and ripe with summer vegetables and sweet corn. His empty, acid-laden stomach growled at the sight of firm summer squash nestled under enormous leaves, red ripe tomatoes and fat cucumbers clinging to frames. There were even apple trees heavy with fruit. Everywhere he looked, fresh fruit and vegetables glowed in the afternoon sun, and not a speck of it had been fermented or pickled. Not since Adam had a man been so tempted.

He pushed onward, following a meandering trail to an enclosed yard of scratching, clucking chickens, and beyond them, a small pasture of cows and a large donkey, happily feasting on the fish-fed greens. After cresting a small rise, he found within a neat picket fence several carved headstones and a white painted cross at the head of a recently mounded grave. He bowed his head and whispered a prayer.

The sound of trickling water caught his attention. He followed it and discovered a pipe heading south and soon found himself peering hesitantly over a precipice, at the penstock plunging into the Healing Sands' famed laundry.

A pulsing and continuous crash, like a wave cresting without end, rose up the cliff, blending with the more distant roar of the ocean. The machinery was hidden beneath the angled roof. As he listened, he began to hear a pattern under the roar that came from the water hitting the paddles of the spinning wheel. He moved on, heading back toward the cliff path, and came upon the old native Henry had mentioned, seated on a boulder, staring out to sea.

Bradshaw approached the old man slowly, keeping a respectful distance. He wore white men's clothing, shoes, trousers, shirt, vest, and jacket, but so worn and filthy they looked as if they'd grown on him. The top of his filthy felt fedora had been eaten away, the brim nibbled at. Yet the old man's ramrod posture and serenity gave him a dignity as ancient as the boulder he sat upon. His skin, like his clothes, was worn and aged, reminding Bradshaw of an ancient cedar tree. A tuft of white beard lined his jaw from ear to ear like moss.

"Good afternoon."

The old man nodded once.

"I'm Professor Bradshaw, staying down below at Healing Sands."

"I am Yoyot." The old man's voice was deep and clear. "It means 'strong' in your language. I was once. Now, I sit." He spoke with the rhythm of a native. "I am known as Old Cedar."

They both looked out at the sea.

Old Cedar said, "You are here because of David."

"You knew him?"

"For many years. I respected him. He respected me. Not many of the young do anymore. Not even of my own people. He often came up here. We talked."

"You heard how he died?"

"I invited him to the sweat lodge, but he believed in your modern science. Now it has killed him."

"Electricity was the means of his death, but it's not to blame."

Old Cedar narrowed his eyes. "In my day, we did not seek to punish those who are already suffering from regret."

"I'm not referring to Dr. Hornsby."

The old eyes flashed wide. "But he was there, he told me so himself."

"Oh, yes, he was there. But he's not responsible. I'm not at liberty to explain." He'd already said as much to Mrs. Hornsby.

Old Cedar turned his face to the ocean again and closed his eyes.

After a quiet moment, Bradshaw asked, "Do you sit here every day?"

"In my youth, I fished," said Old Cedar, opening his eyes. "I made longboats of cedar. I walked the forest. Now I sit. It is surprising how much I enjoy it."

"I believe my housekeeper is surprised by her enjoyment of leisure as well. At home, she never stops moving."

Old Cedar squinted at the beach. "Is she the one under the umbrella who watches the small boys?"

He paid attention to the goings-on below. What else had he noticed? "Yes, that's Mrs. Prouty. I don't know how I'd manage without her."

"She's young yet, and beginning to find work."

Mrs. Prouty would be pleased to know someone considered her young. Today, she'd brought a basket with her embroidery.

"It's the way of a good soul, until nature says it's time to stop. I worked until my eightieth year. Now my hands enjoy stillness. I sit in peace." He turned his head to look toward another section of beach. There, under the shade of an umbrella, lounged Mrs. Thompson in a reclining beach chair. Perched on the edge of the chair near her feet was Arnold Loomis, leaning forward, palms up. His words were lost to them, but his tone appeared beseeching.

Old Cedar said, "That is not her husband, I believe."

"No, you're right."

Mrs. Thompson sat up, reached out to Loomis, touched his face, ran a finger around his ear, then trailed the tip over his lips. Loomis, encouraged, pressed forward toward her, and she pushed him away, sitting back again.

"She spends considerable time with him. And the other one who is not her husband."

"Moss? A stocky man. Walks with a swagger?"

Old Cedar nodded. "In my language there is a word for a woman like her. I don't know how to say it in English."

"Trouble?"

Old Cedar's eyes wrinkled with a smile. "That will do."

Loomis got to his feet, appeared to make one more attempt to persuade Mrs. Thompson of something, then slunk away, defeated. Mrs. Thompson adjusted the umbrella to provide full shade, then reclined.

Curious.

"I've been observing life from this very boulder ever since I can remember. My grandfather would sit here, as I do now, and tell me stories." Old Cedar began to speak of his childhood, and the changes he witnessed over the years. He'd been just five years old when he first saw a white man. The explorer and his team had been welcomed graciously, but they left behind a sickness that took the lives of nearly half the tribe. A quarter century later, another wave of explorers was less eagerly welcomed, but the result was the same. Sickness and death. After that, he'd gone to the city to learn to speak the white man's language. He hoped that if he could converse with the whites, they could find a way to live in health and harmony. White men knew many things; surely they knew how to do this. But it seems they didn't. Their solution was to isolate the natives, put them on a reservation.

"They named it Quinault, as if that would make it more attractive to us. Some of us refused to go. They keep changing the terms, changing the borders, but it does not change it from being a wooded jail. We are meant to roam, to follow the fish and berries. The land provides. What did we give up by not signing the treaty? Blankets and beef?" He swatted the air as if to toss away the pathetic offerings. "We have cedar and salmon. Your people make life difficult for mine, and also for yourselves. Look at that washhouse David built. So much effort to keep clothing clean. Why the fancy dress? The discomfort? Everything for you whites is a fight. You fight against your clothes, your natures, the land, and take anything that strikes your fancy. The guests below take everything: they kill the animals in the forest, empty the sea of life, dig all the clams in the sand. They even take the sand."

"I can't claim to be better than my brethren, yet I agree with all you say." Did that clear him of responsibility, the fact that he agreed with Old Cedar? He might not have written the treaties or marched the natives from their ancestral homes, but as a white man, he lived and worked and benefited from those who did. Didn't his own house in Seattle sit on a deforested hill that natives once freely roamed and hunted?

As they spoke, Martha Hollister had been climbing up to them. When she approached, Old Cedar gave her a polite nod of greeting, then slipped away into the woods. Martha took his place on the boulder, looking out at the ocean. She hadn't looked directly at Bradshaw, and the set of her shoulders displayed a rigid control.

Her voice was flat when she asked, "How is Old Cedar today?"

"He's saddened by your husband's passing."

"He's known too much death." Her words held no emotion. Shock and grief insulated her, held her trapped in a world both numbing and devastating. She turned her head to look at him. "Your machine killed my husband." The grief and accusation in her eyes tore his heart. He felt his eyes sting.

"I'm so very sorry."

She looked away, and he swallowed hard.

She said, "Do you have any answers for us yet about what went wrong?"

He cleared his throat. "No, not yet."

"My mother just told me about how Mr. Loomis conned you, too, but the fact remains it was your machine."

Only the sheriff, deputy, and Doctor Hornsby knew that someone at Healing Sands had deliberately altered the machine to make it fatal. As much as it hurt him that Martha believed him responsible, he couldn't risk his investigation by revealing too much.

"Mrs. Hollister, I promise I will do all that I can to find answers to what happened to David. To do that, I'll need to ask you some questions. I can wait until later, if you want."

"No. I'd rather have it done."

He began to question her gently about events leading up to David's death, but when she began to tremble violently, saying, "It's a dream, it can't be real," he silenced. And when she extended a shaking hand to him, he clasped it between both of his and sat beside her on the boulder, gladly enduring her fierce grip.

He didn't wonder at this sudden intimacy between them. It arose from the same instinct as saving a stranger from drowning.

At first, he didn't speak. But when he felt her grip loosen slightly, he began to talk of simple things. He didn't try to tell her all would be well. He knew such words were useless, even offensive. Worst of all were the platitudes that claimed a devastating tragedy was "meant to be," part of some grand plan devised by a higher power. A man of faith, Bradshaw nevertheless could not bring himself to believe that a loving and powerful entity would devise any sort of plan that could only bring about heavenly peace through human suffering.

He spoke quietly of the ocean, currents, and water flow. He spoke of the time he'd fallen into the Snoqualmie River and found himself clinging to a rock at the edge of the falls.

She looked at him, pulled momentarily out of her misery by his story. But she couldn't sustain the distractive thought.

"I haven't cried yet. I don't know what's wrong with me."

"It takes time. How long had you been married?"

"Seven years. Seems I've always known him. We were children when his family moved to Joe's Creek. That's up the beach a ways. He did a lot of handy work for us. Back then, my father's practice was in Aberdeen and he was only home a few days a week. You think this stretch of beach is empty now, you should have seen it then. Just one other white family within ten miles of us. But we loved it, and we made friends with Old Cedar and some of the young people from his tribe."

"Can you tell me about David?"

A small tight smile brought tears to her eyes, and she let go of his hand a bit shyly, now that her mood had calmed. "David was smart, and gentle, and always working on something. Even as a child, he liked to build things. He was quiet. He wasn't one to need conversation to feel comfortable with other people."

Bradshaw continued asking about David and learned that he had built the washhouse and the machines from reading about them in magazines and newspapers and looking at the designs in journals. "He rolled the old millwheel here from Hoquiam, he and a half dozen friends. It took them a week, and then it was too heavy to mount to the frame he'd built. He had to construct a giant hoist. Over the years, he tried to get all sorts of things running with belts and drive shafts, just to see what sort of motion he could get. When my father announced he was going to build Healing Sands, David was thrilled when he realized how much laundry there'd be. By then he'd built a washing machine, you see, that most of the families on North Beach came to use. They still come once a month. David traveled to Seattle and Portland, and hauled back scrap metal, used parts and motors, and that's the washhouse we have today."

"I'd love to see it, when you're ready."

"I'm ready now," she said.

It took only a few minutes to follow the path down and around the base of the cliff to the weathered washhouse. Inside, the noise of the spinning water turbine was like standing at the ocean's edge on a stormy day, but the drive belts of the laundry system weren't engaged and so the noise was bearable.

Martha raised her voice. "Two years ago, David added the dynamo to the turbine so we could have light at the house." She led Bradshaw past several washing machines consisting of stationary tubs with inner cylinders of perforated staves and reverse motion paddles to prevent tangling. He marveled at the mangle wringers and the massive ventilated drying cabinet with racks that slid in and out, and the starching and ironing machines for shirts, collars, and cuffs. If he hadn't chosen to specialize in electricity, he might have gone mechanical. There was an invigorating allure to a well-designed machine, its parts working smoothly in rhythm and performing a task.

"He changed over the boiler last year to this electric one. We used to dedicate a full day each week to cutting and hauling wood to feed the furnace; but now, the creek does the work for us."

A storage room with a workbench contained David's tools and supplies. Within seconds, Bradshaw found a roll of block tin foil and several spools of wire, although, as with every conductive item in the house, it was impossible for him to determine if anything here had been used to sabotage the electric outfit.

Lastly, Martha showed him David's rotating hot air towel dryer. She said, "This is what has made our guests the happiest. I'd bet we have the softest towels of anyone in the world. The only drawback is the towels don't last as long. They leave a bit of themselves behind as fluff each time we dry them and, so we find we have to budget for new towels."

"All the other buildings here have names. Does the washhouse?"

"No. David never found one that felt right, and then we got used to calling it the washhouse."

"Have any Healing Sands' patients been in here?"

"We give all the guests a tour when they first arrive. David enjoyed that."

"Did any of them come back at another time? The current guests, I mean."

"Mr. Moss and Mr. Loomis were here often. I'm not sure about the Thompsons. I'm in the kitchen much of the time. David would be the one to ask. It doesn't seem possible that we can't ask him."

She looked at David's machines, biting her lip, then steadying herself with a deep breath. "He wasn't what you'd call a social man, my David. He was quiet, like I told you, so I don't think the guests made a habit of coming to speak with him, although he was always happy to answer questions about how his system works. He did mention he spoke to Mrs. Thompson once, not long after she and her husband arrived. She reminded him of someone he once knew in Hoquiam, but it turns out she was no relation. She has that sort of face that seems familiar. Those sleepy eyes."

Bradshaw thought it interesting that women often called such eyes sleepy while men called them sultry.

She said, "I know enough about how it all works to keep doing laundry, but without David, if something breaks, we won't know how to fix it."

It was a problem without an easy answer. There weren't many with the skills to maintain and repair a modern laundry, and those who could weren't likely to want to move to this remote location.

"Does the creek flow all year?"

"Yes, it's fed from an underground spring. Even on the coldest days, we have lights and laundry." She smiled sadly. "Did you ever read the book, *The Time Machine*, Professor? I can't say I much liked it. Very strange. But right now I'd love one of those machines. I'd go back just two months and wait for the mail to arrive with that first letter Mr. Loomis sent to my father, and I'd burn it. Then Loomis would never have come and David would still be here."

Bradshaw wondered how far back in time he'd go. He couldn't undo his marriage to Rachel without losing Justin. After his birth then? And what would he do differently? Have Rachel committed to an asylum to protect her from herself? Who would have believed him? To everyone but him and her parents, she appeared so normal. Could he have prevented her suicide? If he'd stopped her from drinking poison that awful night, would he now still be married to her, living in fear each day of what she might do next?

"Professor?" Martha was looking at him with concern.

He told her what he'd told her father. "What-ifs come unbidden after tragedies, Mrs. Hollister. But they do us no good, and can even do us harm by dwelling on them."

She took a long breath. "I know you're right. But it's so hard now to look back at all that happened and not want to scream about our blindness. It's more than the fact that Mr. Loomis brought that dreadful machine—oh, I'm sorry."

"I understand, and I agree. What more is there to your regrets?"

"Well, Mr. Loomis was impressed with David, you see, and at first David was flattered by his praise and attention. We both were."

"Something changed?"

"Mr. Loomis wanted David to draw up plans for the wash-house, put it all down in diagrams and such and include everything, even the special drive belts and water motor and heated dryer."

"Did he?"

"He wanted to, only he didn't know how. He's never had formal schooling on anything, and as handy as he is—was—with a hammer, he's that clumsy with a pencil. So Mr. Loomis said he'd draw it up for him."

"Did he complete the plans?"

"Oh, yes. They're lovely. I didn't know diagrams could be lovely, but they are. So neat and tidy, with little symbols and elegant script. Made me even more proud to think they represented what my David had built."

"Where are those plans now?"

Her face grew hard. "You'll have to ask Mr. Loomis. He wouldn't let David have them."

"Why ever not?"

"He said that as he'd drawn them, they belonged to him, and he thought David understood that when he agreed to it. He was very pleasant and apologetic about it, but he refused all the same. Is that true, Professor? Does Mr. Loomis own those plans?"

"It depends on what was agreed upon. Did your husband put his name to anything? Sign any agreement or form?"

"No, sir. They just talked."

"Then it's Loomis' word against your husband's."

"And my husband has no word now, does he?"

Chapter Eleven

He should send them all home. Standing on a massive drift log at the top of the beach, Bradshaw was moved by the sight of the boys blissfully engaged. His students had built a makeshift work station and four of them, Knut, Miles, Oren, and Daniel, were carrying out the sand experiments he'd assigned. The younger boys, Justin and Paul, were happily but unsuccessfully digging for clams under Mrs. Prouty's occasionally watchful eye. She was reading a dime novel under her umbrella. Was he selfish to keep them here? Would it be overcautious to send them home?

David Hollister's death was either involuntary manslaughter or murder. Evidence of why David had died still existed, if not in physical clues then in the mind and heart of one or more of the residents. For Bradshaw's money, Loomis was looking particularly guilty.

His students and family were in no danger from whoever had killed David Hollister. His mind told him so. His gut spoke differently. He was a man who trusted instinct above logic, yet he also knew his gut could react out of fear. Was that the case now?

He swept his gaze over the idyllic scene looking for one particular, slender figure. He spotted her in the distance, dress billowing, walking up the beach. He approached Mrs. Prouty. She didn't argue with his request. Being of a maternal nature, she nodded her grudging acceptance.

Before heading up the beach, he turned his pant cuffs up to keep them clean. The wind howled in his ears. He put his head down, and this brought his attention to the transitioning sand, changing from soft and difficult to tread to damp, packed and smooth, easy to walk upon. Rippled patterns etched in the surface fascinated him. The patterns were geometric designs, regularly repeated, created by the action of wind and water. But why were they so even? When the wind gusted irregularly, and the reach of the waves was inconsistent?

His fascination took him to the water's edge where it felt a full ten degrees cooler than up by the house. He hated the howling in his ears.

Missouri stood at the edge of the surf's reach with her bare feet wide, arms spread, face turned blissfully into the wind. "Isn't it heaven?"

He walked around her to put the wind to his back. The roaring dulled. She squinted at him, amused, as usual, at his being uncomfortable. He knew what she thought, that he would enjoy it if he only let himself. If she had her way, he'd be ripping off his clothes and racing into the icy surf. He could see it in the twinkle of her dark amber eyes. She shouted into the wind, "It's so refreshing!"

He said, without shouting, for his voice had the favor of the wind, "It's too loud. Did Henry and Colin head out?"

"Yes, about an hour ago."

"I need you to change your lodgings. There's an extra bed in Mrs. Prouty's room in Paracelsus Cottage."

"I don't want to share a room with Mrs. Prouty."

"You must."

She cocked her head, studying him. "What aren't you telling me?"

He felt sure she was reading his every thought and emotion. He said, "This investigation is more complicated than I anticipated."

She continued studying him, her eyes dancing as if on a treasure hunt through his tangled thoughts. Then her eyes widened. "So there was foul play? Murder?"

"You needn't look happy over the prospect."

"If you remove the twinkle from your eye, so will I. Of course I'm saddened for the family over their loss, as are you, especially since it was your own invention involved, but why deny the appeal of a real investigation? You're only truly happy when you're chin deep in a problem, solving impossible puzzles. You'd be much happier in this world, Mr. Bradshaw, if you accepted your emotions instead of locking them up."

"Been saving that speech, have you?"

"Until the opportune time, yes."

The wind blew her hair across her face. She brushed it back with a toss of her head, and challenged him with a narrowed gaze.

"I don't know who yet to trust in the house. I want you in a cabin. I should probably send you all home."

"Who do you suspect?"

"I don't yet know who's involved."

"You've taken an interest in Mrs. Thompson."

What did she mean by that? She'd never known his late wife, but she'd seen her photo on his mantel. Did she, too, see the resemblance to Ingrid Thompson? Was she alluding to his inner turmoil, the jumble of emotions over his past with Rachel, his future without *her*…?

"I could be of use to you in the house. I could speak to the family, befriend Mrs. Thompson—"

"You will befriend no one."

Her raised eyebrow told him she'd read deeply into that remark.

"Whatever happened here was personal, involving those here at the time. If you and the others stay out of the house except for meals, you won't get involved, and I won't be distracted by worrying about you."

"I don't want to move."

"Then pack your bags, you're going home."

"You can't send me off like a child."

"No, if you were a child, you'd be obeying me."

"Your past skews your judgment, Mr. Bradshaw."

"Yes, it does. You will relocate or leave."

"What has happened to make you feel I'd be unsafe in the house?"

"I won't discuss the case with you."

"I could help."

"Yes, you probably could, but I don't want your help."

"Why are you so angry with me?"

Not you, he wanted to say, at me. But even if he'd been brave enough to say that, opening the door to an honest discussion with her, he couldn't, because galloping up the beach toward them was Deputy Mitchell.

Missouri, unaware of the deputy's approach, said, "You've made it clear, Mr. Bradshaw, by keeping your distance for two years, that you've chosen to suppress your feelings for me. It's not our age difference or the fact that I'm Henry's niece or even the scars of your marriage that worries you because Ann Darlyrope helped you through those—"

His shock must have registered on his face, for she continued, "Yes, I knew about her, and I also know that it's over now. Yes, I was jealous, but she was good for you, I could see that. I might be young, but I understand more than you realize about relationships and a man's needs, and I thought maybe you'd have some sense now, or at least be willing to discuss the very real differences between us to see if we can find a way past them."

He still couldn't look away even though his face burned at the thought that she knew about his affair. The deputy paused on his march toward them, bending to examine a shell, and Bradshaw opened his mouth to say something, anything, while he had the time. But the only thing that came to him was the ridiculous thought that she was a wildflower, and he a boulder, and if he were to act on his feelings, he would crush the life out of her.

"Never mind. I'm tired of pondering your inhibitions, and tired of wondering if you'll ever get over them. You've chosen your path, and I'm striking out on my own."

His heart wrenched. "What is that supposed to mean?"

"You're a college professor, decipher my meaning. Furthermore, you have no call to be angry when Colin shows an interest in me. Sending him off with Uncle Henry—"

"Henry needed a ride into town."

"—and then marching down here pretending your anger is all about your fear for my safety. Do you take me for a fool?"

"Colin's behavior has nothing to do with my frustration with you at this moment." The deputy, now just a few yards away, lifted a hand in greeting that Bradshaw did not return.

She said, "You're jealous of Colin."

Bradshaw's eyes snapped back to Missouri. "Don't play games."

"No. No games. But I'm done waiting. I don't know what sort of future you envision for me, but I assure you, I will not be a spinster or a nun."

He stood dizzy with loving her, paralyzed with the knowledge he was all wrong for her. She was right that his inhibition had nothing to do with their age difference, her being his best friend's niece, nor his being a widower. Those things had mattered to him at first, but not now. What inhibited him was fundamental to their natures. In many ways they were opposites. From afar, he could admire her, be intrigued by her. Love her. But what would happen if they became closer? Could he live daily with their differences? Would they fight over them? Would his stodgy, plodding, regimented ways strangle her free-spirited beauty? He feared so. He knew so. He could no more reach out to her safely than—well, than a coal miner fresh from a shift could safely touch a white silk cloth without ruining it.

He was wounded and bitter, she young and hopeful. He a boulder, she a wildflower. He thought of Henry's insight. He can't both set her free and lock her up. What had he selfishly hoped? That she'd choose a career that left no room for marriage, that kept her free and him ridiculously hopeful they'd age into some sort of compatibility?

All of these thoughts and emotions assaulted him simultaneously with a roar as loud as the ocean, swallowing him, crushing him. And the damned deputy was nearly upon them. The tide surged, sending a sheet of foamy sea sliding up the hard packed sand, flooding Bradshaw's shoes, but Missouri was looking into his eyes with such openness and honesty he didn't dare move. The words were there, on the tip of his tongue. Three words.

"And just so there is no possibility of misunderstanding, Mr. Bradshaw, I'll say it straight out. I love you. I've loved you from the minute I stepped up on your front porch on that rainy night and you opened the door with Justin and the two of you stood there, gawking at me. I knew I was home. You knew it, too, and I believed if I gave you enough time, you'd admit it. But you're more pigheaded than I gave you credit for, and instead of working out the very real differences that stand between us, you plod along and avoid facing them. That's your choice, but it's not mine. So, are we clear?"

And then Deputy Mitchell was there, oblivious to what he was interrupting, greeting them, babbling about something or other. Missouri turned on her heel, heading back to the sanitarium, and he watched her go, numb with emotion.

The deputy had been talking for several minutes before Bradshaw could let go of his own turmoil to comprehend his words. He took a few steps to get out of the surf's reach, and the deputy, who was barefoot with his pant legs rolled up, followed him.

"Professor, now that I've spent time here, I don't think I'll want to leave when the job's done. I'm wondering if they'd want to station a deputy full time up this way. Seems like it'd come in handy, especially once the railroad comes. What do you think, Professor?"

"The county might want somebody with a sharp eye and an aura of authority." Bradshaw snapped, but his sarcasm was lost on the deputy.

"Exactly my thoughts."

"You might get some practice here, deputy. One of the guests might try to flee."

"Which one?"

"I don't yet know, but as there are only four, perhaps you could watch them all."

"Yes, of course, I have been."

"Where are they now?"

Deputy Mitchell shrugged. "Here and there. In the house, on the beach. There's nowhere else, really. You knew Loomis, you said?"

"Yes, I did, and it's my current belief that he's a con artist, so don't trust a word he says."

"He doesn't say much to me, Professor, I—" the deputy rubbed his neck, and looked suddenly thoughtful, "—you spent some time with Martha today, Mrs. Hollister, I mean. How's she holding up, you think?"

"Admirably."

"She's a good woman. She'd be a good mother; it was a shame about David not being able to, you know. She's so strong, still working though her heart is breaking."

Dear Heaven, the man was smitten with Martha. "Deputy, I will soon be speaking with the Thompsons, is there anything you can tell me about them that I might find useful?"

"She wears the pants in that marriage. Mr. Thompson only leaves his wife's side when she orders him away. Or to have a cigarette."

"Any idea why he's so agitated?"

"Well, he's pretty sick. And he seems to want out of here, that's for sure."

"What about Mr. Moss? Any thoughts on him?"

"He's the sorriest rich man I've ever seen. Keeps to himself, mostly. I noticed Mr. Thompson tried to chat him up a few times of an evening, seeing how they have gold in common, you know, Moss digging it up and Thompson melting it down?"

"Mr. Thompson works at the Federal Assay Office?"

"Yes, the one in Seattle. A highly stressful job, it would seem. He's antsy to return yet doesn't want to, if you know what I mean. I'd be looking for a new job, if I were him. Life's too short to stay in a place that makes you miserable. I left a half-dozen good paying jobs because the work didn't agree with me."

Bradshaw refrained from commenting that Mitchell should consider making it seven. "Did he explain what about his work he found so disagreeable?"

"He said it was a huge responsibility and he had to be so careful. I imagine it's a bit like being a lawman. I mean, with criminals always a threat. It's not easy relaxing when you never know if the next man you meet is more determined to commit a crime than you are to keep breathing."

"A long soak in a hot tub followed by a spring shower would help."

"Oh, indeed it does."

"Did you come out here for a reason, Deputy? Something to tell me?"

"Huh? No, I just wanted to ask how Martha was holding up. She's quite a good woman."

"If you'll excuse me, I need to change my shoes and get back to work."

The deputy looked down. "Hey, you got your shoes wet."

"Sharp eye, Deputy." Bradshaw was treated to a pleased grin. As he tromped away, his feet cold and squishing, he muttered, "Heaven help Chehalis County."

Chapter Twelve

The sky had faded to the soft hues of twilight by the time he met Mrs. Thompson on the front porch of Healing Sands. He'd spent the prior few hours in his cabin, taking notes and drawing a chart of suspects. It had been slow-going. One minute, he'd be intent upon recording a thought about the case, the next he'd find himself staring at the cabin wall, Missouri's voice echoing in his head. *I love you. I've loved you from the minute I stepped up on your front porch on that rainy night and you opened the door with Justin and the two of you stood there, gawking at me. I knew I was home.*

The answer to his unspoken question. What he saw in her eyes was love. Incredible. But now what? What did he do with the knowledge? What should he do? He was a man of routine and order and she was unconventional and free-spirited, and open-minded. Did she worry about that, too? Is that what she meant when she said, *"Instead of working out the very real differences that stand between us, you plod along and avoid facing them?"*

The question battled for his attention as he tried to press it away to focus on his notes. He didn't have the energy to face another curdled meal, so he skipped dinner and took a walk to clear his head. He achieved, if not clarity, then at least a physical calm that allowed him to compartmentalize his thoughts.

On his way to the porch of the main house, he passed Zeb Moss, sitting alone on a log with a cigar. The tide was low, the wet packed sand stretching far to the water's edge. Freddie Thompson and Arnold Loomis were together, staring out to sea. The wind whisked away the smoke from Loomis' pipe and Freddie's cigarette. Bradshaw wondered what they were discussing.

His mind was now focused on his job, but Missouri's words, *I love you*, resided in him, in his heart, his chest, his fingers, his toes. He felt her words without thinking of them even as he kept his mind engaged on his task. A man had died here, a beloved man, and it was his job to sort out the truth.

As he climbed the porch steps, he thought of his conversation with Old Cedar, how the old man had seen Mrs. Thompson with both Loomis and Moss. He recalled what he'd witnessed between Mrs. Thompson and Loomis, him seeming to plead, her touching his face before pressing him away. Trouble, indeed. Was Ingrid Thompson simply a flirt? Or was she more than that? What was her interest in Loomis? And Moss?

She sat waiting for him in one of the rocking chairs, keeping up a quick tempo. A small woman, barely five feet, and sturdily built. He thought of peasants in fields when he looked at her, and of Martha's comment that David had said Mrs. Thompson reminded him of someone from his childhood, just as she reminded Bradshaw of his late wife. Was that part of Mrs. Thompson's attraction—the possession of certain features that reminded men of other such women in their lives?

"Good evening, Mrs. Thompson." He removed his hat and sat in the rocker beside her, but he didn't set it in motion.

She gave him a polite nod, but continued to rock, her face turned toward the view. "Evening, Professor." Her voice was pleasant, clear and feminine, with a country not city rhythm.

"Why is it some of your party were allowed to leave this afternoon? They went off in that automobile." She spoke with a charming petulance, a child wanting her way but with a woman's flash of control in her eyes. She stopped rocking and looked him up and down approvingly. It was expertly executed. Even knowing she'd been using her methods on Loomis earlier, he felt foolishly flattered by her positive appraisal.

"None of my party was here at the time of David Hollister's death. We are free to come and go as long as we inform the deputy."

"That hardly seems fair. Will they return?" Her sense of fairness apparently revolved around her own needs. In that way, she was like Rachel. But her bluntness was vastly different. Rachel had had the annoying ability to mention something in a circuitous manner, leaving him feeling vaguely guilty for something not his fault.

He remained silent to see her reaction. She smiled, then bit her lip with a questioning lift of her brow. He allowed a small smile of response. He was aware that after recent events on the beach he would find a cockroach charming. Still, she did possess something that made a man feel singled out, attractive.

A few seagulls exchanged words. She twirled a lock of dark hair that tickled her neck. She licked her lips.

He cleared his throat. "What is your theory about what happened to Mr. Hollister?"

She tipped her head, her expression full of pity. "I didn't know the man. He was the handyman here. Married to the cook, I'm told. Such a shame."

"So you never spoke with him?"

"Only to ask about the laundry and such."

"What about your husband?"

She gave a little sigh. "Freddie talks with everyone. He's hopelessly friendly, a regular gadabout. I've tried being like him, but I'm no good at finding that balance."

"Balance?"

"Oh, you know, if I chat up the maids, they soon stop doing their jobs properly. I don't seem to have an aura of command. No queens of England in my ancestry. Only courtesans and a few indentured servants." She tilted her head and said with mock disapproval, "My grandmother was mistress to some duke or other in Cornwall. I inherited her eyes, but not much else."

"I see."

"I doubt you do see, Professor. You can't know what it's like to be a woman in this world without beauty or wealth."

Mrs. Hornsby said that Mrs. Thompson came from a wealthy home. Did she now resent her choice of husband? Did she regret being tied to a man with a modest income? Is that why she flirted with Loomis and Moss? Hoping for expensive gifts? He said, "Beauty and wealth are subjective, Mrs. Thompson."

She laughed. "I don't know what you mean by that, Professor, but I know what it's like to not have enough of either. Are you rich?"

"Not hardly."

"No? That's disappointing. You're smart enough to be rich, I'm sure of that."

He smiled at her attempt to flatter him as he looked out at the figures on the beach. Freddie Thompson flung down a cigarette end, fished another from his pocket case, and a match flared. "Your husband appears greatly agitated."

She sat back. "I'm not at all impressed with Healing Sands. The curdled meals, the herbal teas. And all those horrid milk dishes."

"You seemed to enjoy your meal this afternoon."

"Yes, well, I've discovered that if you don't breathe through your nose, you don't notice the taste as much. And I must admit my skin has never looked better." She touched her fingertips to her jaw line. "But as far as I can tell those little white pills Dr. Hornsby dispenses, calls it homeopathy, are just milk sugar. Even he says the amount of medicine in them is so small it can't be measured. I ask you? How is that supposed to work?"

Bradshaw could have argued well on behalf of homeopathy, having heard Missouri on the subject many times, and he had witnessed healing that could not be attributed to the so-called placebo effect.

"Your husband is ill?"

"Oh, Dr. Hornsby says he's accumulated toxins and must be flushed, and I won't describe the horrors of that procedure. Freddie felt he needed a rest cure and he refused to go anywhere else but here. He's unsettled all the time, jumpy. His stomach plagues him. He blames the stress of his job, says it's weakening his nerves."

"Why doesn't he quit?"

"He says he must soldier on. I told Dr. Hornsby Freddie wasn't behaving normally."

"Why?"

"Why? Because he's a doctor. He's supposed to make people well."

"I meant, what about your husband's behavior isn't normal?"

"Oh, he's a jangle of nerves. He's always been fidgety and short-tempered and cruel, but now he goes about muttering and pulling his hair. It's disturbing."

Cruel? She'd slipped that word in there so casually—what did she mean by it? "But if it's the strain of his job making him ill, then the doctor can't be expected to provide a cure, can he?"

"He's expected to do something for the amount of money he's being paid." She yawned, and tilted her head back, setting the rocker slowly going again.

"Did you know that Mr. Hollister was having electrotherapy treatments?"

"We were told that Freddie was the only one having electric treatments. Afterward, we were told it had been a secret, that even his wife, the cook, didn't know."

"Your rooms are on the second floor?"

She halted the rocking and lifted an eyebrow at him. "Why yes, the back corner. My room has a view of the ocean out the north window."

"Are you aware of the comings and goings to Dr. Hornsby's office?"

She gave a little shrug, wrinkling her nose. "I'm not in the habit of prying into the concerns of other people."

"Well, then, what about your husband. Did he at any time enter Dr. Hornsby's office before or after consultation hours?"

"I don't keep track of my husband's every move. And he doesn't keep track of mine." The invitation in her eyes couldn't be clearer. He'd forgotten what it was like to be flirted with, or rather, to be aware of being flirted with. He knew it was his awareness that made him different tonight. He took a deep breath and tried to focus.

"Do either of you know anything about electricity?"

"What would we know?"

"That's what I'm asking."

"It makes bulbs light up."

"Nothing more?"

"I tried one of those electric hair curlers that you screw into the light socket, but it burnt my hair so I got rid of it."

"Has your husband had any training with electrical devices? At work, perhaps?"

"Not that he's ever told me."

With her hair over her shoulder, and her eyes half-closed, she looked more than ever like Rachel. Yet unlike Rachel, she was so easy to read, her every thought and emotion verbalized, her attempt at seducing him blatant.

"Your husband is cruel, you said?"

He looked at her, waiting for her to elaborate, knowing she wanted to.

"He hits me, if you must know. Forces me to submit to him. Is that clear enough?"

Her demeanor had changed, hardened. Gone was the playfulness. In its place was what, hatred? No, it was more controlled than that. And colder.

He thought of what he'd observed of them today at lunch. Appearances could be deceiving—his own marriage had looked idyllic from the outside. But the power roles were off here. His own wife in public had fawned on him, not been demanding. Or was that the game of the Thompsons' marriage, in private he dominated then regretted, and in public she had control?

"Why do you stay with him?"

"I could say I made a vow, but that's not why. The truth is I'm afraid to leave him, to be on my own. Who would take care of me? I suppose I'll have to figure it out soon enough. Now he's dying, I'll be left alone."

"His condition is that serious?"

"He took a turn for the worse the other night, I thought he wouldn't recover. He had a reaction to the glowing sand. Did you see it? No, you weren't here. The ocean and sand were blue, all sparkly blue. Frightening and thrilling at the same time. I told Freddie he should stay away from it. A man in his condition, already weak, shouldn't dip his hands in phosphorus. Everyone knows phosphorus is poisonous. But he wouldn't listen. He swam in it. Well, I tried. He was sick in the night, miserable. What did he expect? He must not have swallowed much though, he wasn't glowing."

Anger flashed through Bradshaw. He wanted to tell her not to be so stupid. It wasn't phosphorus in the water that made it glow. Phosphorus was a mineral, a chemical element. Yes, it glowed, but that didn't mean everything that glowed contained phosphorus. What silenced him was the knowledge he would be explaining out of anger, to belittle her. He felt the urge to be mean. He wanted to tell her she was stupid and selfish and ridiculous, her flirtation obvious and unwelcome. But he possessed enough self-awareness to know he was angry at himself, not Ingrid Thompson. Angry that he'd been told what he so longed to hear from Missouri and he still could not decide what to do.

He looked at Mrs. Thompson with a critical eye. "You don't wear the felt slippers provided?"

"Oh, no. They're too flat. I need a heel or my back hurts." She lifted a small foot and rotated her ankle to display the silk house-shoes with the low heel, material unsuitable for street or beach use. They would have been ruined had she worn them on the beach. "Freddie sent for these from Aberdeen. We put felt on the bottom so the doctor couldn't complain." She yawned again without apology. "Are we done, Professor?"

"Yes, thank you, Mrs. Thompson. I'll find you if I have more questions."

She rose from the rocker and headed for the front door. She had a sturdy stride with a feminine swing, making him think again of hardy peasants. He looked toward Freddie, a stick of a man, hunched with illness, arms hanging limp at his sides. If he'd ever forced himself on his wife, surely those days were over.

Chapter Thirteen

That night, he didn't sleep. He sat on the porch of his small cabin, wrapped in a wool blanket, watching the ocean, the white foam crests illuminated by starlight. There wasn't much wind. Gentle steady waves built to a deep rumble, a small crash, and a hiss of withdrawal.

The hotel in Everett near the theater, where he'd stayed with Ann, had been near the waterfront. In the early morning hours when all was still, the gentle wash of the tide would carry through the open window. Just as they were drifting off to sleep, they'd hear the sea birds waking. He'd met Ann while working on a case. She'd been the lead actress at the Seattle Grand, and still was, when she wasn't touring. She had generous curves, a big voice, and a bigger heart. The audiences loved her. And Bradshaw? What did he feel for her? They'd actually talked about love and decided the word didn't fit them, not in the romantic sense. Which made them laugh considering where they were when they made that decision. He said he adored her, and she said good, and they'd laughed again. He'd thought how shocked his friends and colleagues would be if they'd seen him laughing so much. His laughter would likely surprise them more than his affair.

Ann had a colorful and at times troubled life, only she handled trauma with much more aplomb then he did, finding humor in dark moments, and proverbial silver linings in every cloud. Which reminded him of Missouri.

Missouri knew about Ann. He groaned and hugged the blanket more tightly around his shoulders against the cold night wind.

How had she known? And how could she approve? In hindsight, yes, the relationship had been liberating. But Missouri's approval staggered him, as did her pronouncement today. She loved him. Yet it seemed impossible he could ever have with her what he'd had with Ann. He'd had nothing to lose with Ann. He'd not feared harming her or changing her or holding her back from what her life could be.

Missouri was different. With Missouri, everything was at stake.

At dawn, Justin came padding across the sand barefoot, dressed in beach clothes under his wool jacket.

Bradshaw said, "You're up early."

"I'm going exploring," he said, but he squeezed into the rocker with Bradshaw, and they rocked companionably watching the sky brighten and seagulls dive for their breakfast.

"Where's Paul?"

"Sleeping. He snores. Will you have to work all day?"

"I don't yet know. I'm sorry I missed your sand castle yesterday. Did the crabs attack?"

"No, they ran away. Paul and I are going to build a fort with driftwood. Is that OK?"

"Yes, I think that's a fine plan."

"Could you come see it when it's done?"

"Build it out of the reach of the tide, and I'll be sure to see it."

"Did you figure out yet how Mr. Hollister died?"

"No, son. I'm still investigating."

"Did Doctor Hornsby make a mistake with the settings?"

"No, he did nothing wrong."

"Paul said that if the doctor didn't mess up, then Mr. Hollister must have done it himself."

"What do you mean, son?"

"Mr. Hollister must have done something to make the machine deadly. It couldn't have killed anyone otherwise. You showed it to me when you built it. I was just a kid then, only in the first grade, but I remember. Why would someone do that to the machine?"

"That's a question I can't yet answer."

"Paul says Mr. Hollister might have wanted to die. He said that's called suicide."

The dread word caught Bradshaw by surprise. He managed to say, "Paul certainly has a breadth of knowledge beyond his years."

"It's because he's got big sisters. They talk all the time, on and on and on."

"Some people are like that."

"You're not. You don't talk unless you've got something important to say."

"Thank you, son."

"So it's true? That sometimes people do kill themselves?"

What should he say? For the past decade, he knew he would one day need to have such a conversation with Justin. Several times the secret of his mother's suicide had been used as a threat. It would be better for Justin to hear it from him than from anyone else. But now? The boy was too young. He couldn't.

He said carefully, "Sometimes people who aren't well feel so bad they don't want to go on living. There are some illnesses doctors don't yet know how to fix."

Justin turned and looked at him, searching his eyes. "Was my mother one of those sick people who didn't want to go on living?"

It was as if the air had vanished. Bradshaw couldn't breathe. What had he said? How had the boy guessed?

Justin said, "You used the voice you always use when I ask about her."

"I use a different voice?"

"It's real quiet. Like you're afraid of hurting me. Is that why you're always so sad when you talk about her?"

Bradshaw nodded, hating he was admitting it, knowing he could do nothing else. "Yes, son. The doctors couldn't help her." He wrapped his arm around the boy and held him tight, resting his cheek on the boy's fair head.

Justin knew. The horrible secret was out. No details, those would come later. He felt no measure of relief that he no longer had to hide the fact. A weight had sunk like cement to his gut and there he was sure it would remain forever. He was sick that his son now knew something so awful.

Justin said, "You wouldn't ever want to die, would you?"

"No, never."

"What if you got sick? Something the doctor's couldn't fix?"

"I would always want to live to see what sort of mischief you've been up to."

"Promise?"

"I promise. In fact, I think I'll aim for a hundred and two, so that I can see all the mischief your grandchildren get up to."

"A hundred and two! How old are you now?"

"I turned thirty-eight in June."

Justin was quick with mental arithmetic. "That would mean you'll live until 1967!"

"What do you suppose will have been invented by then, son?"

"Oh, flying machines, for sure. Maybe even spaceships."

"You think? That's not just the stuff of fiction?"

"If you can imagine it, you can make it, isn't that what you always tell me?"

"I do. Glad to hear you've been listening." His stomached growled so loudly, Justin began to laugh.

"Maybe we should go up to the house and see if there's any breakfast."

"Oh, it'll be another hour or so yet. How about we go explore the beach together until then."

"Really? You'll come with me?" Justin jumped up. "Come on, there's a gigantic starfish trapped in a pool you've got to see!"

Chapter Fourteen

A rich, warm fragrance greeted them in the dining room, and for a moment Bradshaw silently begged, *please let there be coffee.* The origin of the teasing aroma turned out to be brewed roasted barley. Mellow, slightly sweet, non-stimulating. His taste buds told him it wasn't coffee or Postum, his favored evening drink, but it was better than anything he'd been served thus far.

As Justin was busy dishing up his breakfast in the kitchen, Bradshaw pulled Mrs. Prouty out into the hall. Her broad face showed a touch of color, and the tip of her nose was pink from the sun. Her solid and sturdy no-nonsense stance bolstered Bradshaw even though the red stripes of her bathing costume showed though her shirtwaist. Ten years ago, when Mrs. Prouty was newly arrived from England, he'd chosen her from a lineup of housekeepers, and today he was especially grateful for her unwavering presence in Justin's life.

"What is it, Professor? You look a fright this morning. Not sleeping well? You know how you get when you don't sleep. You black out. Remember when you lost a whole day when you were searching for that peddler's child? You do that here and the tide'll come take you away."

"Mrs. Prouty, it's about Justin. He has learned that his mother's death was self-inflicted."

She gave a small gasp, but otherwise took the news with her usual fortitude.

"He doesn't know any details. He believes she was ill and unhappy and the doctors couldn't help her. I wanted you to know in case he asks questions or he seems quiet or upset."

"Why did you tell him?"

"I didn't, he guessed. With everything happening here, he began thinking. The important thing now is to keep an eye on him."

"As his father, it's your place to answer his questions. What would you like me to say if he asks me anything?"

"If they're general questions, and you feel comfortable, answer them, otherwise, tell him to come see me."

"I'm so sorry, Professor."

"Me, too."

When they returned to the kitchen, false smiles on their faces, Bradshaw tried to bypass the grain portion of the meal, but Mrs. Hornsby caught him with just the barley drink and berries and offered him fat slices of sourdough bread lavishly buttered. It was only after he accepted that he realized the butter today was dark yellow, not pale.

He and Mrs. Prouty joined Justin and Paul. They appeared their usual, boyish selves. Had Justin told Paul, he wondered? And might not that be a good thing? Paul was a worldly little fellow who liked to boast of his acquired knowledge, finding the world's traumas a constant source of entertainment. Yet the more sensational, the more he liked to shrug and take it in stride.

Each boy now sat before a bowl of congealed fermented millet, topped with wild blueberries. The millet was lighter in texture than the oats had been, and slimier. Bradshaw was slightly queasy watching the boys devour it. All the fresh air had made them ravenous and less picky than they tended to be at home. A tentative bite told him what he feared—fishy. Mrs. Thompson's trick of avoiding breathing through the nose helped, but it was far from an enjoyable meal.

The Thompsons ate alone. Freddie served them both while Ingrid sat immersed in an issue of *The Smart Set: A Magazine of Cleverness*. Bradshaw had seen a copy of that once. Once was enough. Long, dreary stories of society and fashion and the sort of events and romantic maneuverings he avoided like the plague. Little quips and jokes and poems of indecisive women longing for hats and men and devotion. He gave a little shudder and continued his perusal of the room.

Like yesterday, Loomis and Moss sat together, eating solitary meals, speaking not at all. Did their silent companionship mean anything? Or did they simply not like to eat a meal in public alone?

The chatter of his students and Mrs. Prouty, along with the clink of utensils, lent a gay normalcy from which Bradshaw felt excluded. Missouri had not come to breakfast.

To quiet his grumbling stomach, he finished his bread and barley tea before heading out to the beach with his students to get them started on their project for the day.

"Look about you," he told the four young men, for Colin and Henry had not yet returned, "and observe a bounty of energy sources. How many can you name?"

"Wind, sun, water, wood," chanted Knut.

"Yes, any more?"

"Chemical?" asked Miles. "Like acids, salts, minerals?"

"Yes, any more?"

"Oil maybe? Or natural gas?"

"Possibly, someone down the coast is hoping so. Any more?"

"Whales," said Oren. "You know, blubber."

"Not easy to secure, but yes. There are even more energy sources, and as you go through the day, take note of any you think of. Your mission today is to harness a source of energy to produce electric power. You may use anything from the crate." He waved his hand over the supply he'd brought of odds and ends from the engineering lab. "And anything you can scavenge from the beach or woods. You are not to take anything that is the property of Healing Sands."

They reached into the crate and began pulling out items, debating about what energy source to use until Knut shouted, "Hey, they're back!"

With a long toot of a ridiculous sounding horn, Henry and Colin inched their way across the shallowest portion of the creek, and once successfully across, raced toward them on the hard-packed sand. The lesson was momentarily interrupted to welcome them back. Justin and Paul came running, and even Mrs. Prouty got up from her beach chair to greet Henry and Colin as if they'd been on a long adventure rather than an overnighter to Hoquiam.

Henry had brought kite kits for the small boys, which earned him hugs, and chocolate for Mrs. Prouty, which earned him a smile. Colin had brought back the makings of a large box kite and asked permission to build it.

"Like the Wrights built a few years ago. The conditions are perfect here for flying it."

Bradshaw considered the request a moment and decided Colin's enthusiasm was the sort that fueled invention. And he liked the idea that this additional project would keep him too busy to make puppy eyes at Missouri. "Yes, but build it near the others so that you can take part in the assignment. The others will explain."

"Someone else is coming!" Paul pointed toward the creek at a horse-drawn wagon.

Henry said, "That's the postman. We came across on the same steamer." He lifted a hand in greeting as the driver leaped from the wagon with his mail bag and gave a hearty hail before hurrying up to the house. He dropped the bag on the porch and was on his way with a wave.

Henry said, "He's gotta get a move on or he'll miss the tide further up. You free?"

"In a minute. I need to get my students set up."

"Right. Meet me at your place."

Henry pulled the Stanley over to Camp Franklin Cabin and disappeared inside. A few minutes later, Bradshaw found his friend in stockinged feet at the small table with a sturdy cardboard box and two fat manila envelopes, being annoyingly perky as he gave Bradshaw an assessing sweep.

"Why the hang-dog look?"

"I didn't sleep."

"Well, I did. Colin and I shacked up at the Grand Hoquiam, that big place at the station? We had a big old steak dinner, and a salmon fillet, a *cooked* salmon, the size of my left arm, lots of *sweet* butter and potatoes, not a bit of fiber or green vegetable or yellow milk to be seen. Topped it off with a few whiskeys. Poor boy said I snored something awful, heard me clean in the next room. Had to push his bed to the other side to get any peace. Ha! Brought us back some contraband, if you're feeling peckish."

"Coffee?"

"And a pot and mugs."

"Henry, I love you."

"Ha!"

They built a fire in the small wood stove and got the coffee percolating. The smell made Bradshaw happily woozy.

Henry said, "I can't make this in my room, I'll come visit you mornings before breakfast. I'll stash the rest of the essentials here, too. Don't hog 'em." He'd brought whiskey, chocolate, tinned cookies, cigars, beef jerky, and Bradshaw's favored evening drink, Postum, which reflected their friendship. Henry never touched the stuff.

"Ben, is that—?" Henry was looking at the urn in the corner. For nearly two years now, Bradshaw had kept it at home as he searched for the proper final resting place, shifting it from one inconspicuous spot to another. One didn't put the ashes of a convicted murderer on display. He'd tried his own bedroom, but its presence haunted his sleep. He'd tried his closet, but that had felt cruel, so hidden away. He'd settled on a shelf in his basement workshop, visible to him and Henry, unnoticed by others, knowing it still wasn't right.

"He wrote of the ocean in his journal," Bradshaw said.

"You're a better man than me."

"No, Henry. It's simply that I knew him, perhaps better than anyone."

"He tried to kill you."

"I haven't forgotten."

Over a meal of coffee, shortbread, and jerky, they began to examine the contents of the manila envelopes that had arrived on the night train in Hoquiam. Professor Hill had exceeded Bradshaw's expectations. In the envelope, he found his diagrams and notes, and a 1901 issue of *American Electrician*, bookmarked at a paragraph in the Anecdote section about a Mr. Arnold Loomis of Seattle, Washington, who had demonstrated a superior electrotheraputic outfit to physicians in Spokane the previous year, taken deposits, and failed to deliver the promised apparatus. The editor had found Mr. Loomis in Portland, Oregon, and was assured production delays would soon be solved.

Henry said, "You subscribe to this magazine, don't you?"

"Yes, but I don't always read it cover-to-cover." He thought of Well's time machine again, and wished he could go back and see this.

Squirrel also impressed him at the speed of his work. He couldn't have had more than two hours to search, yet he'd sent clippings of the announcement of the opening of Healing Sands, the engagement of Martha Hornsby to David Hollister, the arrival of the gold ship bearing Zebediah Moss, and the wedding of Ingrid Colby to Frederick Thompson of Seattle. He'd also found an article that mentioned Arnold Loomis had taken part in a business meeting on developing Washington's resources and that he'd "had keen insight into the potential of the coast with the expansion of the railroad."

"Ben, I can't believe you handed over your outfit to that man."

"I trusted him at the time, and it was his idea to build it. It never occurred to me I was being used. I spent a few pleasant weeks designing and learning something about medical electricity. I wasn't horribly disappointed to find we'd been beaten to market. It happens. Besides, there was nothing new, revolutionary, or patented—other than my coil—it's all been done before and considered public domain."

"It's not like you to be so trusting."

"That's why men like him are called confidence men. He's very good at making others believe what he says."

"Huh. I would've seen through him."

"You would have given him your last dollar."

"I'm shrewder than you realize."

"You're gullible when opportunity is dangled before your eyes."

"You just wait and see, Ben, my old friend. I'll be a success yet. I won't always be living in your spare room."

"You are a success now, if we don't use money as the yardstick. The room isn't spare, it's yours, as long as you please. As for Loomis, just let him talk and try to remember the details. He may have tried a swindle on David Hollister, and he's trying something on Dr. Hornsby." He explained what he learned from Mrs. Hornsby about Loomis' pressure to expand Healings Sands and Martha's regret about Loomis drawing up plans for the washhouse.

"When I was in Nome, there was just one steam laundry and the dirty dogs charged fifty cents a shirt. If you dared complain, they added a two dollar fee to your tab. Some fellers sent their laundry home to be washed. Twenty-seven hundred miles to Seattle and back, it'd take a month, and it was still cheaper than getting it washed local."

"I don't remember you sending your laundry home."

"Nah, I just stayed filthy. Beat my clothes on a rock once in a while to get off the big hunks. David Hollister's fancy laundry—could that be a motive for Loomis?"

"Possibly. But he'd already wrangled the washhouse design from Hollister, so I don't see the point."

"Maybe Hollister got wise and told Loomis he wasn't going to be robbed. What are you going to do?"

"I don't know yet. It will depend on what else we learn."

"What's Loomis got to say?"

"I haven't spoken to him yet."

"Letting him sweat? Good plan. I'd like a chance at him. I've got a claim worth eighty dollars a shovel I'd like to sell him."

"Con the con man? I'd like to see that. In fact…." In fact, interviewing Loomis successfully would require an approach verging on a con. It would require Bradshaw to practice the art of manipulative conversation, which he loathed.

Henry said, "Uh-oh, I know that look. Loomis is in for it. Hey, look at this." Henry handed Bradshaw a clipping from the *Seattle Post-Intelligencer* detailing Zebediah's new life as a millionaire.

"In his mansion on First Hill, Mr. Moss leads a modest life. Wealth has not changed him. He lives there by himself, with no servants, not even a cook. He eats at Seattle's many restaurants, preferring of late the dining room of the Lincoln Hotel, and sends his laundry out. When asked if he ever hires a daily maid, he said, 'What fer? I don't make a mess, do I?'" Henry grunted with disgust. "Waste of good fortune."

"He eats at the Lincoln? Don't the Thompsons live at the Lincoln?" Bradshaw looked again at the clipping on the Thompsons' marriage. "The newlyweds plan to move into rooms at the Lincoln-Hotel Apartments."

"Huh."

"Indeed. I spoke with Ingrid Thompson last night." He told Henry about their conversation, her flirtation, how Old Cedar had observed her with both Loomis and Moss, and how he had seen her with Loomis as well. "She claims her husband beats her and that he's dying of some mysterious illness and behaving erratically."

Henry shivered. "I know the type. Kiss your face while stealing your wallet. Any truth to her accusations? Is Freddie a mean son-of-a-bitch on his last breath?"

"I don't yet know."

"Why'd she tell you? She knows you're looking into a man's death, that you're looking at everyone suspiciously. Why does she go and point to her husband as being unbalanced and violent?"

"Loyal, isn't she?"

"Exactly why I don't marry. Never trust a female. But why would Freddie want to kill David? What's his motive? Or did

Freddie short the machine to kill himself, not knowing David would get it first? What would be the point? Why not just go in there and zap himself and get it over with?"

"Being a coward about it? Maybe he couldn't work up the nerve, so he set it up for the doctor to inflict the lethal current."

"To hell with what he'd put the poor doctor through, eh? I don't know, Ben. He doesn't strike me as that sort of man."

"You never know what people are capable of." Rachel had taught him that. Rachel had taught him insane people could appear rational, that otherwise intelligent people could make stupid decisions. Rachel, through her final ill-thought act, had taught him that insanity could reach up from the grave and hurt the most innocent of victims.

He cussed, a single expletive that hit the cabin walls and made Henry jump.

"What the hell, Ben? What's got into you? Take a nap."

"Justin knows. About his mother."

Henry gasped. "How?"

"Apparently, I have a voice."

"You gonna tell me what that means?"

He explained his morning conversation with Justin. "I've destroyed my son's childhood. His mother's suicide is part of his life now. He'll think about it. He'll question it. He'll want particulars. He'll wonder why."

"I'm sorry, Ben. But he had to learn sometime. It's best it came from you."

"There is no best here, Henry. There is only the awful truth."

Chapter Fifteen

The belt drive was engaged, humming smoothly along the line of washing equipment, sending the machines steaming, agitating, spinning, and tumbling. Fans whisked much of the moisture out of the building, but a damp clean fragrance remained—a blend of soap, bluing, starch, and chlorine bleach. Bradshaw took a moment to admire the laundry in full operation. Well-oiled gears and careful design kept noise at a minimum as the machines toiled.

He hadn't seen Hornsby's daughters, Abigail and Dolley, since he met them yesterday in the library. They'd gone about their work in the main house invisibly, sweeping and polishing, and performing all the daily tasks necessary to keep such an establishment in good order.

He found them now at the far end of the laundry near the drying closet, performing what looked like an elegant square dance. Each held the corners of a pristine white sheet, and after giving it a snapping shake, they moved toward each other, arms held high, touching hands when they met before stepping back to separate, waltzing a quarter circle, then meeting again. After several passes, unfolding and refolding, they met for a final time holding a small flat square, and they bowed to each other. Bradshaw applauded, and the girls bowed to him, then blushed a bit as they laughed.

Bradshaw was glad to see that their youthful, joyful innocence had not been completely obliterated by recent events.

Dolley, a bosomy young woman like her mother and older sister, said, "We used to hate folding sheets, but now it's our favorite part of the laundry. That was our square dance, because we end up with a square. We also have a triangle dance, and a star dance, but we can only do that with the big sheets from our parents' bed. Is it time for you to question us, Professor?"

"If it's convenient for you to take a break."

"You don't have to ask us twice." Dolley led him and Abigail, who was smaller and quieter, out a side door to a cluster of sun-bleached chairs. The girls sat with audible sighs. Dolley told him they'd begun work at five that morning, and without prompting, continued talking about life at Healing Sands and her opinion of the four detained guests.

"We don't visit with guests much, mind you, it's not professional. And Momma says there's a fine line between friendly service and familiar service. When guests get too familiar with you, it's just harder to get them to follow the rules. Mr. Thompson is a decent sort, as far as I can tell. He always says thank you and please, and obeys all the rules, but that Mrs. Thompson is trouble."

Bradshaw smiled at Dolley's choice of description, and she was quick to notice.

"You've seen it, haven't you, Professor? Lazy, is what she is. Isn't that right, Abbie?"

Abigail nodded and added, "She's awful stuck-up with no reason to be. How do the unattractive ones get the good-looking men?"

"She's got a way with her," Dolley countered. "It's in the eyes. She's not pretty, I grant you, but she knows how to use what she's got to get her husband fetching for her. You think Mr. Thompson is good-looking? He's too thin and nervous to be handsome."

"He looks like a driven artist to me," Abigail said. "He should be French."

Dolley wrinkled her nose. "I've never seen him do anything the slightest bit artistic. All he does is dote on his wife."

Bradshaw asked, "Have you noticed any odd behavior by any of the guests?"

"Like what? All our guests are odd, I'd say," said Dolley.

"Did you see anyone where they shouldn't have been?"

Abigail said, "Well, I didn't see which of them took it, but Dolley, do you remember when the fancy cheese disappeared from the larder?"

"You have cheese? Real cheese?" Bradshaw tasted a flicker of hope for future meals.

"Not usually," Dolley said. "Papa says it's too binding for everyday consumption. But a former patient sent it as a gift to Papa. Fancy imported cheese, mind you. Looked like little round Christmas gifts, wrapped in shiny green and gold. We'd served some of it to the guests one evening last week because Papa said the cabbage had been a bit too potent—"

Abigail said, "Dolley!"

"Oh, the Professor is a man of science, he's not embarrassed about such things. Anyway, someone swiped it. Waltzed right in the kitchen and took the last of it. I hope who ever took it doesn't have a movement for a month."

"Dolley! Professor, please forgive her. She's so used to Papa's ease with talking about such matters. And whoever took it must have had a change of heart, or appetite, because I found the cheese the next day on the sideboard in the dining room, unwrapped but the wax not even broken."

"Do all your guests help themselves to the larder?"

"No," Dolley said, "most have better manners. But some get the notion that because they dish out their own meals and wash their own dishes they have rights to all the stores. But really, it's just rude to take without asking. We ought to post a sign on the door."

Abigail tossed up her hands. "Not another sign, the whole place is lousy with them."

"Can you recall the guests being elsewhere they shouldn't have been?"

"You mean like upstairs in the electrotherapy room? No, we talked about that, but we never saw anyone go in when father wasn't there. Of course, we're not upstairs all that much."

"Did you ever notice anyone wearing shoes in the house?" he asked.

Dolley gasped. "Father would have a fit! No, they've all been good about that. Even Mrs. Thompson, in her little heeled slippers. Only the sheriff has dared tromping around in his boots."

"What about the night of the glowing sand?" The question sent them chattering about the strange phenomenon.

"We saw it once before, when we were little. Abigail was afraid of it."

"You told me the sand was haunted and that ghosts were trying to escape."

"Did I? Oh, I am sorry. But it wasn't scary this time, only a bit spooky. What causes the sand to glow like that, Professor?"

He hesitated, trying to decide what information wasn't likely to alter their memories or skew their attitudes toward past events. He settled on saying, "It's called bioluminescence."

"David would have liked that word," said Abigail. "He was so clever. He told us all about the glowing sand being some sort of phosphor. He'd have liked to know the official word for it. He kept scooping seawater on Martha, trying to make her glow like the sand. I remember thinking that I hoped I'd someday meet a man like David." She shook her head, and her face trembled, and she fumbled for a handkerchief.

Dolley patted her sister's arm, and in answer to Bradshaw's question about who else was on the beach that night, said, "Oh, everyone was there. Mr. Loomis, Mr. Moss, but he didn't seem too impressed. Said he'd seen better. Such a sour puss. The Thompsons enjoyed it, splashing about. Mrs. Thompson knocked Mr. Thompson clean over and he went for a swim!"

"She knocked him over?"

Abigail sniffed and dabbed her eyes. "Just horseplay. I was surprised, really. I didn't think she had it in her to be playful."

"She was putting on a show, Abbie. Honestly, you are so gullible. She had an audience." Dolley looked at Bradshaw. "Men. Mrs. Thompson ignores women and plays up to men. Flirts with them shamelessly and they all fall for it. Well, not my father, and she doesn't even try with him. Plays the helpless, concerned wife around him."

"She was playing up to Mr. Moss and Mr. Loomis?"

"And her husband. She splashed them all and they took it, laughing. Well, Mr. Moss didn't laugh, but he looked more pleased than I've ever seen him. None of them attempted to splash her, of course. Can you imagine what her reaction would have been? Oh, she has them trained. And who had to launder their soaked clothing?"

"Did anyone collect any of the glowing sand?"

They shrugged, and Dolley said, "I can't say as I recall. People collect all sorts of things to take home. Sand, shells, driftwood. Goodness knows what they do with it. Make little displays, I suppose, to show their city friends. I wish I'd thought to keep some glowing sand to remember David by."

Bradshaw said, "It stops glowing after a day or so."

"Does it? Oh, well, then it's no matter. What else would you like to know, Professor? Are we being of any help?"

"Yes, you are. Can you tell me more about Mr. Moss?"

"He's forever lurking about. Never doing anything mind you, it's just he's suddenly there, with his sad eyes. He's not been so bad since our tragedy. At least, he doesn't come to the house as much."

"And Mr. Loomis?"

Dolley's expression hardened. "He's too polite. I don't like him."

Abigail blushed. "Oh, I do. He always calls me by name, and he remembers to thank me for even little things."

"Abbie, you watch out for him. A man his age isn't likely to be so considerate of a girl unless he wants something from her."

This was one time Bradshaw gladly added information that would alter the attitudes of those involved. "I agree with Dolley. Mr. Loomis is not a man to be trusted."

Chapter Sixteen

Before tackling the next three interviews, Bradshaw felt a conference with Doctor Hornsby was in order. He found him in his office, holding a clipboard and scratching his head over his array of colorful bottles.

"Good morning, Professor, or—" he glanced at the wall clock, "—yes, still morning. I have no concept of time these days. And no memory for detail either." He scowled again at his bottles.

"Something wrong?"

"Oh, no. I just keep misplacing things. Stress-induced memory loss. I can diagnose it, but I can't seem to cure it. Now my tincture of gentian is missing. It'll turn up in the most unlikely of places. I found my hairbrush in my sock drawer earlier. What can I do for you, Professor?"

They both sat, and Bradshaw gave him full details of his past association with Arnold Loomis.

"It came as quite a shock to hear you say you'd built the Luminator."

Bradshaw cringed at the name. "I apologize for surprising you in the library."

Hornsby nodded. "Loomis. I wish to God I'd never heard the name. He's staying here gratis, did I tell you that? I'm not really sure how that happened. I can't recall offering. He's been trying to get me to build more cabins, hire more help, says he envisions Healing Sands being as famous as Kellogg's place in Battle Creek, Michigan. But I don't want fame. I don't even want fortune. I want to help people heal in my small sanitarium in this beautiful place. He wants to turn it into a zoo. Martha said she told you about how he drew up plans for David's washhouse? He can't sell the plans, can he?"

Hornsby was sounding both weary and frantic. Bradshaw found a drinking glass, filled it from the tap in the electrotherapy room, and gave it to the doctor, who took a sip. Bradshaw prodded him as if he were a child until he'd emptied the glass.

"Doctor, what did Loomis charge you for the outfit?"

Hornsby rubbed his mouth then sighed. "Too much. I'd trade my bank account for what that machine cost me."

Bradshaw strode to the window and for a moment watched the waves wash in. Then his eye fell nearer to the house and the lounge chair under the umbrella. Mrs. Thompson was there again, reclining. "Doctor, did you say that Ingrid Thompson is in her late twenties?"

"I did. I take it by your question you doubt that age? So do I. But she stuck to it when I probed. She came here to find peace and healing, and while it's my personal belief that living a lie isn't conducive to either, it's her secret to keep. Between you and me? I treated her medically as I would any woman between the ages of thirty and forty."

"Does her husband suspect she lies about her age?"

"I think he believes whatever she tells him. He's that sort, led through the nose. Well, he's happy, so I suppose it harms no one."

"But he isn't happy, he's severely agitated, maybe even suicidal."

"Oh, no, I wouldn't go so far as that. His gastric upset is due to the release of toxins. It doesn't originate from his relationship with his wife, hard as it is to believe. He's devoted to her."

"Can you tell me if you've seen any evidence of physical abuse?"

"Oh, my, no. She doesn't hit him."

He pondered that a moment. It was interesting that Hornsby's first thought had been of Ingrid abusing Freddie. "I meant does he hit her?"

"No, no, gentle as a mouse is Mr. Thompson. Poor man. He suffers from a toxic condition all too common these days that manifests in a digestive disorder, decreased weight, and what is commonly referred to as the fidgets. He has every sign of lead poisoning. You know he works at the Federal Assay Office? Lead oxide is a major component of the flux used in the melting process to separate the gold from the ore. Since coming here, I've been slowly flushing his system. It's dangerous to flush too quickly. Even so, occasionally, the body will release large doses into the bloodstream, and that's what happened the other night. He was taken violently ill, and I considered transporting him to the hospital. But the symptoms abated, and he seems to have turned a corner. It's that way, sometimes. The body reaches a crisis point, and becomes stronger for the experience."

Bradshaw turned back to the window. Zebediah Moss now sat perched where yesterday Arnold Loomis had, at Ingrid Thompson's feet.

"Could you show me the books and magazines you mentioned? The ones on electrotherapy?"

"Certainly." Hornsby rose slowly and led Bradshaw downstairs to the library. The materials on electrotherapy were shelved together, the magazines neatly stacked beside the textbooks.

"Did the Thompsons, Moss, or Loomis read these?"

"I can't say I ever saw Mr. Moss reading in the library, but Mr. Thompson, yes, he was curious about the treatment I was administering, and I encourage my patients to educate themselves."

"What about Mrs. Thompson?"

"Oh, I doubt if she's read them. You could ask her of course, but I've never seen her with anything so substantial. When she found nothing in the library to her liking, she mailed for some fashion magazines."

"What about Mr. Loomis?"

"Loomis? He has no need to examine my materials, does he? He seems so knowledgeable." Hornsby stared at Bradshaw. "Professor, I am well versed in electrotherapeutic devices and I can tell you, he has a thorough knowledge of the subject."

"I'm sure he is quite believable, but four years ago he was merely a salesman hoping to find fortune bringing a new outfit to market. He knew nothing of the science himself. He's had plenty of time to learn, of course, but it's possible he has merely learned the language of the field, not the actual science."

Hornsby picked up a magazine and leafed through it absently. "He did like to peruse the new journals when they arrived. He said he could have written many of the articles himself."

"Where was he the day before and the morning of David's death?"

"Oh. It's hard to say. His habits here are the same as everyone else's. At any given time, he could have been in his room, eating, on the beach. I didn't *interrogate* everyone before you arrived, Professor, but I did talk to them to see if anyone could shed some light on the tragedy. Of course, I believed it to be just that, a tragic accident. I'm still holding out hope you find out it was an accident after all." Hornsby's expression was so pleading, Bradshaw felt it best not to encourage false hope. He shook his head, and the doctor's face fell.

"I'll study these for awhile, Doctor. Thank you for your help."

Hornsby nodded and wandered off, leaving Bradshaw alone to concentrate. He examined the materials systematically, reading the tables of content, flipping each page for relevant images or diagrams.

In a well-thumbed *Fischer Magazine*, he found a diagram of the internal components of a typical cabinet style diathermy outfit, consisting of a coil and Leyden jar capacitors. The text explained the danger of the primary and secondary coils shorting because of inefficient insulating distance between them. It also explained the function of the Leyden jars in the circuit, saying, *"without them, the full force of the supply current would be delivered to the patient with damaging or fatal results."* The journal was written as a warning for would-be coil makers, amateur engineers, or physicians attempting a do-it-yourself: *"Why risk injury to you or your patients with a home-built? Buy Fischer!"* Had Loomis read this? Had he grasped it well enough to know that the Leyden jars could be bypassed by creating a short with a conductive material across the carbon tops? Could anyone else here make that deduction?

Chapter Seventeen

"Professor, we know you can't discuss your investigation, but could you talk in general terms about electrotherapy?"

Bradshaw's students had pressed two tables together in the dining room so he could sit with them at lunch to discuss their morning's work. They'd argued over the energy source to harness. Oren and Colin advocated wind, Miles championed chemicals to build batteries, and Daniel felt the tide's constant movement should be tapped. Knut wanted to use them all, which was too complicated for today's assignment but did address industry needs for backup systems. They discussed the pros and cons of each over slices of a meatless-loaf made of grains, sour pickled cucumbers, and bowls of Greek yoghurt, a sour creamy food, topped with fresh blueberries. Bradshaw had eaten until his mouth refused to open, but it was enough to stave off pangs. His students had nearly licked their plates. He admired their fortitude. Now they looked at him, awaiting an answer to Daniel's question.

Oren said, "It doesn't really work, does it, Professor? Isn't electrotherapy quack medicine?"

"Some of it is, certainly, but ever since the discovery of natural magnets, men have been applying electrical fields to the body in hopes of generating healing. With each advance by men like Galvani, Volta, Franklin, and Faraday, and now Nikola Tesla, new techniques and apparatuses have been tried. The medical experts at some of the country's most prestigious hospitals have been impressed with the results of some techniques. And there's no doubt that Roentgen's x-rays have proved valuable."

Oren crossed his arms over his stocky chest. "I thought all those advertisements for electric belts and whatnot were quackery, a good way for a fool to lose his money. That's what my granddad says."

"I agree with your granddad, but there's a world of difference between the devices sold to the public through advertisements and those used by medical professionals."

"Professor," asked Miles, "why doesn't the university have any electrical medical devices in the lab, or classes on their uses?"

"Because we have no school of medicine and no faculty experts in the field of electrotherapeutics. I can teach you how to avoid injury when working with electricity but not how to apply electricity to the body for medical purposes."

"Shouldn't there be? A medical college I mean? Seattle's one of the biggest cities on the whole West Coast."

"It's been proposed, but it's costly to properly set up and maintain a first-rate medical school, and we're state funded."

He told them what he knew of the field of electrotherapeutics and the various devices, from static generators to Kinraide coils. As he lectured, the dining room emptied, and he was fully aware of Missouri's departure. She'd eaten with Justin and Paul, and he'd tried not to be distracted by her laughter mingling with theirs.

Daniel said, "You sure know a lot about the devices."

"Oh, only surface knowledge of their medical uses. The sort that gets many men in trouble because they assume it's enough to go on."

"But you designed the outfit that's here." This was said by Colin, quite seriously. They all waited silently for Bradshaw's explanation.

"I did. I built it in accordance with published medical papers about the various techniques and devices used by physicians. I improved on a few safety issues of earlier models, and made the operation of it as simple and mistake-proof as possible. I built an outfit that could provide the voltage and frequency output required, but I am not a man of medicine and I have no opinion as to the efficacy of electrotherapy."

Oren nudged Miles, who said, "Uh, Professor. Can you tell us—do you know yet if something went wrong? With your machine, we mean?"

Again, they watched him anxiously.

"Is the machine's design to blame? No. The design was not a factor, and that's all I can tell you regarding the investigation."

They all appeared relieved at his reply.

"Will we get a chance to see it?"

"It wouldn't be appropriate for me to show it to you under the circumstances."

They asked why it never went into production, and he explained that competition was fierce, and it seemed other similar machines had beat his outfit to the market.

Colin said, "You must have been disappointed."

"Disappointment is part of the inventor's world. For every patent I've been granted, I have another dozen creations stored in my basement that never made it to the patent office. I like to think of all I learned in the process, rather than patents not attained." He could have added that his few patents brought him a healthy income, which he mostly saved and invested for his son. But he didn't like to give the young men under his tutelage the idea that invention was an easy road to wealth. Invention need be a labor of passion, indeed obsession, but not a path chosen for fame and fortune.

Oren Springer said, "Gosh, Professor, how many patents do you have?"

"A dozen or so," he said. The number was actually twenty-nine, which satisfied him personally but was nothing compared to the hundreds held by men like Edison and Tesla. He'd chosen years ago to forego the mad race to the patent office in favor of being a sane and devoted father, teacher, and more recently, investigator. Occasionally, an idea did drive him to his basement, but he was careful to monitor his obsession lest he bring on the wrath of Mrs. Prouty.

Oren asked, "What's your favorite one?"

"I'd say it's a toss up between the coil and the microphone."

"What? The Bradshaw Coil is yours?"

Knut Peterson rubbed his knuckles on the top of Oren's blond head. "Kid's a genius. Three guesses what the microphone's called, first two don't count."

"The Bradshaw detective microphone!" Oren said. "It was in the last issue of the *Electrician*. And quit razzing me, Nut. It's a common enough name. How was I supposed to know? I thought all the famous inventors lived on the East Coast."

Bradshaw knew he was far from famous, but he supposed to this young man, newly introduced to the world of electrical engineering, having a mention in a magazine qualified.

"Time now for dishes and for you to return to your work."

"Can you spare Uncle Henry for a bit this afternoon?" asked Colin. "To help with the kite? He told me about a few specialty knots that would speed things up."

Knut elbowed Colin and said, "Uncle Henry, is it?" And the other boys laughed.

"I realize circumstances are unusual and we've adopted a less formal tone with this summer course, Colin, but Mr. Pratt is my colleague and your elder."

"Yes, sir. I meant no offense."

"I'm sure you didn't." Bradshaw picked up his dishes and carried them into the kitchen, resisting the urge to hurl them against the wall.

Chapter Eighteen

With his hat mashed down tight against the expected breeze, Bradshaw climbed over the drift logs, tromped through the soft low dunes, and crossed to the band of hard-packed wet sand, narrowed by high tide, until he reached Freddie Thompson.

Thompson was barefoot, with his trousers rolled to his knees and his white shirt rolled to the elbows. His head was bare. The wind lifted his thin hair like a small sail and whipped the smoke away from his face with each drag of his cigarette.

"How are you feeling, Mr. Thompson?"

Thompson finished a long draw on his cigarette, then exhaled with a slight cough. "Now there's a loaded question."

"I'll try a simpler one. When did you arrive at Healing Sands?"

He took another draw before answering. "On the fourth. We were supposed to leave three days ago."

"You work at the Seattle Assay Office?"

"Yes, that's right."

"Has it made things difficult for you, having to stay? Does it put your job in jeopardy?"

Mr. Thompson threw down his cigarette and ground it into the sand with his bare foot. "Could very well be."

The sun was nearly directly overhead, beating down and giving the breeze stiff competition. Bradshaw loosened his collar a bit and decided removing his jacket was more dignified than dripping sweat.

"Why?"

"What do you mean, *why?*"

"Why wouldn't your boss understand the circumstances?"

"They're rigid, OK? It's the federal government. I thought you were going to ask me about that infernal machine."

"Tell me about your experience with electrotherapy, then. About the last session with Dr. Hornsby before David died. Did anything unusual happen?"

"No. It went fine. He zapped me with those electrodes, told me to bury myself and calm down."

"Bury yourself?"

"On the hot beds. You lay down in the cot and the doctor covers you with sand. It's very soothing." He said the words through gritted teeth.

"Do you know anything about electricity, Mr. Thompson?"

"About as much as most. I know how to screw in a bulb."

"Do you know how to short a circuit?" He looked into Mr. Thompson's literally jaundiced eyes and was met with a narrowed glare, but no evasion.

"I don't know how to short a circuit or long a circuit. I do know the damn things are deadly and I sure as hell am never going near one ever again."

"Did you notice anyone going into Dr. Hornsby's office or the electrotherapy room, other than the doctor?"

"No."

"The morning of the incident, when did you arrive at Dr. Hornsby's office?"

"Just before my appointment. He came and got me."

"Is that usual?"

"No. I felt like hell. Death would have been a welcome relief. My wife fetched him to my room, and he said my usual treatment might help."

"Why didn't you go directly into the electrotherapy room?"

"He told me to wait, and besides, I don't go barging in on other people's appointments."

"So you knew he had another patient in there?"

"Hornsby wasn't talking to himself."

"Who was he talking to?"

"I thought you were some sort of genius investigator? Hollister. He was talking to David Hollister."

"Are you sure? Did you recognize his voice?"

"Not at the time, no. I heard voices, but I couldn't hear what was being said and I didn't try. It was all I could do to sit upright. About a quarter hour later, he came out looking like he just saw—well, what he saw, a man die right before his eyes."

"Were you surprised David had been getting a treatment?"

"I was surprised he was dead. The revelation that he was getting treatment couldn't compete with that."

"And how did that make you feel?"

"How the hell do you think it made me feel? God-awful. He was a nice fellow, alive one minute, dead the next. And Hornsby was all tore up, they all were. They're a close family."

"Did you think about the possibility that it could have been you?"

"Killed you mean? I did later. I was still a bit shocked when my wife started sobbing that it could have been me. Then the damn sheriff showed up and put us all under house arrest—"

"You're not under arrest, you're being detained."

"What the hell's the difference? Can I leave? Haven't you got an answer yet? Didn't you examine the machine?"

"I examined it."

"So it was an accident, right? Why are you dragging it out talking with everyone? Tell the sheriff it was an accident and let us go!"

"I'm not convinced it was an accident."

"I don't believe it! Are you getting paid by the hour? Whatever Hornsby's paying you, I'll double it."

"No one is paying me."

"What? You're in it for the glory? And I thought Loomis had an ego." He pulled his cigarette case from his trouser pocket and shoved one in his mouth.

"You don't like Mr. Loomis?"

He jerked the cigarette out. "Oh, my God, don't go reading into every word I say. Mr. Loomis is a perfectly lovely individual, I do not believe he killed David Hollister or anybody. I don't believe anyone here killed David Hollister, it was a horrid, god-awful tragedy, and I just want to go home."

"I'll try to be as quick about it as I can. It's not such a bad place to be held captive."

"I curse the day I ever set eyes on this coast."

"Have you been here before?"

He hesitated. "Not to Healing Sands, no."

"But to the coast?"

He took the time to light his cigarette before replying. "Came down a few times, the wife and I."

"Where did you stay previously?"

"Not many places to stay, are there? Copalis Hotel, Iron Springs."

"That's all? Nothing further north?"

"There is nothing further north, no hotels, at any rate, though I hear there soon will be."

"Have you been further north?"

Freddie swallowed, then cleared his throat. "Took a day trip up a ways. My wife wouldn't hear of camping."

"How did you travel? On foot?"

"Hornsby keeps a little donkey cart for the guests."

Bradshaw recalled the donkey grazing with the cows up in the pasture. "Did you spend any time with David Hollister?"

"Why would I?"

"You tell me?"

"I talked to him a bit." He looked off into the distance. "Nice fellow." He cast a glance at the main house. "All of them, nice folks. It's a shame."

"What did you talk to him about?"

He shrugged. "This and that."

"Be specific please."

"Oh, for Pete's sake. Marriage, if you must know. They were happy and I'm miserable. Is that what you want to know? It turns out there's no magic answer, unless it's in choosing the right wife, and it has nothing to do with your investigation, Professor."

"Have you ever hit your wife?"

His incredulous face matched his reply. "Of course not."

"How old is your wife? Near forty?"

"Where did Hornsby find you? An ad in the funny papers?" He closed his eyes and shook his head and mumbled. "I'm a dead man."

"Why do you say that?"

"She's twenty-seven. I'm thirty. We have no children. We have no personal grudge against anyone here, and we didn't kill the handyman. Are we done? Can I go now? I'd like to have a moment of peace before I die."

Chapter Nineteen

Deputy Mitchell stood at the front desk in the foyer reading a Tacoma newspaper, a small brown paper package tied with string at his elbow.

Bradshaw asked him, "Anything exciting been happening in the world since we've been here?"

The deputy shook his head. "Just the usual."

The package was addressed to Ingrid Thompson c/o Healing Sands Sanitarium, Ocean Springs, Wash. The return address was Frederick & Nelson Department Store, Seattle. On the corner of the box was an order reference name: Z. Moss.

"Deputy, are you holding this package here for some reason?"

"Me? No. It's for Mrs. Thompson. Doc just sorted the mail."

"You weren't going to ask her about it?"

"No. You think I should?"

"One never knows what useful information might arrive in a package delivered to a crime scene."

The deputy got up, setting the paper aside. "Oh."

A shuffling sound caught Bradshaw's ear. He looked down the hall and spied Zebediah Moss lurking outside the Healing Sands room, chewing his lip, as if unsure of entering. When he noticed Bradshaw watching him, he scurried into the library.

"Hold onto this, Deputy." Bradshaw nodded at Ingrid's package, then followed Moss and found him arms crossed, staring at the bookshelves. "Good afternoon, Mr. Moss."

Moss nodded, not meeting his eye.

"Have a seat. It's time we talked."

Moss sat stiffly at the nearest table, arms still crossed, eyes on the shelves, jaw tight. Bradshaw sat across from him.

"Did you know the Thompsons before coming to Healing Sands?"

He gave a noncommittal shrug.

"Yes or no."

"He works at the assay office in Seattle, don't he?"

"Is that where you met him?"

"Mighta been."

"He was working the day you brought in your gold?"

"That's right."

"How did that go?"

Moss shifted his eyes to Bradshaw's face quickly, then looked away again. "What do you mean?"

"It's something I've never had the pleasure of experiencing. You arrived by ship with other miners; there were crowds to greet you and cheer your success, and you hauled your bags up to the federal office. I've seen miners come in, it's quite a production."

Moss said, "I hired a hack to haul it up the hill."

"A memorable day. Any trouble?"

"With what?"

"The process? Paperwork?"

"No trouble. It was fine."

"Fine? I'd expect the experience to be more than fine."

"Yeah, well, I expected I'd brought home more."

"Your haul wasn't worth as much as you anticipated?"

"It was pert near. You always hope for the high end of the estimate. Disappointing when it ain't." He pinched the crease of his trousers. He had thick, stubby fingers and strong, meaty hands.

"Who makes the estimate?"

"Oh, well, the experts up in Alaska. They tell ya it'll bring between this and that, and you hope for that."

"But you got this, the low estimate."

"Pert near."

"Near the low? Not even reaching the low? The estimates were off?"

"Close enough. I'm rich, ain't I? If you've got a problem with the estimate or assay office, go talk to them. I'm happy and satisfied with my take."

"Mr. Moss, I've observed you here at Healing Sands. You appear neither happy nor satisfied."

"Well it ain't got nothing to do with estimates, Professor."

"What's it got to do with?"

"None of your damn business."

"You're probably right, but I'd like to know anyway."

"Don't mean I got to tell you."

"Is it to do with a woman?"

Moss looked up at the ceiling, as if hoping it would fall down on him.

"When did you first meet Mrs. Thompson?"

Moss twitched, and his eyes shot to the library door. "I can't rightly recall."

"Really? I would have thought meeting Mrs. Thompson an unforgettable event."

"Why?" Moss pursed his lips and brought his narrowed gaze to Bradshaw.

"She's hardly an ordinary woman."

Moss glared at him.

Bradshaw said, "Some women are like that. They demand you take notice."

Moss looked away, toward the door again.

"At the assay office? In Seattle? On the train?"

"What?"

"Where you met Mrs. Thompson?"

"I can't rightly recall."

"You made an order by letter from here last week? To Frederick & Nelson Department Store?"

"Mighta done."

"You had it delivered to Mrs. Thompson. It's in the foyer now, on the desk."

"Don't mean nothing. No crime in doing a favor for a lady."

"Are you in the habit of doing her favors?"

"I don't know what you mean by that."

"Or is it that she does you favors?"

"Now see here, Professor. I don't like your questions. I'm not the smartest man on this earth, but I know when a women's virtue has been insulted."

"What did you buy for her?"

"Not my place to say."

"I'll find out."

"Not from me. And if you were a gentleman, you wouldn't ask her, neither. Truth is, I don't know. She wrote down what she wanted, asked me to send for it."

"Do you mean she asked you to pay for it?"

"I got an account at the store, don't I?"

"You must know her well to be trusted with such a delicate favor."

Moss' ruddy complexion deepened.

Bradshaw asked, "Does her husband know about this favor?"

"He's a mean son-of-a-bitch. Doesn't like her ordering nothing."

"Do you know he's mean through observation? Or is that what you were told?"

"He just is." Moss set his jaw and turned his eyes back up to the ceiling.

"Did she repay you for the purchase?"

"Money ain't no concern to me."

"Where were you from around ten in the morning Monday until the time of David Hollister's death?"

That got his attention. He looked with fury at Bradshaw. "Me? I had nothing to do with that handyman dying. What are you saying? You saying it wasn't an accident?"

"I don't yet know. Where were you?"

"I wasn't in that room upstairs poking around no wires."

"Why do you mention wires?"

"It's an electric machine, ain't it? Got wires, ain't it?"

"Oh, yes. It has wires. Have you ever been in the electrotherapy room, Mr. Moss?"

He hesitated, his mouth scrunched. He looked as if he were weighing his answer against what Bradshaw might have learned from others. He said finally, "Mighta been."

"For treatment?"

"No way in hell I'd let anybody put electricity in me."

"Then why did you enter the room?"

"To have a look around, why else?"

"Was Dr. Hornsby with you?"

"No."

"Someone else with you?"

"No."

"When was this? When did you enter to have a look around?"

"I dunno, long time ago, when I first got here."

"How did you get in?"

"Watcha mean? I walked in, didn't I? You expect I climbed through a window?"

"I mean it's kept locked."

"I don't know about that, it wasn't locked when I went in."

"And how many times did you enter the electrotherapy room?"

"Just the once. Ain't been near it since."

"Good, then you have nothing to worry about. How do you spend your days here, Mr. Moss?"

"Same as everyone else. I eat, wash my dishes, walk the beach, eat, wash my dishes, walk the beach. That's pert much all there is to do here, in case you haven't noticed."

"I hear there was a spectacular natural phenomenon the evening before David Hollister's death."

"Huh?"

"The glowing sand on the beach?"

Moss twitched again, and cleared his throat. "The sparky sand. Yeah. I seen better down the coast, near Mexico. But it was something."

"Mrs. Thompson dunked you in the surf?"

He wiped his hand over his mouth. "So? We was all acting like kids. I, uh, noticed Mr. Loomis forgot to put on his shoes. He wore his slippers out on the beach. Danged stupid rule about slippers."

"Why are you telling me this?"

"I dunno, just thought of it. Might be a clue."

"A clue about what?"

"I dunno! We done here?" Moss got to his feet.

"Just a few more questions, Mr. Moss. Did you have occasion to speak with David Hollister at any time during your stay?"

Moss remained standing, his eyes on the door. "I can't rightly recall."

"Take your time." Bradshaw settled back in his chair.

"Mighta spoke with him up on the cliff a time or two. He showed me that powerhouse and laundry he built."

"Did he ask you to finance him? And don't say 'he might have done,' did he?"

"He's got a right money maker in that wash system. Yeah, he asked me could I back him if he wanted to make a business of it, you know, selling the plans and whatnot."

"Did you agree?"

"Mighta—I didn't say no. Hadn't made up my mind, truth be told. Yeah, I got money, fat lot a good it does me. Mighta done him some good if he hadn't gotten himself fried by that machine."

"Did Mr. Loomis know you were thinking of backing Mr. Hollister?"

"He didn't hear it from me. Hollister wanted to keep it quiet. Loomis did those fancy drawings, and Hollister was afraid he was gonna make off with them."

"So Hollister was trying to establish rights to his washhouse design before Loomis had the chance."

"Well, Loomis owns the drawings. Hollister had to act fast."

"Loomis might own the drawings, but not the design. Nothing was agreed legally. What does Loomis plan to do now that David Hollister is dead?"

"I dunno, ask him."

"You've spoken with him, what did he tell you?"

"Says he'll be sure the widow gets looked after."

"And you trust him?"

Moss grunted. "Hell, I don't trust no one." He stomped out of the room, his felt slippers slapping the polished floors.

Chapter Twenty

Professor Bradshaw and Deputy Mitchell located Mrs. Thompson in the sunny sand room, fully clothed in a fashionable gown, not a grain of sand on her. She lounged with her feet up in the shady breeze of an open patio door, browsing through a French fashion magazine.

She looked up as they approached, and her expression shifted from bland boredom to coquettishness. She gave them a pouty smile, and her appreciative gaze lingered so long on Deputy Mitchell, he blushed. He pushed back his hat and squared his shoulders, and Bradshaw thought seriously of taking the man's gun for safekeeping.

She turned her full attention to Bradshaw, her eye dropping to the package in his hand. "Is that for me?"

He said, "Would you open it, please?"

She gaped at him. "What, now? In front of you?"

"Yes."

"No."

The deputy dipped his head with apology. "Ma'am, I'm afraid I'm going to have to ask you to do what the Professor wants."

"I don't see why. This is simply rude. Being nosy parkers for the sake of it. You've got no right to see what's in my private mail."

"We know Mr. Moss placed the order for you."

Her pout was genuine this time, and angry, and this drew attention to her square jaw and showed little wrinkles around her lips. In the bright light of the lamp, every flaw was revealed, every small sag at the jaw. In their mid-thirties, many women's facial features sharpened, the softness and plumpness of youth receding to a more mature profile. Could she be just four years older than Missouri? If so, what had aged her so prematurely? Previous illness? Unhappy marriage? Disappointment? A hard life? He did not presume that growing up wealthy, as Mrs. Hornsby said Ingrid Thompson had, sheltered one from all of life's cruelties.

She wiggled, resumed her playful pout and said childishly, "I haven't got a knife."

"I have." The deputy flipped open a wicked-looking knife that Mrs. Thompson took without grace. She slit the string and cut the paper with a few strong flips of her wrist, then tossed the knife aside. It fell from her lounge chair with a clatter to the floor, and the deputy retrieved it. She withdrew from the straw packing a blue glass bottle, elegantly curved, with a corked top and thrust it at Bradshaw, then turned her face to glare out the open door.

He held the cool glass gingerly and read: *Fountain of Youth Lotion, Restore Youthful Fullness to the Hands and Face. Satisfaction Guaranteed. Imported.*

The deputy cleared his throat and said he'd be off now to check on the others.

Bradshaw returned the blue bottle to Mrs. Thompson.

"Are you happy? Why, I've never been so humiliated. A woman is entitled to her beauty secrets."

"How old are you, Mrs. Thompson?"

"What possible reason could you have for asking?"

"Are you refusing to answer?"

"I just don't see the point? Are you almost done with your little investigation here? When are you going to set us free?"

"I'm not holding you here, the Chehalis County Sheriff is. It's not a bad place to be detained."

"Oh please, it's a nightmare. To think we paid to come here and eat sour food and endure dangerous treatments."

"How did you learn about Healing Sands?"

"Oh, I don't know. Freddie found it." She ran a finger down the curve of the bottle. "He says the sand here is perfect."

"How old are you?"

"That again? Why is it so important to you?"

He waited silently for an answer.

"You are persistent, aren't you? I like that in a man."

He waited.

"Twenty-seven."

"You're sure?"

"I was fairly young at the time of my birth, but that's my understanding."

"And you've lived in Seattle all your life?"

"Are you trying to tell me you know me from somewhere?"

"No, we've never met."

"How can you be sure?"

He wasn't about to tell her she reminded him of his late wife and could never forget meeting her. "What is your maiden name?"

"Colby."

"No protest at the question?"

"I'd like to be done with this conversation. You're spoiling the relaxing mood of the room."

"Have you been making use of the sand beds?"

"I most certainly have not. Have you seen them? Go have a look!"

He'd seen them, but he looked again at the beds placed discreetly behind screens of white cloth and placed to take greatest advantage of the southern exposure.

He turned to Mrs. Thompson. "Too restricting?"

She stiffened and clutched the fabric above her breast. "You must completely disrobe, and I mean completely, before you're buried in sand, and you are not alone. Mrs. Hornsby buries the women. Doctor Hornsby buries the men."

He glanced at the beds again. "Oh."

"Yes, oh."

"Couldn't your husband cover you?"

"I mean really! What sort of people disrobe in front of strangers?" She seemed to belatedly hear his suggestion. "Freddie? My husband has never seen me in my altogether and trust me, he never will."

The fierce look in her eyes as she continued to clutch the fabric of her dress was in such sharp contrast to her usual provocative flirting. He was momentarily thrust into the past, to a conversation with his wife on their wedding night, when her provocative flirting came to an abrupt halt at the bedroom door and only reappeared when in public, when the possibility of following-through was impossible.

Poor Freddie. Poor Zeb Moss. Poor Arnold—no, he could not bring himself to pity Arnold Loomis. But Moss? He was chasing something he'd never get. Freddie wasn't apparently getting much either. Like Old Cedar said, she was trouble. She enjoyed looking her best, fine clothes, perfume, and being admired and flirted with. But she didn't want what she promised. She used a man's desire to tease from him those things she truly wanted. Had she brought one of her suitors to the edge of reason with her teasing? Had Moss or Loomis so wanted what she promised he'd attempted to kill to get it? Had Freddie been the intended victim and David Hollister killed by mistake? Or was Freddie Thompson so miserable in his marriage he'd rigged the device to kill himself and failed?

"Mr. Moss is in love with you." He'd hoped to startle her, but she didn't blink an eye.

"Nothing wrong with having an admirer. Many society women have them. They're useful, but don't think it goes beyond that."

"Useful?"

"Mrs. Mills has one. You know Mrs. Mills, surely. Her husband is manager of Puget Sound National Savings. Her admirer is a good deal younger than her and forever bringing her flowers, and he takes her to the theater. Her husband doesn't mind because he hates the theater."

"Does Mr. Moss bring you to the theater when you're home in Seattle?"

"Good heavens, no. He's not that sort of admirer. Can you see him at the opera?"

"What sort is he?"

"He mopes about, looks at me like I'm something to see, does me favors if I ask. Buys me things. I don't see the harm in it."

No harm? At best, a man was wasting his time, his heart, and his money. At worst, he may have killed an innocent man while trying to kill her husband.

"And what does he get from you?"

She puffed up a bit, saying, "I give him my opinion as to dress and art. He has no taste or culture." She spoke as if she represented Seattle's upper class, yet she was the wife of a Federal Assay Officer, a public employee. Hardly among the upper echelons of Seattle society. The magazines she pored over, as well as her attention to fashion in her dress and hairstyle, told him she aspired to more. With Moss, she must have found someone she considered beneath her, yet his wealth gave him prestige and gave her gifts.

"What does your husband think about your relationship with Mr. Moss?"

"I don't know that he has an opinion."

"It doesn't make him more violent toward you?"

"That's ridiculous. Freddie does what I tell him."

Yesterday, she'd claimed he beat her and forced her to submit to him. He didn't challenge her change of tune. She'd shown herself to be a liar, a manipulator, a user of men. It was now his job to learn if she'd also played a part in murder.

Chapter Twenty-one

He found Henry on the beach, assisting Colin with knots. "Henry, come with me."

Henry handed his knotted string to Colin. "Under, over, tighten, slide."

Colin nodded. "Got it."

Bradshaw led Henry up the beach along the transitional sand just below the wrack line, where clumps of seaweed and shells and debris were daily deposited at high tide. When safely beyond observation by anyone from Healing Sands, he hunkered down and scooped up a handful of damp sand, spreading it over his palm. The grains were mostly black, mixed with bits of white, brown, and speckles of rusty red.

He said, "Mrs. Thompson told me that Mr. Thompson said the sand here is perfect."

"Perfect for what?"

"You tell me."

Henry grabbed his own scoop. "Placer sand? They think there's gold here?"

"The Thompsons have been on this coast several times since they first took a holiday on the North Beach a year ago. We can have it verified, of course, which is why Freddie admitted they did a tour. They stopped for a night or two at the few hotels along the beach, at Copalis and Iron Springs. That's when they discovered Healing Sands."

Henry rubbed the tip of his finger across the grains in his palm. "You're thinking Freddie noticed a similarity between this sand and what he's cleaning from the gold deposits from Nome?"

"Or he came in search of such sand, and found it."

"And so he and the little woman came back to—what? Drive Hornsby out of business so they can buy the property?"

He shook his head. "The gold's in Seattle, at the assay office."

Henry's eyes widened and he whistled. "He's shorting the miners. He adds a bit of this to the ore, I'll wager, and pockets a bit of gold dust. When it's all weighed out, the ore plus gold equals the original weight, and so it all looks hunky-dory to the auditors."

"It could be part of what's ailing him. Hornsby thinks Freddie's got a touch of lead poisoning, but if he's been stealing from the Federal Assay Office, he's got to be living in a constant state of fear. He doesn't appear to have the constitution for thievery. If a boat from Nome arrives in Seattle before he's back on the job, there will be a discrepancy from previous hauls and the auditors will take notice."

Henry whistled again. "And it was Mrs. Thompson who pointed out Freddie's fondness for the sand? First she tells you he's mean and crazy, and now she tells you he's a sand man. Helluva woman. Looks like I'm heading back to town. Who am I tattling to?"

"Wire Captain Bell of the Secret Service in Seattle. And update Sheriff Graham. He might want to send more men."

"Deputy Mitchell not up to dealing with a gold thief?"

"Deputy Mitchell hasn't found his true calling in life."

"Ha! Should I take Colin again?"

His instinct was to say yes, but he thought of Missouri accusing him of intentionally sending Colin away yesterday. "Take Knut. He's familiar with the vehicle, too, if it acts up or you get stuck." He glanced out at the tide. "It'll be an hour or two yet before you can head out. While you're in town, see if you can find me a pair of suitable boots."

Henry looked down at Bradshaw's shoes, discolored from yesterday's saltwater licking.

"Caught you unawares?"

"If only you knew."

Henry lifted his brow but asked nothing. They wiped the sand from their hands and turned back toward the sanitarium.

"If Freddie Thompson didn't kill David Hollister to put Hornsby out of business," Henry asked, "do you suppose he's suicidal and rigged that machine to end it all? Only David got it by mistake?"

"Freddie knew someone was in the electrotherapy room with Hornsby, both he and Hornsby told me so. Would he sit quietly waiting his turn if he'd rigged the machine?"

"Maybe he didn't sit. Maybe he paced the room, not sure what to do, working up his nerve to interrupt Hornsby and confess, but he let it go too late."

"He doesn't strike me as a man now suffering from the guilt of having killed an innocent man. I'm not convinced he had anything to do with David's death. He's worried, yes, and sick, but there's more anger than anguish in him. Being detained may have cost him his permanent freedom. If he's destined for jail, he has good reason to fret. But if I were him, I'd be glad for the time away from my wife."

Chapter Twenty-two

Bradshaw informed Deputy Mitchell, who sat rocking on the porch swing, of Henry and Knut's imminent departure, giving him no explanation, receiving no complaint or even curiosity.

"Have you seen Mr. Loomis?"

The deputy shook his head. "Not for an hour or so. Do you need him?"

"Only to interrogate. When you find him, would you ask him to meet me after dinner at my cabin?"

"Certainly. Be glad to help in any way I can."

"Good to know." Bradshaw failed to keep the sarcasm from his voice.

Once in his cabin, he closed the door, opened the windows, and stretched out on the bed above the covers, his hands behind his head. The steady rhythm of the ocean drifted in, with the intermittent call of sea birds. He didn't force his thoughts, just gave them time to settle and shift. He didn't sleep, but he drifted in and out of a restful state. When his stomach growled, he checked his pocket watch to see dinner had begun. That made him smile. He got up and stoked the stove coals and set water boiling. With Postum and shortbread, he reexamined his suspect chart, adding gold theft to Freddie Thompson's motive column. Then he added it to Ingrid's. If her husband was guilty, she likely knew about it. And Zeb Moss? How did he fit in with this new knowledge? As one of the miners cheated, had he confronted

Freddie? Discovered the truth? Had Freddie pulled him into the scheme somehow? Was Moss being used to disguise the stolen gold? What bank would be suspicious of a known millionaire depositing a few ounces of dust?

Or was Moss being used unwittingly? Is that where Ingrid was involved? Was she using Moss' infatuation with her to keep him from going to the authorities? Or to get him to deposit gold dust for her?

If he were right about the sand, if Freddie Thompson had come here to collect more in order to mask his gold theft at the assay office, was that theft connected to David Hollister's death? Or was there more going on here, another get-rich scheme connected with David's laundry? Or something more personal between those here, between Freddie Thompson and Moss and Loomis, perhaps motivated by Ingrid Thompson's merciless teasing? And what role did Loomis play, if anything? It was hard to imagine Loomis was simply a not-so-innocent bystander and David's death merely a coincidence.

Footsteps alerted him to Loomis' arrival before his knock. Bradshaw folded his graph and joined Loomis on the porch with Henry's tin cups and whiskey. Loomis' eyes opened wide with appreciation, and he accepted a generous splash.

They sat, the bottle on the porch between them. About an hour remained until sunset, and for the first time since they'd arrived, clouds gathered in the distance, meeting the lowering sun. A band of pale gold began to deepen toward red on the horizon.

He must tread carefully. Gaining the confidence and extracting truth from a con man was no easy feat. Loomis could read phoniness and was immune to flattery—both subjects he excelled in himself. Bradshaw would have to feel his way carefully.

"I'd begun to think you'd decided not to question me. I'm sure you know I had nothing to do with poor Mr. Hollister's unfortunate demise."

"Mr. Hollister would be alive today if you'd never arrived, Mr. Loomis. You are inextricably involved."

"I can't be blamed for the misuse of a product I represent, Professor. Doctor Hornsby was well instructed, and he signed a legal document assuming all responsibility for its use."

"Are such documents valid if you had no legal authority to sell the machine?"

Loomis laughed. "My authority is well-established. You gave it to me."

"You know very well I understood my machine was to reside in a medical office in Seattle."

"That was my understanding as well, Professor, but circumstances change rapidly in the medical fields, and a salesman must be prepared to shift with the times."

With a hiss of steam and a honk of its ridiculous horn, the Stanley Steamer shot by, Knut at the tiller. Besides him, Henry lifted his hat in salute as they swooped by and made for the shallowest portion of the creek.

"Your associate is going again to Hoquiam?" Loomis' face reflected a questioning interest, which Bradshaw had no intention of satisfying.

"Mr. Loomis, tell me the truth about my outfit bearing your name. What happened after you supposedly delivered it to the doctor in Seattle and we parted ways. If I believe you, we might discuss what happens next."

Loomis opened his mouth, his shoulders raised, his palms up, and Bradshaw sensed the whitewashing to come.

"I will be learning the full truth, so you might as well save yourself the effort."

"I am wounded, Professor. We had such a good rapport when we worked together, a solid team!"

"Yesterday, you hardly knew me."

"Nonsense. I merely strived to minimize your involvement. You should have followed my lead. The sheriff was none too pleased by your revelation. I saw him drag you into the hall. If I'm responsible, then so are you, and he's well aware of it."

"You were trying to protect me?"

"Why, of course. I thought we'd be better off sorting through this predicament together."

"Without the sheriff's knowledge."

"I've got nothing against Sheriff Graham, a decent man by the looks of him, but that deputy? Where'd they find him, the Sears & Roebuck?"

"He has hidden depths," Bradshaw said, not because he believed it, but because he wanted to cast Loomis in doubt about the incompetent lawman.

"You are far too generous, Professor."

"A bad habit, I know. For instance, I trusted you when you asked me to design that outfit in Doctor Hornsby's office. I even included my coil in the design. My patented coil."

"A beautiful piece of craftsmanship, truly. And one I have not reproduced in any way. In fact, if you'd cease in your accusations for a moment, I'll share with you some very good news."

"Let me guess. Over the past four years, you've collected hundreds of deposits from unsuspecting physicians who've now given up on ever receiving their orders."

"You wound me, Professor. I regret time has slipped away from me more swiftly than anticipated, but it has proved to be in our favor. The other outfits that beat us to the market are far inferior, while your creation has stood the test of time. Why, the trail of cures I have paved from demonstrations of our unit is as long as the Columbia River. We'd have no trouble lining up a manufacturer now, and the money will be rolling in."

Bradshaw pretended to mull this over, his gaze toward the ocean. After a silent moment, he poured more whiskey into Loomis' cup, not meeting his eye. But he saw the corner of Loomis' mouth twitch up.

"Why, thank you, Professor. Hornsby's cupboards are decidedly dry."

"No trouble with the outfit in all this time?"

"Not a lick."

"And the Leyden jars? You removed them before transporting?"

"Each and every time. I only had one break, and that was at the hands of an overzealous porter. I ordered a new one from Fischer, and it matched perfectly. Tell me, Professor, truthfully. What do you think of the name? The Loomis Long Life Luminator? Rather fun to say, easy to remember?"

"Bit too snake-oil for me. It's a legitimate medical outfit, not a quack device. The original name, the Bradshaw Complete Portable Electrotherapy Outfit, is more dignified and more informative to physicians."

"Well, we could change it back, if you feel it would boost confidence in the product."

Bradshaw sipped the whiskey, letting it warm his tongue before it slid down his throat.

"You're a clever man, Mr. Loomis, so I know you're aware of your predicament. You are in possession of what men like me call the holy trinity. Means, motive, and opportunity."

"I protest all three! I can talk all day about the glories of the Luminator, and satisfactorily educate a physician on its uses, but I don't truly understand how the damn thing works and I surely wouldn't know what setting combinations would make it lethal."

Setting combinations? Bradshaw wondered. Did Loomis truly believe David had been killed by someone simply setting the machine's combinations in a lethal manner, or was he misdirecting?

"As for motive, I fail to see how David Hollister's death in anyway benefited me. Yes, I drew up his washhouse designs, but had no intention of profiting by them. It was my goal from the outset to serve as Hollister's marketing guide."

"What about opportunity?"

"That my dear Professor, is the most confounding. Only Dr. Hornsby had opportunity. Dr. Hornsby administered the treatment. How could anyone else have changed the unit's settings before Hollister's treatment without the doctor noticing? Did he simply flip the switch and apply the electrodes without checking the settings? Inconceivable. And yet his son-in-law is dead."

"The sheriff has told me flat out that if I don't find anyone else to blame, you and I, and Dr. Hornsby will face a judge."

"That's preposterous. We must work together to find a solution."

"You betrayed my trust, Mr. Loomis."

"I'm sorry that's how you see it, Professor. I truly am. I wish you'd give me a second chance. What can I do?"

"I don't know. I've been lied to so much since I arrived, I don't know whom to believe."

"You think Hornsby is lying about what happened?"

"Would he? You've been here a few weeks, long enough to get to know him. What's your impression?"

"Why ask me? You don't trust me."

"I trust your ability to assess other men. You pegged me about right." He lifted his tin cup in salute, and Loomis laughed, then wiped his mouth, as if considering which way to go, truth or embellishment? Bradshaw could see he was weighing which would win Bradshaw's trust.

"All right then. I never met a more honest, earnest, fellow. He's intelligent, careful, considerate. He's in it for the healing, not the money. And by gum, I've tried to convince him to go big and he flat out will not do it. The railroad's coming, you know. Passengers will be able to ride from Seattle to this beach in a single train ride. Do you know what that means, sir? Six hours! Six hours, maybe a bit more, from Seattle to Healing Sands. Hornsby is sitting on a fortune if he expands. I want him to partner with me to make this a destination, a Mecca for the rich, but he won't hear of it. Not getting bigger or raising his fees. Says he built what he was capable of personally overseeing, he wants no other doctors, and he won't cater to the rich. The man is unbribable. He likely made an honest-to-goodness mistake when he administered electrotherapy on his son-in-law and truly didn't realize it."

Loomis sat back, satisfied with his delivery, having neatly explained any schemes Bradshaw may have gotten wind of since his arrival, and having placed the blame of David's death squarely with Hornsby.

"David Hollister's laundry system—does it have something to do with your idea to expand Healing Sands?"

"Of course, it's the heart of this place. Have you felt how soft the towels are? Pure luxury. But poor David. A fine young man, such a tragedy about his death. That laundry is a brilliant scheme. Hotels, hospitals, schools. I see them all wanting such a setup."

"Tell me about Mrs. Thompson." He asked just as Loomis was raising his cup. The cup stalled, for just a second, before Loomis took a big swallow.

"Professor, I'm not sure how to say this."

Bradshaw waited.

Loomis shook his head. "I've met my fair share of women, Professor. And, that one? She makes a man feel like a hungry fish."

"Am I supposed to understand that?"

"I don't know how to put it delicately."

"Then put it indelicately."

"I don't like to speak poorly of a female."

"You must realize that in such a small place your relationship with Mrs. Thompson isn't a secret."

"My relationship with her is no different than Moss', or her husband's, for that matter. She's tempting bait at the end of a nasty hook, Professor. She shamelessly flirts to get her way, earnestly flirts if you get my meaning, but she has no intention of delivering on her promises. Sometimes she flirts with all three of us at once. Why, one night before you arrived, we were all out here on the beach," he said, lifting his whiskey toward the ocean, "the water and sand were glowing blue, I kid you not. Some sort of phosphor in the tide…."

Loomis continued to talk, but Bradshaw's eyes were locked on the whiskey, and his thoughts were suddenly so loud and demanding he couldn't hear him. Bradshaw grabbed the bottle and stared at the golden liquid. Snippets of conversations about the glowing sand echoed in his brain, and a series of events he previously considered unrelated lined up like one of Justin's jigsaw puzzles revealing its picture. He'd been so focused on the electrical aspect of the case, he'd completely missed what else was happening. He jumped to his feet, startling Loomis into a gaping silence.

Without taking the time to explain, Bradshaw leaped off the porch into the soft sand and ran toward the main house. Heedless of the rules, he hurdled past the slippers and raced inside to the library where he dropped to his knees at the hearth and scooped up a handful of the kindling. Amidst the larger, irregular pieces, tiny, precise bits of wood trickled over his fingers.

Matchsticks. Dozens of them, the heads broken off. He'd seen them the day after he arrived, even noted their matchstick size, and not realized what he was looking at. Dear God. He raced upstairs, shouting, "Mr. Thompson!" Banging on his door, bringing forth not Freddie Thompson, but the Hornsby's from next door, and Mrs. Thompson from her room, her hair down.

"Where's your husband?"

"I don't know. Isn't he in his room?"

Bradshaw threw open Freddie's door, but the man wasn't inside.

Mrs. Thompson said, "Maybe he went for a stroll. What's wrong?"

"Doctor, come with me."

Hornsby didn't question, he followed Bradshaw down the stairs and outside to the beach without stopping for his shoes. The sun had dipped below the clouds, plunging the world into an early twilight. The low tide extended into the far distance. There, barely visible against the gray clouds and ocean was a figure, Freddie Thompson, bent double.

Bradshaw broke into a run. Freddie crumpled, dropped, and fell within reach of the bubbling, frothy fingers of surf. When Bradshaw reached Freddie, he turned him over, and held up his head. Hornsby came panting, his stockings soaked, having lost his slippers when he began to run. He dropped to his knees and pressed his ear to Freddie's heart.

But Bradshaw knew there was no heartbeat to hear. Freddie's eyes were open, glazed, unblinking. Hornsby slapped lightly at Freddie's cheeks, his wrists, and repeated his name. "Mr. Thompson. Mr. Thompson!"

"Doctor," Bradshaw said gently. "We couldn't have saved him. He's been a walking dead man since the night of the glowing sand."

"What?" Hornsby shook his head, not understanding.

"Phosphorus, doctor. Freddie Thompson was poisoned."

Chapter Twenty-three

"No, no, you must be mistaken, Professor. I saw no evidence of phosphorus poisoning! It was lead. He works with lead, and his symptoms were that of lead poisoning. Depression, abdominal pain, severe mood changes. I didn't know it was this severe. He didn't show signs of being near death."

"Because he wasn't near death until he ingested a fatal dose of phosphorus."

"He was violently ill the night before David died, but it couldn't have been phosphorus, Professor. With phosphorus, there's a distinct and unmistakable luminescence. Mr. Thompson displayed none, I swear to you!"

"The luminescence was neutralized. You are missing a tincture from your office?"

Hornsby stared at him.

"I'm not a chemist, Doctor, but I'm familiar with common poisons. The luminosity of phosphorus can be temporarily negated with certain alcohols, and there are other substances that permanently destroy the glow, without affecting the toxicity."

Hornsby gasped, slapping his hand over his mouth. When his hand dropped, he uttered, "Dear God. My gentian tincture." He slumped to the wet sand. "But phosphorus? I keep none in my supplies."

"I found an entire box of broken matchsticks in the library hearth."

Hornsby's brow narrowed in deep thought. "Phossy jaw," he mumbled, likely recalling the many incidents of disfigurement incurred by workers in match factories. Some countries had banned white phosphorus for use in matches because of its toxicity to workers and because of accidental and intentional poisonings, but no such laws had yet been passed in the United States. Safety matches were available, the sort that required the match tip to be struck against the box where a strip of non-poisonous red phosphorus had been applied, but the cheaper "lucifer" matches made of white phosphorus were still common. And commonly used by those attempting suicide. And less frequently, murder.

"I should have guessed. I should have seen. I'm a sorry excuse for a doctor. I don't recognize the sound of a fatal current, I don't recognize the signs of poisoning. I should have dosed him with oil of turpentine the night he was so ill. I might have saved him…I should have saved him."

"You are not at fault, doctor. Someone deliberately hid the signs of danger."

"I was sure it was lead. It never occurred to me he'd taken poison. It's never happened before. And he was getting better. After that severe attack, he'd gotten better."

"That's often the case with phosphorus poisoning. Death can come in a half hour, or after many days or weeks, but most commonly, after violent purging, the victim becomes asymptomatic for a day or so before organ failure begins."

"I did know that about phosphorus. Of course, I knew that. Yet it never occurred to me. It never…what is happening here, Professor? Has everyone gone mad?"

Chapter Twenty-four

Deputy Mitchell resigned. That Bradshaw hadn't the authority to accept his resignation didn't seem to matter to him.

"I don't know what I'm doing. Two months, that's all the experience I had before coming here. It's not what I expected. Police work…I thought the bad guys would be obvious, that I'd see them coming with guns drawn. But nothing here is what it seems. Now someone's poisoning us? I feel ill. Really, I'm sick to my stomach. And look, my palms are clammy. I can't breathe!"

Bradshaw snatched the deputy's hat off his head, pushed him down onto a chair, and shoved his face into the hat's hollow. "Breathe, you're having a fit of hysterics."

Once the deputy had regained his composure, if not his dignity, and downed a full glass of water that Bradshaw filled himself from the kitchen tap, promising him it wasn't poisoned, he agreed to stand his post and honor his badge until the sheriff returned.

"I wouldn't have abandoned the Hornsbys or Martha—Mrs. Hollister. I just don't want to be the one in charge here. I don't know what I'm doing."

"I'll take charge until the sheriff arrives in the morning. Your job until then is to simply watch those three and don't let them talk to each other." He nodded toward the library where Ingrid Thompson, Zebediah Moss, and Arnold Loomis sat silently, with Doctor Hornsby keeping watch. Two hours had passed since Freddie's death. In that time, Bradshaw had assisted Hornsby with moving Freddie's body from the beach to the Manipulation Room and helped with the unpleasant tasks associated with tidying a fresh corpse. Afterward, Hornsby had questioned the need for Mrs. Thompson to be pulled from her room and forced to sit in the library.

"She just lost her husband," Hornsby said, the pained expression in his eyes revealing the depth of his empathy. His own daughter had been in this very situation just a few days ago.

Bradshaw felt the sting of Hornsby's words, but answered, "It's necessary to my investigation."

Mrs. Hornsby, Martha, Dolley, and Abigail were in the kitchen, brewing tea and baking cookies: for the shock, they said. He wondered if they were using flour and sugar, and if the taste would match the delicious smell. He wondered if he was being insensitive, even morbid, to think of food at such a time. But there was something comforting about the scent of warm cinnamon that softened the harsh reality of death.

Once he felt confident that Mitchell was capable of maintaining order and silence in the library, he brought Hornsby up to the doctor's office to conduct an experiment. Hornsby found his jar of dried gentian and medicinal alcohol in order to make a fresh tincture like the one that had gone missing.

"It's vodka," Hornsby said, "The best alcohol for making tinctures." He crushed the gentian with a mortar and pestle, then blended it with the vodka. "It should sit for two weeks. Ideally, I would make it on the night of a full moon, then filter it with a new moon."

"Is that science or folklore, Doctor?"

"I don't know if science has yet proved this traditional method, Professor. But you've seen the power of the moon with each tide, and my instincts tell me if the moon can move oceans, it surely imparts some stimulating action on smaller liquid bodies."

"It's not necessary for our purposes to wait for the moon. We'll fill a second jar with plain warm water and compare the results when lucifer tips are added."

This was done, and several dozen match tips added to each. Bradshaw flipped off the electric light, plunging the office into darkness. As their eyes adjusted, Bradshaw agitated the jar containing plain water to introduce oxygen, and it began to emit a slight green phosphorescence and a whiff of garlic-like odor. He repeated the agitation with the gentian jar, but produced no glow, no garlic odor, only the bitter, weedy scent of gentian.

"You may turn on the light," he said, and Hornsby flipped the switch. "We won't put it to the test, but my guess is that even the taste of the phosphorus has been negated by the gentian."

"Professor, I've been dosing Mr. Thompson with gentian since his arrival. Do you suppose he knew it would mask the phosphorus? Working at the assay office, he must know something of chemistry."

"Doctor, we don't know that it was Mr. Thompson who added the match tips to the tincture."

Hornsby's face registered surprise, and then dismay. From below his wash basin, he lifted a clear bottle marked "French Oil of Turpentine" and shook his head. "It's the French oil that is said to work with cases of phosphorus poisonings. Resinified turpentine works, too, if the French can't be found. A few drops of this, floating in hot water, and I might have saved him."

"It's not a certain cure. You mustn't torture yourself. You were given no clues to phosphorus poisoning. You couldn't have known. No one could have. There's nothing more we can do this evening. It's time now for rest. Tomorrow, you'll need your strength. My associate will be returning with the federal authorities."

"The federal…that's where Mr. Pratt went today? Is this a federal matter?"

"Tomorrow more information will be revealed. For now, it would be best if you and Mrs. Hornsby tried to sleep."

Hornsby looked near collapse. He held out a trembling hand to Bradshaw. "I'm glad you're here, Professor. I don't know how I would have managed on my own."

"We shall have answers. Get some rest."

Hornsby left to find his wife, and after checking on the deputy and his detainees, Bradshaw went to see his son. In a small bedroom in Paracelsus Cottage, Justin and Paul were asleep in their beds, snuggled down beneath woolen blankets. He left them to their dreams after a careful, quiet examination of their peaceful faces. He told Mrs. Prouty about Mr. Thompson's death and left it to her to tell the others as she thought best. He knew she could do so without alarming them while also verifying that each and every one of them was of sound health. He didn't believe any of them had been poisoned, but to presume and be wrong didn't bear contemplating. As he left the cottage, a framed quote by the door caught his eye: "Poison is in everything, and nothing is without poison. The dosage makes it either a poison or a remedy."

Before returning to the main house, he entered Moss' small cabin, Hippocrates Hut, without bothering to ask permission. Moss' habits were tidy enough for a bachelor, his clothes slung over a chair, his wash basin filled with fresh water. An effort had been made at pulling the bedclothes up, but the rumpled result wouldn't have passed Mrs. Prouty's inspection. There was nothing else in the cabin to see, other than framed quotes: "Let food be thy medicine," and "Opinion breeds ignorance." Bradshaw had always been fond of Hippocrates.

Moss possessed no personal items other than a shaving kit. No photographs, no reading materials. A pen and ink, but no writing paper. Bradshaw got down on the floor to look under the bed and found Moss' leather suitcase, unstrapped.

He hauled it out and discovered, beneath several new union suits, a child's school journal with the letters A-B-C on the cardboard cover. Inside, the paper was wide-lined for a young hand. At the top of each page simple words were printed, meant to be copied. And they had been copied. Page after page of careful lettering, well executed but for direction and order. Some letters faced the wrong way, despite the clear example. Some words were scrambled or backwards. Occasionally a few accurately spelled words emerged, but their occurrence was random. Bradshaw had not pegged Zeb Moss for a genius, but this evidence of illiteracy, the struggle with the simple words and shape of the letters, meant the miner was incapable of understanding the complicated electrical materials in the library. Or the inspiring quotes on the walls.

He slid the suitcase back under the bed, felt under the mattress for any hidden objects, and when he found none, he returned to the main house. By now, the cookies and chamomile tea had made their appearance in the library with the confined guests. Bradshaw stepped in long enough only to snatch a warm cookie and confirm that Deputy Mitchell was competently guarding the trio. Moss never looked up from his slippered feet, and Loomis offered his help. Ingrid Thompson glared at him, a handkerchief clutched in her hand, telling him he was heartless. She wasn't sobbing or being overdramatic. She appeared genuinely upset. Hers had not been an ideal marriage, but she must have been fond of her husband once, and now he was dead.

Hadn't he been in a similar situation once? He felt a pang of empathy followed by doubt. Was he being cruel to keep her here rather than letting her return to her room to get through this time of shock privately? Wouldn't he have preferred to be let alone on the night his wife died, rather than hauled down to the police station and forced to answer humiliating questions?

But he had not had a hand in Rachel's death. He had not put the carbolic acid on the sideboard or encouraged her to drink it.

Could he say the same of Ingrid Thompson? Had she had a hand in Freddie's death? Had she poisoned the tincture of gentian on the eve of the glowing sand and offered a dose to her unsuspecting husband?

He left without comment, feeling cruel but not knowing how else he could fairly and systematically proceed. He devoured a cookie as he went upstairs. It was unlike any cookie he'd ever eaten, dense and moist and chewy. But it was sweet and spicy, like pumpkin pie, and he hoped there'd be more later.

Loomis' room resembled Moss' for level of tidiness, but with far more possessions. As a traveling salesman, he carried his home in a pair of suitcases, and his room looked as if he'd lived there for years, with framed photographs on the dresser, adventure novels beside the bed, and an array of souvenirs from towns he'd visited on display.

He apparently wasn't so confident about his rights to David's washhouse designs that he left them out in the open, but the small padlock on his metal cash box was meant only to discourage honest men. Bradshaw had it open in seconds. He leafed through carbon-copy deposit receipts written to dozens of physicians throughout the West and as far east as Chicago, letters of interest from others, and much literature on the rich potential of Washington's coast. The washhouse designs were neatly rolled, and as Martha said, beautifully drawn. He tore the designs in two, enjoying the ripping sound, then tore them again, until the pieces fit easily in his jacket pocket. If the design didn't exist, there could be no dispute over possession. He left all else intact and locked the box.

A thorough search of the room revealed no food or drink or medicine, tainted or otherwise, and no empty matchbox. He lastly got down on his knees to check under the mattress, expecting nothing, surprised when his fingertips met something. About the size of an egg, but rougher and more solid. He pulled it out. It was a crumpled ball of tinfoil. Flecks of green glimmered in the dull silver.

What had Dolley and Abigail said? Someone had taken cheese from the larder. Cheese wrapped in colorful tinfoil. He attempted to pick loose a corner. Tinfoil, unlike aluminum, was high in lead and very soft. When balled tightly, it almost melted to itself.

He crossed to the electric light, and after a few moments of careful peeling, he could just make out the words "Zuyder Zee." The Hornsby girls said the guests had been served this cheese in the library. That's how they knew about it. So it had been Loomis that entered the larder and helped himself? Loomis that stripped off the foil wrap, changed his mind about the cheese and abandoned it untouched on the dining room sideboard? And then balled up the tinfoil and shoved it under his mattress?

Why would he try to hide the foil rather than simply leaving it with the cheese, or throwing it in the wastebasket?

Tinfoil made an excellent conductor. Loomis knew that, surely. Unraveled, there would be enough to extend over the tops of the Leyden jars inside the electrotherapy outfit, or prop against their sides to connect them. The tinfoil could be the conductive material that had shorted the machine and killed David Hollister.

For a few minutes, Bradshaw sat on the floor beside the bed, pondering the tinfoil, where he'd found it, and all the implications. This discovery pointed to Arnold Loomis as David's killer. And yet…Loomis was a confidence man, dishonest to his core. But a murderer? Over the years, Bradshaw had met several murderers, and each of them had surprised him in some way. It was a fact he knew about himself, that despite his cynicism, he had difficulty believing the worst of people. He was more like poor Deputy Mitchell than he cared to admit, always thinking the bad guy should look the part. Well, in this case the bad guy being a con man, he did look the part, and Bradshaw still didn't want to believe it. He pocketed the foil and got wearily to his feet.

He moved on to Freddie Thompson's room.

Entering a dead man's bedroom is never a pleasant task. Bradshaw had experienced it several times in his investigative work, and it never got any easier. It made him think of his own habits and wonder what others would one day think of him when they had to sort through his belongings. And who would that be? Mrs. Prouty? His son? Henry? Missouri? He stood very still, for a moment trapped inside his emotions.

He shook himself, whispered an apology to Freddie Thompson, and began to search. The room was obsessively tidy, the bed so tightly made a coin would bounce if dropped upon it. Freddie's reading choices, literary novels and poetry, were stacked spine to spine and his toiletries arranged with geometric precision. Bradshaw found a cedar box with hundreds of hand-rolled cigarettes, each perfectly and precisely formed. He found two full boxes of nontoxic safety matches, and one half-full box. He found no food or drink or tinctures of any kind.

The only item of interest, which he left in place for authorities to see, was a ten-pound bag of black sand in the bottom of Freddie's trunk.

He moved lastly to Ingrid Thompson's room. The door was barred from swinging fully open by clothes strewn upon the floor. The bedspread hung from the rumpled sheets. Every surface of the room was cluttered with toiletries, jewelry, and fashion magazines. In the wardrobe, freshly laundered clothes were hung or folded with a precision that told Bradshaw they'd come from the Healing Sands laundry that way.

A blend of scents perfumed the air, feminine and flowery. He made a systematic search of the messy room, finding discarded magazines and empty bottles of lotion, but nothing that hinted of poison. He realized as he grew frustrated that he wanted to find evidence of Ingrid's guilt—he wanted to find soggy match tips and Hornsby's missing gentian. He wanted to find proof she killed her husband, and he knew such a want could undermine his clarity and objectivity. Evidence shouldn't be gathered to prove a theory but to create one.

There were no matches or makings of poison here. No evidence she'd killed her husband.

His search had turned up nothing to help explain Freddie Thompson's death. But in his pocket he had the Zuyder Zee tinfoil.

He returned to the library, sat in a chair visible to all those present, pulled the ball of tinfoil from his pocket, and began to pick it apart.

He asked, "Who can tell me what this is?"

Deputy Mitchell leaned closer.

"Not you, Deputy. Let's see what these three have to say."

In a few minutes, several inches of shiny green foil glinted in the lamp light. Loomis sucked his teeth and fidgeted, clearing his throat. Ingrid Thompson gave the foil a single glance, then looked away, burying her face in her hands.

Only Zeb Moss watched Bradshaw painstakingly unravel the foil. "Cheese," he barked out, his craggy face beaming with pride at having guessed. "That's a cheese wrapper."

"How do you know, Mr. Moss?"

"I seen it before, haven't I? They served it one night, here in this room. A treat, I tell you. Loomis was doing parlor tricks, and used that foil off the cheese to pull electricity from everybody's clothes! It was the dangdest thing. He rubbed it off of us and put in a water tumbler, and it sparked so loud you could see it."

A Leyden jar. Arnold Loomis had built and charged a Leyden jar using a drinking glass and tinfoil, revealing a thorough knowledge of the device and a possibility of passing that knowledge to the others.

Loomis had gone pale. He shrugged and lifted his hands innocently and said, "The old static trick. A harmless little bit of science. Child's play, really."

For Bradshaw's child, yes, it was a favorite trick. Justin often delighted his schoolmates by building Leyden jars and discharging them with toy tin soldiers so that it seemed their rifles fired. But he was the son of an electrical engineer. Most adults thought it was a magic trick, not science.

"Anyone care to guess where I found this cheese wrapper?"

Moss sat forward, legs jumpy with excitement, like a child wanting to win a game.

"What about you, Mr. Loomis?"

"I don't understand what you're getting at, Professor. It's garbage as far as I can tell."

"Are you in the habit of storing garbage in your room?"

Loomis guffawed. "I know we have a disagreement about the Luminator, Professor, but that is no justification for framing me."

"How does a bit of tinfoil frame you?"

Loomis shot to his feet, and Deputy Mitchell stood, putting a hand on his holster, looking surprisingly like a capable lawman.

"Now listen here, Professor, you can't do this to me! You know very well you didn't find that wrapper in my room. Deputy, I want you to pay close attention here; you are the authority in this room, and I'm telling you this man is attempting to frame me for David Hollister's death."

Mitchell looked to Bradshaw for direction.

"That's an excellent idea. Deputy, it might be prudent to make an official record of my finding and Mr. Loomis' response."

The deputy found paper and a pen and scratched out a statement from each of them.

Bradshaw then asked, "Mr. Loomis, why do you believe this tinfoil connects you with David Hollister's death?"

Loomis glared at Bradshaw. "Everyone here saw me perform that parlor trick."

"That doesn't answer my question. How does the tinfoil connect you with David's death?"

"You did not find it in my room!" He threw up his hands. "That's it!" He sat down and crossed his arms and legs. "I'm done speaking until my attorney is present."

"Make a note of that, too, Deputy."

Mitchell's pen scratched across the paper again, and then Bradshaw announced, "The deputy will now escort you upstairs to your rooms. Mr. Moss, I will fetch your nightclothes from your cabin, and you will be spending the night here. You will all remain in your rooms until you are otherwise notified. Deputy Mitchell will be on guard in the hall for the night should you need anything."

Moss bit his lip, and his ruddy complexion deepened. He cleared his throat. "My nightclothes are in my case, under the bed."

Bradshaw knew that, just as he knew Moss' embarrassment came from the belief his illiteracy would be revealed by the other contents of the case.

"I'll bring your suitcase to you."

Moss nodded. "Oh, good. Thanks."

When Bradshaw returned with Moss' suitcase a few minutes later, they all marched upstairs. Moss gratefully took his bag into an empty bedroom. Ingrid disappeared into her room without a complaint, and Loomis marched into his, still seething, and slammed his door. The house fell deathly quiet.

On guard in the hall Deputy Mitchell whispered, "What if they go out a window?"

"It's a long way down. And it's a long way to anywhere from here."

"I won't fall asleep. I promise."

"I've got a solution that will allow you to get some rest."

The solution required only string and a bell and a few minutes of arranging.

"If Mrs. Thompson or Loomis or Moss opens their door even the slightest, the bell will ring and wake you if you've fallen asleep."

Deputy Mitchell looked visibly relieved. It was not an alarm likely to block a serious escape attempt, but Bradshaw had arranged it for a reason he would not tell Deputy Mitchell. The deputy was armed. Two men had already died here at Healing Sands. He didn't want a bullet from the deputy's gun to kill a third. If any of them tried to leave their room, he wanted the deputy awake.

Chapter Twenty-five

After gathering a few necessities from his cabin, Bradshaw returned to the main house and chose the vacant room next to Loomis', leaving his door wide open to the hall. Fully dressed, minus felt slippers, he stretched out on the bed to rest and think, and he spent the hours until dawn drifting in and out of sleep. When the window lightened from black to soft gray, and the birds began to sing, he got up and looked into the hall. Deputy Mitchell was puffy eyed but awake. A rap on each door, and a demanded response, ensured him no one had escaped.

Well. He'd made no deductions, but his mind was clear and he felt refreshed, and he had the makings of coffee in his cabin. When he brought the deputy a smuggled-in mug of the real stuff, tears welled in the lawman's eyes.

"Bless you, Professor."

Mrs. Hornsby and Martha Hollister, in the kitchen sliding plump, dark loaves of bread into the oven, agreed to serve the guests breakfast in their rooms and Deputy Mitchell in the hall, just this once.

Bradshaw then decided to sneak in a bath. In one of the private bathrooms, he shaved and showered, and he found the towels to be as soft and luxurious as promised. He emerged into the main hall feeling clean, smelling of lemon soap, holding his bundle of clothes and toiletries, and he met Missouri.

She, too, held clothes and toiletries for a bath.

He didn't say good-morning. Their eyes met, and it was as if the intervening hours since they last spoke had never happened. Her words were there, her declaration of love, the revelation she was done waiting for him. But there was an appeal this morning, too. A worry that transcended their personal concerns.

She said, "Was Mr. Thompson really poisoned?"

He nodded.

"How?"

"Phosphorus."

Her mouth opened with a small, quick intake of breath, and her eyes flashed with pain. "Matches?"

He nodded again.

"I knew someone…." She shook her head. "Her baby—he'd just learned to crawl. He'd only sucked one match, but…those matches should be outlawed."

He agreed. "I believe Mr. Thompson was poisoned before we arrived and he only succumbed last night, but I'm taking no chances."

"You're sending us home? It's for the best. For Justin and Paul, especially. Are you in any danger?"

"Me? No." No more than he ever was when deeply involved in a criminal investigation. There was always someone who didn't want him to discover the truth. He'd been threatened, hit, kicked, nearly drowned, nearly electrocuted, and nearly run over by a streetcar. He'd not yet been nearly poisoned, and he wouldn't allow this case to be his first. "No," he repeated.

She nodded, and he could see she didn't believe him, but not arguing was her way of saying she trusted him to look out for himself. She moved past him, and he reached out to her, putting a hand on her shoulder. She turned her head to look at him. Was there ever a time he didn't love her?

He said, "Will you look after Justin until I get back? Can you stay at the house?"

Her brow furrowed. "Of course," she said, but her eyes begged, "Why?"

"He knows about his mother's death. He learned yesterday morning. Not the details, just that she chose to end her life because she was unwell."

Her face registered all he felt in his heart for his son, love and fear and sorrow that such a horrible thing was now part of his boy's life. Her eyes glistened with unshed tears. He felt his own eyes well. He cleared his throat.

"I've informed Mrs. Prouty, of course, but Justin—he sometimes will speak to you about matters he doesn't want to discuss with anyone else. I would feel better knowing you were at the house."

"Yes, of course I'll stay. Try not to worry."

"Thank you." His voice was grave with emotion.

She stepped up to him and kissed him on the cheek, then quickly turned toward the bath and slipped inside. He heard the door lock click.

He didn't have an opportunity to see her alone again before she left.

The same low tide that took her and the others away brought Henry and Knut in the Stanley with Sheriff Graham and Captain Bell of the Secret Service, along with a half-dozen men in a hired wagon.

For a few minutes the beach was a busy transfer station. He'd hugged his son fiercely and told him to take care of Mrs. Prouty until he returned home. He shook hands with the others, and only Knut complained because he had to do an about face and return from whence he came, without the Stanley Steamer. Bradshaw commandeered it, sending money with Colin to pay the owner for another week's rental as they passed Copalis. He'd also given Colin a letter to deliver to the university president, Thomas Kane, explaining his absence. When he returned, he would contact his students and complete the course before the start of the fall term.

He watched the wagon take his charges safely across the creek, his heart heavy at their going, and yet relieved. At last, he turned to the newly arrived lawmen, who'd climbed from their vehicles and already begun assessing the scene.

Although sixty-two and nearly bald, Captain Bushrod Bell, head of the Northwest Division of the Secret Service, exuded the strength and energy of a much younger man. He fanned his face with his hat, squinting into the hot sun as he and Sheriff Graham approached Bradshaw, and he said, "Well, Professor, I hear you've found a thief."

"Our thief is dead, Captain. Freddie Thompson was poisoned."

Sheriff Graham pushed back his hat and rubbed his jaw.

Captain Bell ceased fanning his hat. "Huh. Where's the body, Professor?"

Chapter Twenty-six

Captain Bell removed his boots on the porch of Healing Sands, and slid his feet into felt slippers. Bell's men followed suit, but not Sheriff Graham. He again used his handkerchief to wipe clean the bottoms of his boots, and marched inside with a clomp of authority.

Bradshaw and Captain Bell had worked together a few times over the past couple of years in Seattle. Bell was a man who wore his authority quietly. Although his experience had shown him the worst of men, and he never trusted at face value anything he was shown or told, he retained a refreshing sense of humor and held a genuine fondness for his fellow men. Even when arresting them. He'd seen much in his years of experience, and had grown philosophical about the human species.

"So Professor," Bell said, once he and Bradshaw and Sheriff Graham were settled in the library. "You've uncovered a nest of foul play here at the edge of the continent. Start from the beginning, and let me know what you prefer to keep off the record."

The telling took a full hour, during which Captain Bell and Sheriff Graham listened without interruption, and one of Bell's men took notes. Wanting to hear the opinion of the experienced detective, Bradshaw did his best to give facts only, not opinion, but Bell was a shrewd man and picked up on the undercurrents.

"You trust Doctor Hornsby and his family?" Bell asked.

"Yes."

"I will investigate them."

"As well you should."

"And you believe Mr. Thompson was poisoned before your arrival?"

"His symptoms indicate that, yes."

"One of my men served as a medic in Cuba. He's experienced enough to perform a preliminary autopsy. Phosphorus poisoning is, unfortunately, routinely seen and well understood. Could we have two separate, unrelated cases here, Professor?"

"It's possible."

"I tell you right now, Bradshaw, my money's on Arnold Loomis for the Hollister death. I've dealt with him before. He's not likely to be pleased to see me." Bell cocked his head. "You don't agree? Not Moss, from what you've told me, he's not got the brains, or a motive, unless he'd been trying to kill Mr. Thompson. The woman, then, Mrs. Thompson? It's true women do tend to choose poison when they turn their hands to murder, so if we've got separate cases, she's likely guilty there. Unless it was suicide. But electricity? More of a man's weapon, wouldn't you say?"

"You know my dislike of presumptions, Captain."

"It serves you well, Professor, as my instinct for criminals serves me. We certainly have no shortage of motives. We've had our eye on the Seattle Assay Office for some time now, and your telegram was the final straw. We suspected somebody in the office was skimming from the deposits from one particular region, but we didn't know who or how. Clever business with the sand. On the way down here I added up what appears to be missing. Seventy-five thousand dollars worth of dust at today's prices. If honest men were as clever as thieves, there'd be a lot more millionaires in this world."

Bell got to his feet, followed by the sheriff. After a slight hesitation, Bradshaw also stood, wondering why. He hadn't been told anything yet; they hadn't discussed theories about what might have happened, about what should be done next. Where were they going?

Bell further confused him by extending his hand and saying, "I appreciate all you've done here, Professor. If I have any questions, I'll find you."

Bradshaw accepted the Captain's hand, hoping he had misread what was happening. He said, "I am here at Doctor Hornsby's request, Captain. I will continue with my investigation."

"Let me know if you come up with anything more on how your electro-outfit killed David Hollister. That tinfoil wrapper you found in Loomis' room is circumstantial. We need something concrete that can be used in court, otherwise, we'll be in touch when we need your expert testimony. It will take one of your best lectures to explain to a jury how a subtle change in sound means the difference between an accident and murder."

He hadn't misread anything. The Secret Service was now in charge, and Bradshaw's had been demoted to expert witness.

Chapter Twenty-seven

"We've been summarily dismissed, Henry. Did you bring any information?"

"What, me? I had the good sheriff and a captain of the Secret Service with me. I was obligated to turn over any information about the case that came my way. I was told so in no uncertain terms."

Bradshaw held out his hand, and Henry broke into a grin, producing a fat manila envelope.

They were in Camp Franklin, and it was feeling decidedly less spacious now that Henry had moved in his things, which thankfully included a fresh supply of contraband. The sheriff said they needed all the rooms in the house since more men were on their way. Digging had already begun above the berm, beyond the reach of the highest tides and storm waves.

"I got the feeling when Bell stepped off the train," Henry said, "that we were about to lose our status at this fine institution. He has that federal air about him. Figured we'd be demoted to expert witnesses. It's hell taking a case this far then being told to shove off."

"I don't like it any more than you do, but two murders and a federal crime are beyond the scope of private investigators."

"But? I hear a *but* in your voice."

"But I didn't think we'd be dismissed so quickly."

"Well, Bell can't stop us from doing our jobs. Hornsby's the one that hired us. Let's open the envelope and see if Squirrel sent something to cheer us up."

They sat at the small table and began to sort through the newspaper clippings and Squirrel's meticulous notes. The man wrote in a small print so precise it looked typewritten, and it emerged from his hand at nearly the machine's speed.

Henry read a few articles about Zeb Moss with grunts of disgust.

"Waste of good fortune. Now Arnold Loomis, he's not the nicest feller in the world, but you've got to admit he makes good copy. Listen to this. 'April, 1902. Spokane. Mr. Arnold Loomis of Seattle was acquitted today of charges of swindling. He told the judge, 'Sir, it was merely an unfortunate misunderstanding.' Captain Bell of the Secret Service in Seattle had no comment."

"What was the swindle?"

"Doesn't say. Just hints with 'non-delivery of promised items.'" Henry picked through the clippings in search of details.

While Henry studied Loomis, Bradshaw read through Squirrel's notes on Ingrid Thompson, formerly Ingrid Colby. Unable to find any relatives, Squirrel had gone to her home, the Lincoln Hotel-Apartments, and hadn't found a single person who admitted to being a close friend. Many said they knew her, but they knew nothing about her. Shop owners either detested her or were smitten with her. She'd lived briefly at a fancy boarding house in Seattle before marrying Freddie, and Squirrel had included the landlady's remarks: "A bit of fancy work, that Ingrid was. I don't trust women who can't keep a clean room. Attracted mice, she did, and I've never had mice in my home before. She didn't like women, but oh, did she have an eye for the men. To her credit, she didn't try to bring none of them back here. Mind you, I don't allow that sort of nonsense."

Bradshaw got up from the table and stood at the window, staring toward the ocean, thinking of Ingrid Thompson's messy habits and her resemblance to his late wife. He pulled the cheese wrapper from his pocket and held it up to the sunlight.

Henry said, "What you hoping to find?"

"Some indication the foil has been subjected to an electric current."

"If you don't find anything, does it mean it wasn't?"

"No."

"Maybe Loomis was just hungry."

"The cheese wasn't eaten. The wax wasn't even cracked. What's that smell like?" Bradshaw pressed the foil at Henry.

"Cheese? Roses?"

"Mrs. Thompson's youth potion smells strongly of roses."

"What are you thinking? You said the foil was under Loomis' bed."

"How did it get Mrs. Thompson's lotion on it?"

Henry shook his head. "Maybe…maybe he held her hand helping her over a log on the beach? Maybe he got covered in it while making passionate love to her."

"Or maybe she helped him prepare the foil for use in the machine. Or maybe she's the one who stole the cheese, rigged the machine, then hid the foil in Loomis' room to frame him. Loomis is left-handed, Henry, and the only prints on the doorknob of the electrotherapy room were right-handed."

"Even left-handed people sometimes open doors with their right hands, Ben."

"You see the finger marks here?" He tilted the foil so that the light reflected off the smudges. Not a single clear print. "Like she pressed the foil down on a hard surface, spreading it open, spreading it flat."

"But how, Ben? Even I wouldn't have known a cheese wrapper across the capacitor would make that machine deadly, and I've been watching you tinkering for years. I know you said Loomis did that parlor trick with it, and there's that article in the library journal for all to see, but seriously? Could she have figured it out? Mrs. Thompson does not strike me as a particularly intelligent individual. And most of the women I know are jumpy about electricity, don't even want to screw in a light bulb."

"She's not well-educated, but she's clever and determined, and not the nervous type. I believe she could have put the information together and made a guess."

"What about Moss? You say he's in love with Mrs. Thompson. Maybe the two of them schemed to off Freddie, then hid the foil in Loomis' room."

"He hasn't the cognitive skills, she does. He couldn't have read the journals, and it's highly doubtful he could intuit the mechanics of the circuit simply by observing Loomis' parlor trick."

"Loomis still seems more likely than Mrs. Thompson. Maybe the feds are right, maybe he agreed to do it, or he showed Mrs. Thompson how to do it for a share of Freddie's stolen gold. Then poor David got the zap instead, Loomis panics, hides the evidence under his mattress. What's that face for?"

"Nah."

"Nah?"

"It's too blatantly criminal. Loomis doesn't work that way. He skirts the law; he works in the gray areas. Captain Bell implied as much. Why would he suddenly change his mode of operation? Part of the thrill for him is that he gets away with legal theft. He wants to flaunt and spend and be beyond reach. He's too smart to get pulled into a murder scheme, and he's too smart to dispose of evidence under his own mattress."

"People are stupid when they panic. And he's a con man, Ben. It's all about the con. Maybe he got greedy."

"He's always been greedy. He wouldn't have risked it."

"I hate it when you get cocky, Ben. Makes me want to prove you wrong."

"I'm not wrong."

"So you think he *accidentally* told Ingrid Thompson how to kill her husband with cheese wrappers? And the handyman got it by mistake?"

"That's my working theory, yes."

"Huh. How can you be sure David Hollister wasn't the real intended victim?"

"The only one who had the slightest motive to kill David Hollister was Loomis in order to secure the designs to David's wash system. He wouldn't have taken the chance."

"So you say. But you didn't trust him."

"That's not the point."

"Well, I just can't see Mrs. Thompson doing it all on her own. It's so cold-blooded."

"She's cold-blooded."

"Don't mean she did it. And you don't know for sure that wrapper's what shorted the machine. There must be dozens of things here at Healing Sands that could have done the job. You do realize there's more evidence against Loomis or even Freddie Thompson? In fact, the more I think on it, I believe Freddie's got my vote. Between guilt over stealing and having Ingrid for a wife, he's the most desperate to end it all."

"She's involved."

"You sure that machine just didn't have some sort of surge? Couldn't it have had a momentary fit or something? Maybe the only criminal death here is Freddie's poisoning, and maybe it was suicide."

Bradshaw's jaw tightened.

"I'm sorry, Ben. You know I think you're a genius. You say that machine couldn't have killed unless it was shorted, and I believe you have the expertise to make that call. I just want to be sure you're being completely honest with yourself. You want Mrs. Thompson to be guilty. Admit it, you want to see her locked up. But her rigging that machine makes no sense. You said yourself Freddie took or was given poison the same night the machine was rigged. If it wasn't suicide, if she gave him the poison and rigged the machine too, why? Why would she try to kill him twice?"

"I can ask you the exact same question, Henry. Why would Freddie both rig the machine and take poison? Why try to kill himself twice?"

"That's a whole different situation. He was half-mad with guilt and desperation. He likely felt if one didn't kill him, the other would. People aren't always logical how they go about suicide. You know that better than most."

"You can't see her the way I do. She's skilled at manipulation. She's calculating, deceptive, greedy, insensitive, and selfish."

Henry snorted. "You've had some experience with that sort of female. But that don't mean she's homicidal. Ben—your wife killed herself, she didn't kill you."

"Didn't she?"

He didn't need to say more. Henry knew what he meant. For eight years following his wife's suicide, he'd lived a circumscribed existence, unable—unwilling—to participate in anything but the tasks he penciled neatly onto his desk calendar. He'd fallen into dour, plodding ways, even down to his mannerisms and gait, which had been, to his utter dismay, captured in flickering images by the engineering students on a Kinetoscope. It had only been in the past couple years, since he'd added electrical forensic investigator to his credentials, and since Missouri Fremont appeared on his doorstep, that he'd begun to feel human again. He would never be active in society, but he rarely plodded anymore.

Henry said, "Well, you're alive now."

"But David Hollister and Freddie Thompson are dead."

"She just don't seem smart enough to pull it off. It's just too far-fetched, Ben."

"When all other possibilities are eliminated, the far-fetched must be considered."

"But the other possibilities aren't eliminated. You've got no proof it wasn't Loomis or Freddie or Moss, for that matter."

Bradshaw carefully tucked the flattened foil between sheets of paper, setting it beside his suspect chart. He turned to Squirrel's notes to reread the information on Mrs. Thompson.

Henry cleared his throat. "With them eyes, she does look like Rachel."

"She's nothing like Rachel. That's what I failed to see before. She's a different sort of evil altogether."

"Ben, you know I trust you. But couldn't it be you're not seeing things clearly. The minute you laid eyes on Ingrid Thompson she reminded you of—"

"This isn't about my past, Henry."

"So you say. Hell, I'm game if you want to keep poking around. I just don't want you chasing after something that ain't there. You can't strangle a dead ghost."

Chapter Twenty-eight

After thoroughly examining Squirrel's materials and taking notes, Bradshaw gathered all of his files to give to Captain Bell.

"We've been dismissed," Henry complained as Bradshaw headed out the cabin door. "Why be so generous?"

"We're on the same side, Henry."

"You want me arrested for withholding evidence?"

"No, that's why I'm handing it over."

Bradshaw found Captain Bell at the top of the cliff, alone, watching his men below dig. Bell silently accepted the fat envelopes, and after a glance inside said, "Squirrel?"

"He's thorough."

"Are you expecting anything more from him?"

"Not unless I ask."

"You've been extending the scope of your investigations of late, Professor, but you seem to know when turning matters over to the proper authorities is required. Your associate could use a reminder."

"He's loyal to me, and devoted to justice."

"As long as he knows this is the Rural West, not the Wild West."

Below, Deputy Mitchell was bringing a bucket of water and tin cups to the diggers. "Deputy Mitchell has chosen to stay?"

"He gave me and Sheriff Graham a full confession of his incompetence, but decided to stay on to help out. I expect he'll resign once this assignment is over."

"You noticed his interest in Mrs. Hollister?"

"He confessed to that, too. He has us confused with his parish priest."

"He's not yet found his calling in life."

"Well, if he stays here, I hope he has an iron stomach. I wish you'd sent a warning along with your summons, Bradshaw. The men have made it clear I'll have a mutiny on my hands if meat and potatoes don't soon appear."

Bradshaw thought of his and Henry's secret stash of coffee and edibles, but quickly decided he'd been generous enough sharing Squirrel's information. Captain Bell could get his own food.

"Has everyone in the house been informed of Mr. Thompson's theft?"

"It is now known in the main house and will soon be known along the entire coast that the federal government of the United States is searching for stolen gold dust. No one will be able to claim finders-keepers."

"Are your men digging randomly or is there some method to their selection?"

"I'm not at liberty, Professor."

"I don't think you'll find the gold here."

"Where do you think it is?"

"If it's not sitting in a bank or already exchanged for stocks or property or diamonds?"

Bell didn't reply, but the very fact that his men were digging revealed that his department's examination of the Seattle Assay Office employees up until now hadn't turned up evidence of the Thompsons having deposited or spent the ill-gotten gold.

Bradshaw said, "I'd look to the Thompsons' past. Places they were familiar with, had access to, and are fairly private. It could be in several hiding places, but my guess is they chose one, and I don't think it's here on the coast. This is where they came for sand, not where they came to bury their stolen treasure."

"We've had a stroke of luck with their residence. They've lived at the Lincoln Hotel since the day they married, as I'm sure you already know, and the Lincoln keeps accurate records.

The Thompsons only left Seattle a half dozen times since moving in, and each time they told the hotel they were traveling to this area. We've now begun verifying that. The gold is either here or there, or somewhere along the way. We'll find it."

"What of the deaths here, Captain?"

"What of them?"

"If David and Freddie's deaths aren't related to the gold theft, if there were more personal motives at work, shouldn't the investigation dig more deeply into the lives of all of them? The clues to murder often lie in the past."

"Not in this case. Luckily, the players in this mess only recently met. It's safe to say we need not probe beyond the beginning of the Thompsons' marriage and Loomis' affairs since acquiring your outfit. I can see you want to argue with me, Professor. If you've got something you want to say, say it."

"There's more here than simple greed, Captain."

Bell cocked his head and studied Bradshaw. "I'll keep that in mind. I appreciate your sharing Squirrel's files." He tipped his hat and strode to the zig-zagged path down the cliff. Bradshaw sighed. He'd been dismissed again.

Chapter Twenty-nine

It was the shouts that woke him. Bradshaw opened his eyes to utter darkness and lay tense, listening, at first hearing only Henry's soft snoring. Then shouts erupted again, Henry snorted awake, and a light streaked by the front of the cabin.

Bradshaw leaped out of bed, shoved his legs into his pants, and ran barefoot out of the cabin, Henry not far behind. The darkness was less intense outside, the edges of the ocean surf glowed white, and lanterns flickered as they swayed in the hands of the men shouting and running after the Stanley Steamer. The automobile hissed and huffed, gathering speed on the damp flat stretches.

Deputy Mitchell led the chase, his white hat reflecting the meager light. Captain Bell shouted to his men, "Stop him!"

The Stanley raced on toward the shallowest part of the creek. But the tide had not yet dropped low enough, and the steamer plunged into a swiftly flowing current several feet deep. As the driver—a man—Loomis?—stood on the seat and leaped, a sharp crack sounded a single explosive "pop." A gun shot.

Mid-leap, the man flailed his arms, then dropped like a boulder, splashing into the creek. He got up spluttering and stumbling, but then collapsed, and the current began to carry him and the automobile toward the ocean.

Bell and his men were there now, wading in, and Bradshaw and Henry followed. Two men got hold of Arnold Loomis, and the rest of them grabbed the Stanley, hauling it up onto the beach.

Dripping, Bradshaw and Henry joined the circle of lanterns where Captain Bell stood over the prone figure of Arnold Loomis. Doctor Hornsby, in his robe, knelt beside Loomis, feeling his neck for a pulse.

Bell leaned toward Bradshaw. "Did you see who fired the shot?"

"No."

Loomis' mouth opened, and Hornsby put his ear low. A moment later, he sat back. Loomis' eyes stared unblinking at the black sky. Hornsby looked up at Captain Bell, then at Bradshaw.

"He said, 'I didn't mean to.' That's all. Just, 'I didn't mean to.'"

Deputy Mitchell bumped up beside Bradshaw. He'd lost his hat. His right arm hung at his side, his hand wrapped around his revolver. The wavering lantern light turned his shocked expression into a frightened mask.

"He's not dead. Right? He's not."

Bell exchanged a worried glance with Bradshaw before asking, "Deputy Mitchell, did you fire your weapon?"

Mitchell said, "You said, 'Stop him' and I couldn't catch him, so I-I, I meant to shoot the Stanley."

Bell put a hand on Mitchell's shoulder. "Well, son, you shot Arnold Loomis in the line of duty. It's the hardest part of the job."

"He's not dead," Mitchell said again.

"He is, and it's his own damn fault. He was fleeing the scene of a crime. I ordered you to stop him, and you stopped him. You did your duty."

Mitchell looked at his revolver with repulsion, then shoved it at the captain, who pressed the barrel down and took control of it. Then Mitchell tore off his badge and handed it to Bell before turning, walking away, a hand clamped over his mouth.

Chapter Thirty

"With the attempted escape of Mr. Arnold Loomis, we are closing the investigation into David Hollister's death. There is sufficient evidence to prove that Mr. Loomis lethally altered the electrotherapy machine he peddled in order to steal Hollister's washhouse design, which may be worth a considerable amount."

They had all gathered in the library. The Hornsbys, Martha Hollister, Deputy Mitchell, Zeb Moss, Ingrid Thompson, as well as Henry and Bradshaw.

The Hornsby family sat closely together, clenching hands. With the pronouncement, Doctor Hornsby dropped his head and quietly sobbed. He blamed himself, Bradshaw knew, for bringing Loomis into their lives and for not seeing the lethal clues.

"Arnold Loomis was one of the most cunning con artists I've come across in my professional capacity. He spent the better part of the last two decades skirting the law and capitalizing on his fellow men by violating their trust. Here at Healing Sands, his greed finally brought about his demise."

"Autopsy results have confirmed that Mr. Freddie Thompson's death was the result of the ingestion of phosphorus. Barring the presentation of any evidence proving otherwise, his death is being considered a suicide, the act of a man driven desperate by guilt for having committed a federal crime."

Bradshaw couldn't fault their reasoning. Loomis fit the crime. He had means, motive, and opportunity, and in attempting to run away, had revealed himself to be guilty. Of something. But murder? He was tangled in the crimes here, that was certain. So tangled he'd thought running away in the dead of night was his best option. So tangled he'd told Hornsby, "I didn't mean to."

But murder? Had Loomis been such a good con man that Bradshaw couldn't believe him capable of murder?

As for Freddie Thompson…suicide fit. It made sense. It all made sense. Bradshaw's logical mind understood, but his gut screamed no. His gut asked, Where did Ingrid Thompson come into it? Merely as seductress?

He watched her now, sitting alone at the edge of the room wearing a somber but elegant dark frock, her hair carefully done up. Her face was a blank mask, her eyes glazed. He recognized that expression; he'd lived that expression. Shock, grief, confusion, uncertainty, maybe even mingled with a hidden, guilty relief. Yes, he'd been there, through no fault of his own. It had taken him years to understand he couldn't have prevented his wife's death.

Could Ingrid have prevented Freddie's death? Did she have a hand in his death? Bradshaw had to admit to himself Ingrid Thompson fascinated him. She had the looks and personality of his late wife, yet she was living his own trauma. She was his marriage embodied in one person. Or was his judgment of Ingrid in this moment clouded yet again by his own experience? Hadn't he decided that Ingrid's evil was nothing like Rachel's?

And Moss? Zebediah Moss was the only one of the three men who'd paid attention to Ingrid Thompson at Healing Sands who was still alive. Moss now sat across the room from her, head hung low.

Bell said, "Mrs. Thompson, you may leave at any time. Given the ongoing investigation into your husband's theft, you will be accompanied by one of my men. I know you must be anxious to return to Seattle to bury your husband. I must ask that once in Seattle, you remain in the city until you hear from me. Is that understood?"

Mrs. Thompson nodded but her expression remained blank.

"Mr. Moss, you are also free to go."

Moss got up and left the room as if the information had been a call to action. Everyone else except Bradshaw and Henry followed. They sat beside the cold hearth.

"Well," Henry said. "That's it then. Can I drive?"

Bradshaw stared at the matchsticks among the kindling. "I'm not leaving yet, but I'd like you to go home and keep investigating."

"You heard Bell, both cases are closed."

Yes, both cases were closed. But Bradshaw didn't like it. Something was wrong, something nagged at the pit of his stomach that important answers had not yet been found. He said, "Then just go home, Henry."

"Ben...."

"I need the Stanley. You can ride back with the others."

"Don't sulk, Ben. Makes you look old. Do you want me to keep poking around?"

Bradshaw looked at Henry. He was gruff, rough—in badly in need of a shave—intelligent, and his most trusted friend. "Are you satisfied that all is known about what happened here?"

"As Moss would say, pert near."

"Pert near isn't good enough for me."

"I was afraid of that. So what more can you do here?"

"I don't know. If I find nothing here, I'll go home and keep looking."

"Ah, hell, Ben. I'll look at home. Just tell me where. You pay better than the outfitters and the work's easier on my back."

"Thank you. Look into the past, as far back as you can with Ingrid Thompson and Zeb Moss."

"Not Loomis?"

"I know you disagree, but I believe Loomis is a victim in all this. Although not an innocent victim."

"But he confessed."

"He said 'I didn't mean to.' That could be a confession, or a plea for Hornsby to understand he was lured into something he hadn't anticipated. It's possible he showed remorse for the part he played, and for the sake of his soul, I hope that's so."

Chapter Thirty-one

The wind direction shifted during the night. Bradshaw was awake when it happened, working by lantern light in his cabin. The shift rattled the windows and pulled him from his notes. He added more wood to the small stove and made another mug of Postum.

In the morning, he opened the door to a cold, thick fog that turned the porch and sand dark with dampness. With typical Pacific Northwest speed, summer weather had vanished overnight. It didn't matter that the calendar said it was still August. Bradshaw layered his jackets and pulled on the new boots Henry had brought him, then trudged up the cliff. The main house was quiet, though lights glowed in the kitchen and a few rooms. The diggers had not yet begun. Up top, the view was no better than it had been below, and the wind was stronger, but he found whom he hoped to find. Old Cedar. Dressed in the same old clothes he had worn when the weather was warm, he seemed immune to the damp fog.

Bradshaw said, "I have a favor to ask."

They made arrangements to meet in the afternoon when the tide would be outgoing. By then, the fog had risen to form a low ceiling. Pant legs rolled up to his knees, Bradshaw waded barefoot in the surf to the cedar longboat manned by two young native men. He carried the white ceramic urn he'd brought from home. He set it gently in the boat, then grasped the edge to climb in.

His awkward boarding brought smiles to the faces of the two young natives, but he didn't take a dunking. Old Cedar sat with dignity in the bow as the younger men paddled out to sea.

Once past the breaker zone, Old Cedar signaled. The natives shipped their paddles. Bradshaw cleared his throat. He'd planned to say a few words, a prayer, but now that the time had come words escaped him and his throat was too tight to speak. He held the cool urn and felt his palms warm the ceramic.

His eyes welled.

He'd been the only one who attended the young man's hanging other than those officiating. It had been done in semi-secrecy to avoid any ugliness or any public celebration. Bradshaw had inherited all of the young man's possessions. His family had wanted none of them. Amongst the things now stored in a trunk in Bradshaw's basement were textbooks, poetry, assignments, and childhood toys. And a diary. The pages within revealed a short life, from troubled innocence to ingenious assassin. The pages held the key to the design of a revolutionary device now at the bottom of Elliott Bay. The pages were filled with sadness, fear, yearning, and madness.

As he held the jar and the longboat rocked gently, Bradshaw thought of madness and the fragility of the human mind, and the inner forces driving one's actions. Why was one young man a brave soldier and another a condemned assassin? Why did one woman who thrived on applause and attention become a celebrated actress, like Ann Darlyrope, and another woman who craved attention and sympathy, like his late wife, stage a fatal play?

We are dealt a hand at our birth, he thought, consisting of strengths and weaknesses, talents and handicaps, physical and mental. When our time is done, when choices have been irrevocably made, then what? For those who were dealt a weak hand, did they spend the rest of eternity being punished for their behavior? Was the Almighty, who'd created all and thus created the flaws, that unforgiving? Did evil reside in the soul or in the chemical makeup of the body and brain? Was there a chance, at the end of human life, for peace?

He hoped so. He prayed so.

He removed the lid from the jar and tipped the ashy contents into the sea.

Old Cedar began to chant in his ancient language, his voice a low rumble more of nature than man.

Words then came to Bradshaw, and under the music of Old Cedar's chant, he spoke them for the young man whose ashes he set free, and he spoke them for his late wife, forgiving her at last. "Peace be with you."

The jar was empty. He let go.

Chapter Thirty-two

Bradshaw spent the remainder of the day in the Healing Sands barn drying out and firing up the Stanley, a plan developing.

With the early tide the next morning, he packed a small bag into the Stanley, told Doctor Hornsby he planned to return that evening, or the next morning if he missed the tides, and headed north. The weather remained gray and misty, the clouds low; but the wind was mercifully absent, leaving only the movement of the steamer to buffet him with mist.

The white-crested, steely ocean spread endlessly on his left, and virgin forest loomed from the cliffs and bluffs to his right. Seabirds swooped and cried, razor clams spit from thousands of tiny holes in the wet sand, a seal hauled himself into the water with a throaty honk. A bald eagle, curious perhaps about the new red hissing creature, dove down with a screech, its wings spread eight feet tip to tip.

At first, Bradshaw was alone with nature at the edge of the continent, but upon reaching Joe's Creek, human activity intruded. As Mrs. Hornsby had explained, here was the newly named and freshly platted town of Pacific Beach where the Northern Pacific depot was under construction. Preparations had begun for the railroad to travel along the beach northward to Moclips. Trees had been cleared, a service road plowed, and freshly milled lumber awaited the hammer.

As he drove on, figures appeared that proved to be diggers. Not clam diggers catching the low tide, but gold diggers—treasure seekers—searching the dry sand and cliff bases and the wooded verge that dipped low to meet the sea.

He waved to the diggers. If they waved back, he drove out of the reach of the incoming tide to talk to them. If they ignored him or dispersed for trails up into the woods, he continued on. Captain Bell had spread word in the area by way of the mail carrier that volunteer diggers were welcome but must first check in with him or send him a letter of intent. The unfriendly diggers had likely ignored that request.

The coast, he knew, was sparsely populated. Yet he counted no less than a hundred diggers. Those who spoke with him said they'd come from the logging camps, the mills, the canneries, from Aberdeen, from Tacoma, even Seattle. Those who'd abandoned logging or railroad construction jobs had come through the forest following logging roads and railroad spurs as far as possible. Others had traveled on foot from Oyehut after catching the steamer from Hoquiam. He'd not seen them pass Healing Sands on their way north, but last night as the tide began to drop, they must have been silently marching past his cabin as he slept.

He arrived at Moclips—a cluster of shacks and modest new buildings—just as the tide threatened to force him off the beach. He drove the Stanley up out of reach of the waves, prepared to eat the meager supplies he'd brought. But his arrival was hailed by a friendly housewife of Mrs. Prouty's proportions and years who invited him to share a hot meal with her husband—a man as small as she was large—who'd just come in from fishing on the river.

Inside a tidy clapboard house named "West End," he was served what he considered the first real meal since his arrival on the coast. Roast duck, clam chowder, fresh garden vegetables, fresh white bread, and a home-brewed ale the same amber as Missouri's eyes. He was profuse with his praise.

The pair had spoken to Captain Bell the previous day, they said, and they had no information to share for they'd not seen the Thompsons when they made their daytrip up to Moclips. They knew the Hornsbys, had often made use of David Hollister's washhouse, and wondered if it would be impolite to ask about resuming monthly washings. Bradshaw doubted they'd be allowed until Captain Bell completed his investigation.

He thanked the couple for the fine meal and made his leave, spending the next few hours retracing Captain Bell's footsteps and getting the same results. The Thompsons had not been seen in Moclips.

Bradshaw returned to the Stanley to await the tide. His thoughts wandered as he stared at the ocean. To the north, seastacks, vertical formations of rock formed by the forces of erosion, rose near shore. He wondered what about their jagged shapes gave them such an eerie, alluring quality. He wondered what it was about Missouri Fremont that so possessed him. He dug into his supplies, found paper and his pencil, and wrote a letter to Missouri that he didn't intend to mail. And then he wrote out, for himself, every word he could recall of what she'd said to him on the beach. He studied her words, especially the part where she said, *"I thought maybe you'd have some sense now, or at least be willing to discuss the very real differences between us to see if we can find a way past them."*

What were those real differences?

She was young, he was not. He was a man of habit, she was spontaneous. He felt at peace with organized routine and she lived each day anew. He was a man who found solace and stability in attending Mass. She considered nature God's cathedral.

He set down his pencil and stared, unseeing, at the ocean. The wind gusted, fluttering the paper beneath his hand.

Why had it not occurred to him before? He was Catholic. Was she? He'd never asked. Henry, while not a man of regular church habits, was Catholic, and he'd assumed Missouri, being his niece, was too, although lapsed. She was of a spiritual nature but felt no compulsion to follow the organized prescriptions of any church. He'd supposed she was, like many young people, exploring religious and spiritual ideas on a voyage of self-discovery that would eventually lead her back to the church.

But what if her voyage took her elsewhere? Was she Catholic? Would she be Catholic—for him?

The very real differences between us.

She must have been referring at least in part to this.

His chest tightened. She was right. Of course, she was right. While he dragged his feet, ignoring his feelings for her, it kept him from seeing this very real difference. This obstacle.

But if it were an insurmountable obstacle, would she have declared her feelings, told him she was done waiting, chastised him for wasting so much time rather than figuring it out?

And yet, what was there to figure out? While a mixed-marriage between a Catholic and someone who practiced another form of Christianity was possible with a special dispensation, it was frowned upon and highly discouraged. Marriage to a person of any other faith, or non-faith, was forbidden.

When the tide had dropped enough to set out for Healing Sands, he did so, attempting to distract his thoughts by constructing physics lessons from the forces of nature—wind, temperature, granular matter, liquid, solids. He wondered if the emptiness and uncertainty he felt, and the ache in the pit of his stomach that threatened to reverse the direction of the digesting duct, were about his investigation. Or Missouri. He knew it was very possible he was avoiding returning home and facing her.

And yet he also knew this case was not over. Even Captain Bell had declared there were yet unknowns. Captain Bell could live with them, Bradshaw could not.

Chapter Thirty-three

The next morning, he was off again with the low tide, this time driving south with all his belongings in the Stanley.

He'd been welcomed back to Healing Sands by the Hornsbys like a long lost relative although he'd only been gone the day. As darkness pressed against the windows, they'd all gathered in the dining room, drinking chamomile tea, and telling him what had had happened in his absence.

Sheriff Graham had returned to Hoquiam, and Captain Bell had returned to Seattle, leaving a trusted man in charge of his crew to continue the search along the North Beach. Mr. Scott Mitchell, no longer a deputy, remained. He'd asked Hornsby if he could work for room and board, and his request had been granted. Being neither handy nor skilled, he was not being called the handyman, but his humble presence was appreciated by all. He was still visibly shaken by having killed a man. The depth of the family character was revealed in the fact that he was being treated with sympathy, not as a hero.

They had accepted Captain Bell's pronouncement of Loomis' guilt. Knowing who killed David gave them some measure of relief and was allowing them to begin to move forward. Bradshaw didn't want to disturb that with uncertainty.

But he couldn't pretend he was done searching for answers.

When he announced he was leaving the next day, Martha asked if he was going home.

"Not yet," he said.

She understood what he was saying. The effect of his simple reply was reflected in her eyes. He'd reopened the wound that had only just begun to heal by putting her back into that horrible place of uncertainty. That hadn't been his intention, yet he couldn't bring himself to lie and say he was satisfied with Bell's conclusions. Ingrid Thompson's involvement in what had happened here obsessed him. He knew it. Just as he knew that while at first he'd been distracted by her resemblance to his late wife, now it was Mrs. Thompson herself that attracted his attention. He couldn't rest until he learned what role she played.

He would be retracing her route from Healing Sands back to Seattle, and once there continue to delve until he found answers. There was one slender thread of information Martha had told him that he'd begun thinking about on the drive back from Moclips. David had thought he recognized Ingrid Thompson from his childhood. Her name then would have been Ingrid Colby. She had denied they knew each other. Had she told the truth? Or was that a small clue, which combined with her lying about her age, might point him somewhere?

He asked, "Can anyone draw a portrait?"

He now had that portrait tucked safely inside his jacket. Abigail, it turned out, was an artist, and she'd captured Mrs. Thompson's likeness with remarkable skill.

He stopped at the modest hotel and health resort at Iron Springs. More diggers were there on the beach and searching the surrounding woods. He asked about the Thompson's stay the previous year; their answers came easily for the staff had sorted their memories for Captain Bell the previous day. They didn't know of an Ingrid Colby or any Colbys from Hoquiam. The answers were the same in Copalis, where he returned the Stanley Steamer to its owner and intercepted the mailman, who carried a letter from Henry.

Ben,

Met a guy who's known Moss since boyhood. I bought him a drink and he sang me a tune. Says Moss was a quiet kid, not very bright. Could never get the hang of reading. Always been uglier than sin and denser than dirt, but not mean. Worked his parents' farm until he headed up north. No wife, never had the prospect of one. Resigned bachelor.

When he got home loaded with gold and made his deposit at the assay office, he was not a happy customer. He grumbled loudly and profusely to George, that's the friend's name, that he'd been cheated. George told him he ought to make an official complaint, but Moss went instead to confront Frederick Thompson at his domicile.

After he paid that visit he shut up about being cheated. Said not another word. George asked what happened and Zeb said nothing, he'd been mistaken. Then he suddenly started acting strange, getting regular haircuts, had fancy suits made. George said he thought Zeb was sweet on Mrs. Thompson.

For the first time in his life, a woman begins paying him attention? He's likely to have serious lapses in judgment.

I can't get near the Lincoln. Every reporter and gold-digger in the state is camped on the sidewalk, waiting for Ingrid Thompson to lead them to the loot.

I started following Moss. No one seems to be paying him any attention except one professional-type. I realized on the danged trolley we were both following Moss. I wanted to know who hired this guy so I tailed him until he got bored watching a moping millionaire, and he led me to 117 Cherry Street. I know you recognize the address of our old friends, the Pinkerton Detectives. They were feeling charitable, hoping for a clue from us I reckon, and said they were helping the feds. Looks like Moss was one of the cheated, but he's not wanting to get involved and they think that's suspicious. They think maybe he was helping Freddie Thompson hide the stolen gold, depositing it in his own accounts (no one would question him having a few bags of dust, would they?) but they can't find any evidence to support that theory. And why would he help Freddie? Moss has got more gold than he knows what to do with.

    I can't find a dang thing on Ingrid Thompson or Ingrid Colby going back any earlier than about a year before her marriage, and we already know all that. I set Squirrel on it. How are you faring? What you up to?

Your humble servant,
Henry

Chapter Thirty-four

By late afternoon, Bradshaw was in Hoquiam in the records department of the county courthouse searching for the name Colby and not having any luck.

The clerk, a young fellow with an expansive mustache twirled at the ends, asked if he knew about what year he was hoping to find the Colbys. "Are they newcomers, I mean to say, or first settlers?"

If David had known Ingrid Colby as a child, then that would have been twenty years ago. "Early eighteen-eighties?" Bradshaw ventured.

"Well then, that's a might easier. Not so many people here then, not nearly so many. And the only business was logging. Let's check the old mill records."

They checked the mill records, and the earliest tax records, the homestead filings, and the marriage records. Not a single Colby in the city. He tried another angle.

"How about Hollister?"

"David Hollister?"

"You knew him?"

"Read about him in the newspaper. Was killed out at Healing Sands." They turned back to the old records and quickly found several Hollisters listed, including David, and the address of the original homestead.

"A main road runs by that old place now."

"Do you have a map?"

"To see or keep? We got some for sale."

"I'll take one of those. Can you show me how to get there?"

The title clerk pointed him in the right direction on his rented bicycle, out of the city and up a well-maintained country road bordered by acres of logged land stubbled with massive stumps and an occasional farm scraped from the rubble. He found the peddling easy enough and the exercise welcome, and he appreciated the cool breeze of the overcast day. In Seattle, he cycled daily from his home on Capitol Hill to the university and back. It was his favorite mode of transport.

After awhile he came to a cluster of red-painted buildings all belonging to a general mercantile that served as a farm and feed store and post office. A few wagons were parked, their horses tethered. His was the only bicycle.

He wiped his face with his handkerchief and went inside the mercantile, the bell above the door announcing him. He was greeted warmly by a portly man behind the counter who said Bradshaw looked as if he could use a soda.

"What do you have?"

"Only the best. Take your pick."

Four cool bottles were removed from an icebox and placed before him. Being associated with a university at times had its benefits. In this case since Bradshaw had heard a colleague lecture at length on food adulteration, he knew the brand of orange soda offered contained no orange, the ginger ale was possibly contaminated with ethyl alcohol, and the root beer colored with coal tar. But the sarsaparilla bore a local label he knew to be reliable. He happily bought a bottle and quenched his thirst, then asked about the Hollisters.

He said, "They used to have property on this road, I'm told."

"Oh, sure. In fact, you just passed the place. No Hollisters there no more, they moved closer into town."

"How long have you been here?"

"Oh, going on a quarter century. I was one of the first settlers."

"Do you recall a family by the name of Colby?"

"Colby? No, no, I don't think I do."

Bradshaw showed the man the sketched portrait of Ingrid Thompson.

"You're not looking for the Colbys, you want the Voglers. That's the Vogler girl."

"Vogler?"

"Oh, yeah, that place goes way back. One of the first to settle. A married couple ran a chicken farm."

"They had a daughter? Ingrid?"

"Never heard of an Ingrid. No, they had a son, but he died when he was a young man not yet twenty. That girl in the picture was their niece. Marion. She lived with them. Orphaned, I believe."

"Where is she now? Does she still live on the farm?"

"Not for a few years, I don't think. She took over after her aunt died and tried to make a go of it, hired a few managers over the years. Don't know where she found them, they never worked out. Well, young men these days all have gold fever, don't they? Don't want to put a shovel into the ground unless there's a promise of riches."

Bradshaw produced his map, and the fellow gladly traced a fat finger along the route.

He said, "The farm's north a piece, oh, a few miles, I'd say, from where this county road ends. Never was much of a road, and it must be overgrown by now. Doubt you can get a wagon through. What kind of rig you driving?"

"Bicycle."

"That'll do part ways if you don't mind hills. Likely have to walk some. It's a good two hours if not more."

"Who lives there now?"

"Nobody, far as I know. You know who you might want to talk to, if you're wanting to know more about the Voglers, is old Doc Hathaway. He knows everybody around here, treated us all, and our children. If you continue on up the road you'll find him just past the cemetery, the little red house."

◇◇◇

Nestled in a small clearing edging virgin forest and smack dab in a ray of sunshine poking through the clouds, the little red house had white trim and window boxes overflowing with nasturtiums in a rainbow of colors. A stone path wound through a front garden that freely mixed decorative flowers with practical vegetables and ended at the white-washed covered porch where old Doc Hathaway snoozed in a rocking chair. A lanky man, dressed for yard work, he looked all of eighty. He snorted awake at Bradshaw's approach, and welcomed him, calling into the house, "Evelyn, we've got comp'ny!"

A petite white-haired woman came through the screen door, drying her hands on her apron. She looked closer to seventy, with a full face and rosy cheeks.

After introductions were made, a glass of well water gratefully accepted, and Mrs. Hathaway excused herself to return to her sewing, Bradshaw brought up the reason for his visit.

"Oh, indeed," breathed the doctor, sucking his teeth. "I remember the Voglers. I didn't like 'em. Not a one of them."

"Why not?"

Doc shook his head. "Hard to put a finger on it. You know how it is with some, the minute you meet 'em you get to talking and swapping stories, and you feel grateful you've found a new friend? That wasn't them. In all the years I knew 'em, I didn't know 'em. They didn't let you in, if you know what I mean. Mr. Vogler, now he never spoke unless it were to complain. Carried around a Bible, but I think he only read the parts about hell and damnation. He worked in the logging camps most of the year. That's what eventually killed him. Mrs. Vogler ran the farm; she was the one with the brains, but she had no softness in her. No nonsense at all. Now me? I think a little nonsense is good for a body. Ain't that right, Evelyn?" He shouted the last with a wink at Bradshaw, and his wife said she wasn't eavesdropping, but yes, he was full of nonsense.

"They had a son?"

"That's right, just the one child." Doc's smile faded as his eyes narrowed in recollection. He sucked his teeth again. "Shame about him."

"What do you mean?"

"Oh, what can you expect, growing up in that sort of house? He was a rambunctious youth. I treated him for the usual cuts and bumps, got bronchitis once. Nice looking boy, only he knew it, and it didn't take him long to think the world ought to treat him special for it. His mother put that notion in his head. Between her telling him he deserved the world, and his father telling him the devil was in him, it's no wonder things turned out like they did."

"And how was that?"

Doc cocked his head and studied Bradshaw. "Why is it you're asking after the Voglers? It can't have nothing to do with Healing Sands." Doc laughed. "Don't look so surprised, Professor. Your name's been in the paper more than once with all the killing going on at the sanitarium."

"I can't give you the details just yet, but the Voglers might be involved."

"Don't see how they can be, they're all dead."

"Marion's not."

The doctor's eyebrows shot up. "I haven't heard about her for a few years now. She moved away. Where'd she go? She in trouble?"

Bradshaw showed him the sketch.

"That's a good likeness, you draw that?"

He shook his head. "If you don't mind, I'd prefer not to answer any questions just yet, but I do have more to ask."

"That's all right, I'm happy to talk, though you do have me curious. When you find out, will you come back and tell me?"

"I will. What do you know about Marion?"

Doc took a moment to speak. A bee buzzed in the flower boxes then darted out to the garden. The sweet scent of late summer wafted on the breeze. The warm scent of the woods, the pine and fir and cedar, mixed with the heady scent of garden flowers.

"She wasn't their child, but a niece on the mother's side. Went to live with them after her mother died, in Portland, I believe. Rumor had it the mother wasn't married, but nobody was giving out any details when they settled here. She fit right in with them, though. Far as I could tell, she took after her aunt, no warmth to her. I really shouldn't judge since I never saw her professionally but the once. What she lacked in sweetness she made up for in hardiness. I felt sorry for her, being sent to that family." Doc Hathaway looked away, fixing his gaze on the garden. He sat up a bit and took a deep, nasally breath.

"I don't know if this signifies to what you're investigating, Professor, but it's nagged at me all these years and sometimes I wonder if I acted rightly. The one and only time I doctored Marion she came here to my house in the night all by herself. She was but fourteen years old. She'd been hurt bad and was bleeding." He glanced up, and Bradshaw gave a nod of understanding.

"I had to stitch her up. I told her she didn't have to go home, she could stay right here with the missus and me, but she wouldn't stay. I thought of going to the sheriff, but the wife said that would just make the girl's shame public."

"Was it her uncle? The cousin?"

The doctor wiped his mouth; the rough skin of his hand rasped against the shadowed stubble of his jaw. "Well, the next day I got a message saying I was needed urgently up at the Vogler place. I went up there with my bag, expecting to find the girl collapsed, thought maybe she'd had internal bleeding. But it was the boy ailing."

"How old was he?"

"Nineteen. He'd taken to his bed with a bellyache, and when the nausea and vomiting started his mother got worried and sent for me. He was senseless when I got there, and when I examined him I found scratches on his arms and neck and a nasty bruise on his leg. He'd been in a fight, and I knew who'd fought him. He never came 'round."

"Did you tell his parents about Marion visiting you?"

"Nope."

"Why not?"

"When I saw their faces...they were in shock. For all their harsh ways, and their cold manner, they loved that boy. Spoiled him. Ruined him. But they loved him. I knew what that boy had done to the girl, but I didn't think his parents should suffer for it. He was gone and wouldn't hurt her again. What was the point in telling them?"

"What did you put on the death certificate?"

"Kinked intestines."

"What really killed him?"

"Oh, his intestines were kinked, that wasn't a lie. But there's one detail I didn't put down and it haunts me to this day." He struggled, having kept the secret for so long he couldn't bring himself to speak of it.

"I think I know, Doc. The boy's vomit and breath were luminescent. They glowed green."

"I dread to think how you know that."

Chapter Thirty-five

By the time Bradshaw climbed back on his bicycle the clouds had rebuilt, filling in the patches of blue and threatening to lower. It would be dark soon. There was no sense in going to the old Vogler place until morning.

He returned to town and booked a room at the Grand Hoquiam, finding it as luxurious and the food as good as Henry had reported. He contemplated contacting Captain Bell but decided to wait until after he saw the house and gathered more information. After all, even if Ingrid Thompson was Marion Vogler, it proved nothing regarding the deaths at Healing Sands. He needed hard evidence, and the chances of finding it were slim. But he did send Henry a telegram asking him to come at once.

Bright and early the next morning on the red eye, Henry arrived, eager to hear the news. As they left the depot and headed into town, Bradshaw, pushing his bicycle, said, "We need to find you some wheels."

"A bicycle? For what?"

"It's the best way to get to the Vogler Farm."

"I can't ride a bicycle."

"Yes, you can."

"You ever seen me on a bike?"

"Not since college. It'll come back to you."

"Hire a horse, you cheap skate."

"Because you're too lazy to pedal? Horses need food and water, and I don't know how long we'll be gone."

"Horses eat grass, and in case you hadn't noticed, there's plenty of grass out in the country." Henry put a hand to his back, and though Bradshaw knew the gesture was meant to play on his sympathy, he also knew his occasional flare-ups were painful.

"You can get a motorized bike."

Henry's eyes lit up. "No fooling? Hot damn, I've always wanted to try one of them."

◇◇◇

The shop owner's thorough lesson on the art of operating a motorized bike took the better part of an hour. It was a complicated machine that required precision in the timing of the start-up procedure, but once it was alight and chugging, it hummed along beautifully. They strapped their supplies, Bradshaw's tool bag, and food and water, to the machine and were off.

Henry delighted in racing ahead, charging up hills, then turning back around to rejoin Bradshaw.

"You'll run out of fuel and then have to pedal," Bradshaw warned, and this put a stop to Henry's circling.

The weather was once again with them, cool enough to be comfortable, the sky a blanket of drabness, but with no rain threatening.

A mile after passing the doctor's little red house they came to a handsome farm carved out of the forest, with a cedar home, outbuildings, cows grazing, fields of corn ripening. Bradshaw hailed the farmer, a lanky gentleman in overalls, who crossed his field to greet them.

"We're going to the Vogler place, do you know it?" Bradshaw asked after introducing himself and Henry.

"Oh, aye," said the farmer, "But there ain't nobody home. The place is empty."

"Do you know the people who own it?"

"Marion Vogler, you mean?" The farmer scratched his weathered cheek thoughtfully. "Can't say I know her, but I know who she is when she passes by."

"Does she pass by often?"

"Ah, no. She don't live round here no more."

"When was the last time you saw her?"

"Oh, that'd be just a few weeks past. It was a Sunday, as I recall, and early morning. I was in the milk barn," he said, nodding toward the barn closest to the road. "And the cows all perked up their ears and turned their heads, so I looked out and there she was."

"Was she alone?"

"Far as I can tell. I only saw her. Riding a donkey."

Henry guffawed. "They eat grass, too, Ben."

The farmer said, "If you're thinking of making an offer for her property, you'll be disappointed."

"Why is that?"

"She swears she'll never sell. I've made an offer every time I seen her since she inherited the place. I'd tear down the house but the land is good for farming, and there's timber. Can't be she's sentimental over the place. The Voglers weren't what you called warm people. Well, we'll see. The new railroad line they're building to the beach passes not more than a mile from her property. Somebody will make an offer high enough, I suspect."

Bradshaw showed his map to the farmer, who confirmed they were heading in the right direction and warned them the road was maintained only about another half mile. Bradshaw thanked him, and he and Henry started out again.

As warned, the road maintenance came to an abrupt end. There were visible marks where the plow turned. From there, the road became a path, decent enough for their bikes, then an overgrown trail, with brush and saplings attempting to reforest where loggers had felled giants two decades ago. For the last half mile, they walked, pushing their bikes to avoid being unseated by low hanging branches or bucked off by ruts.

Finally, the trail opened to a small clearing backed by towering Douglas firs and western hemlock, where stood a sagging house, a dilapidated barn, and a string of weathered and disintegrating chicken coops

The house was a two-story farm style. The roof hung low over the offset porch, casting the entrance in deep shadow. The white clapboard siding was streaked black and peeling, bisected by an oddly positioned red brick chimney. The windows on the first floor had been boarded over, and the porch steps lost in a tangle of weeds. From the eves of the upper story hung delicate lace trim, making the place look tawdry, like frilly bloomers on a streetwalker.

Henry said, "This place gives me the creeps. I don't have to go in, do I?"

"You wouldn't let me go in alone."

"Like hell, I would."

"Let's look around outside first."

They examined the yard, the chicken coops, the barn, looking for signs of something recently hidden or moved or changed, without disturbing anything themselves.

The kitchen garden had years ago gone to seed and was a tangle of wildflowers, vegetable greens, weeds, corn stalks, even a few cedar and fir saplings. The coal shed was missing its heavy door.

A broken rail fence marked the boundary to a field tall with grass. A doe and her two fawns lifted their heads, ears alert, then resumed grazing. Henry grunted but made no comment.

The tangle of weeds and layers of grime in the yard were marked only by the trails of insects and the footprints of wild creatures. An experienced tracker might have been able to say if a human had recently been here, but neither Bradshaw nor Henry could.

Bradshaw looked at Henry. "What do you think?"

Henry stomped his foot. "We could spend a hundred years searching out here. But goldarn her eyes, I betcha the gold's in the house."

They approached the small back porch with a sense of curious dread. Weeds grew up between the boards. The wind shifted, rustling their clothes, suddenly flooding the house and yard with sunshine that revealed in greater detail the weeds and peeling paint.

Henry hung back, giving Bradshaw a small shove.

"Henry, there's nothing to be afraid of."

"You trying to convince me or you?"

Bradshaw gripped the bronze knob. The door was locked.

Henry said, "That's telling. Country folk don't usually lock their doors."

"They do if they no longer live there and want to discourage tramps from moving in."

"Got an answer for everything, don't ya? Well, come on then. Pick it."

The lock easily gave way to Bradshaw's pick. He pushed the door open. It squeaked on its hinges into the dim interior. A tunnel of sunlight poured through the open door and narrow chinks slipped in through the boarded windows revealing a scarred table and chairs, a sink with a pump handle faucet, an icebox, and an ancient coal range. Dust and cobwebs coated the shelves, corners, abandoned oddments, dishes, pots, and canisters.

The moldy smell of the place wafted out to them. Not the pleasant mustiness of the cabins at Healing Sands, but a sour stench of things left too long in damp and darkness.

"Not much of a housekeeper, our Mrs. Thompson," whispered Henry.

"Shh."

"Why? No one's here."

"We are."

Henry rolled his eyes but remained silent as they stepped inside. He'd been often enough with Bradshaw on investigations to need no reminders about watching where he stepped and what he touched.

With slow deliberation, Bradshaw moved about the room. Unlike the yard, here was ample evidence of human movement. Scuffed footprints in the dusty floor, and swaths of table and drain board recently wiped, as if they'd been swept clean by shirtsleeves, revealed someone had been here fairly recently.

The footprints were small, slightly turned-in with a narrow heel and toe, most certainly a woman's. They led to a cellar door.

Bradshaw wondered if his own face reflected the same foreboding that he saw in Henry.

"It's just another part of the house, Ben."

"A dark, underground, spider-filled, airless part of the house."

"And you call yourself a Professor."

"I don't profess to like cellars. You go down, I'll check up here."

He turned away and headed into the parlor, Henry defiantly on his heels. There they found a photograph of a young woman with a square jaw and sultry eyes.

Henry whispered, "Spitting image of her."

They discovered a moldering family Bible inscribed with a list of births, marriages, and deaths.

1855, Jacob Herbert Vogler married Cordelia Colby, West Virginia.

1861, son born, Jacob Herbert, Jr., California.

1866, Marion Ingrid Colby, born out of wedlock to Helen Colby, sister of Cordelia.

1871, Helen Colby died, Oregon.

Henry said, "That makes our Mrs. Thompson thirty-seven. Kind of them to put her illegitimacy right there on the page. We got our proof. Ingrid Thompson is Marion Vogler."

"If those are her footprints in the kitchen, we know where we need to look first."

Bradshaw returned to the kitchen, to the cellar door.

Henry followed, but he didn't reach to open the door. He swallowed hard. "Let's look around upstairs, first."

"At twenty dollars an ounce, seventy-five thousand in gold dust weighs over two hundred pounds, Henry. Do you think they piled it upstairs?"

"Why not? They got it in small doses over more than a year. You know, I was thinking, Freddie must have had days when he walked out of that office with five pounds of dust on him. How in the Sam Hill did he get away with it?"

"It's why his nerves were shot."

"I don't want to go down there."

"Neither do I." Bradshaw found a lamp with a bit of oil, struck a match to light it, then pulled open the door. They were hit by an updraft of sour rot.

Henry coughed. "Smells like a bushel of rotten potatoes."

At the bottom of the stairs they found an upturned crate that had been used as a table. Piled on it were mason jars and lids, a pair of scissors, and scraps of white cloth. They both examined the scraps that appeared to be garment seams and laces.

Henry said, "Are you thinking what I'm thinking?"

"She sewed the gold into her underclothes and wore it here."

"Then cut out the pockets of gold and stuffed them into jars? But where are the full jars?"

Armed with the lamp, the explored the sour cellar. They found no rotting root vegetables, but they did find steps dug into the earth floor that led down to a squat padlocked door.

Henry whistled. "That's the door missing from the coal shed. Frame and all."

It looked as if someone had carved a space to fit the frame, then packed earth solidly around it.

"I don't like this. Goldarn it, the hair's standing up on my arms. Look."

Bradshaw was too busy picking the lock to look. The heavy iron at last yielded to the pressure of his tools. He removed the lock and placed a hand on the latch, but didn't pull.

He said, "It's probably just the gold inside."

"Then why do you look like a scared rabbit?"

"Oh, shut up."

The smell hit them as Bradshaw pulled open the heavy door. It was the same as upstairs, only fouler, riper, more potent.

Inside was a dungeon-like space, too short for Bradshaw to enter completely upright. He thrust the lantern in and crouched, burying his nose in the crook of his sleeve. He took only two steps before he saw the four mounds of dirt, each about six feet long and three feet wide. The mounds were dimpled and lumpy. From the nearest one jutted a familiar shape.

Bradshaw backed out, nearly knocking Henry over and swung the door shut.

They staggered up the steps, through the kitchen, and out into the yard. Henry coughed until he almost vomited, but then finally got in a good breath and let out a deep rumbling belch. They sat far across the yard from the house in the fresh air.

"Ben—that wasn't gold buried in there."

"Not unless gold can grow feet."

Chapter Thirty-six

"Who are they?"

"I don't know. Henry, I need you to get Captain Bell."

"Hell, we need the whole damn army."

"No, just Bell and a few of his men. Plain clothes. Don't be followed."

"You don't expect him to ride a bicycle here, do you?"

"However he wants to come. Don't be followed."

"You already said that."

"It bears repeating. Everyone is looking for Ingrid Thompson and the gold. The doctor and the neighbor know we're asking questions about Marion. It's only a matter of time before they make the connection. If word gets out, the gold-diggers will be swarming the house and woods. I want every scrap of evidence I can find."

"How much evidence you need? You got four corpses!"

"Evidence she's responsible for the deaths at Healing Sands."

"You going back in there?"

"Not the cellar. But I still need to inspect the rest of the house."

Henry got up, coughing again and clearing his throat. He screwed up his face, shaking his head. "I don't get it, Ben. She hides the gold in her underthings but leaves the evidence out in plain sight."

"I think she feels safe here. No one knows she's Mrs. Thompson, wife, now widow, of a gold thief. If we didn't know about her connection with stolen gold, we wouldn't have guessed by simply finding the scraps of cloth and jars. I find it far more troubling that she can set up a worktable just outside the room where four bodies are rotting."

"Something wrong with that woman."

"She has no conscience."

"I'll vote for that."

"Leave me my tools and the food."

Once Henry had gone on the motorbike, Bradshaw reentered the house. He moved through the rooms systematically, startling a few mice back to their nests. Spiders occupied every corner and he hoped they stayed there.

Upstairs, he found Ingrid's room. There was no mistaking it. The room was a filthy shrine to her obsession for riches. Advertising posters of foreign castles and pages of fashion magazines covered the walls. The floor was strewn with discarded garments and mouse-nibbled magazines. In a jewelry box he found three men's pocket watches, a pair of gold cuff links, and a pocket knife. He picked through the mess and found a writing desk with several years' worth of correspondence, receipts, telegrams, and letters.

There was no order to any of it, and for an hour he sorted, pausing to read the personal letters completely. The most telling, the most damning, was dated three years ago.

Dear Miss Vogler,

I received your letter and am happy to provide all you ask. Yes, it was in response to your classified advertisement that I first wrote. A woman in your position must of course go about seeking a farm manager and prospective husband with the utmost care. I assure you my intentions are noble, and should I satisfy you as to the former and not the latter, I shall gladly serve in that capacity as long as needed.

I am thirty years of age, in the best of health, and have been employed in farm management for the past ten years. I have no close kin and very much would like to marry and have children. I am a man of frugal nature and have

saved a tidy sum in hopes of one day buying a small farm
of my own. Your situation near the coast of Washington
State appeals to me greatly. I am prepared to make a down
payment on the purchase of your property to show you I am
earnest in my desire to ease you of the burden of responsi-
bility. If you will let me know where to have the funds sent,
I will do so immediately via Western Union.

I look forward to meeting you next month,

Sincerely,
Reginald R. Fowler

Reginald R. Fowler.

Bradshaw closed his eyes and whispered a prayer for ever-
lasting peace for Reginald Fowler and the others whose letters
revealed a similar pattern and whose bodies, he was almost
certain, now lay buried in the cellar.

Had she tired of the game? Of luring men here, taking their
money and lives? She must have thought in a big city like Seattle,
she'd find wealthier men. Had she been unable to get their
attention? Come up with a new plan? Met Freddie Thompson
of the Seattle Assay Office and decided he would steal gold for
her? Had it been her idea?

She must have realized that getting rid of a husband with a
public job in a big city was far more difficult than getting rid of
a farm manager no one knew in a remote location. She couldn't
simply bury his body in the cellar and hope no one asked where
he'd gone. No, his death had to be as public as his life.

And homely Zebediah Moss? Where did he fit in? As a pack
mule for the gold? A way to disguise the stolen dust? But if Ingrid
had been hiding the gold somewhere here in jars, then Moss
hadn't been passing it through his accounts for Freddie. Ingrid
had wanted Moss for herself, not to help disguise the gold, but to
get his gold once she got rid of Freddie. Bradshaw imagined what
that moment might have been like when she opened the door
of her Lincoln Hotel apartment to Zeb Moss, the millionaire
miner who came to accuse her husband of theft. It must have

been a dream come true for her. A millionaire—uneducated, illiterate, inexperienced with women—knocking on her door.

He set the letters aside to go in search of the gold. He began in the attic and worked his way down to the kitchen without finding a glint. But he found lucifer matches. Dozens of boxes, some of them empty, some full, piled haphazardly in the bottom of a linen closet.

He recalled what Ingrid Thompson said on the porch of Healing Sands about the phenomenon of the glowing water, or rather, about Freddie being made sick by it. She said he couldn't have swallowed much because he didn't glow. She must not have known that by soaking the match tips in the tincture of gentian she would negate the glow of phosphorus. She had simply chosen it because Doctor Hornsby had been dosing her husband with it. What had happened that night of the glowing sand?

He was convinced she'd poisoned Freddie. But had she been the one to kill David Hollister? He now knew her motive, but was she capable of it?

One scenario played in Bradshaw's mind. While her husband, Loomis, and Moss were occupied changing into dry clothes that evening after she'd playfully dunked them, and Doctor Hornsby and the others were still on the beach, she could have slipped upstairs to the electrotherapy room and placed the cheese foil across the Leyden jars. This she must have been planning for several days. Her intention was to kill David Hollister because he'd recognized her.

She killed him to keep secret what was in the cellar of this house. How had she known about his electrotherapy sessions? It seemed reasonable she feared being unmasked and so had watched David, followed him, eavesdropped on his conversations in case he told others about the Voglers. She could easily have seen him enter Doctor Hornsby's office each morning before her husband's treatments. She could have listened at the door and heard a treatment in progress. Would she have cared if her timing was off and Freddie took the fatal current? No. So much the better for her.

How had she known how to make the machine fatal? Loomis. Loomis and his parlor trick. Had Loomis shown her more than that trick? Had he been playing some sort of perverse seductive game with her? Had she asked him questions about the machine, asked for a private viewing of the working components, even hinted at the dangers to her husband? Is that what he meant when he said with his dying breath that he didn't mean to?

And had the glowing sand that same evening given her another lethal idea? An idea that had pleased her so much, she'd been uncharacteristically giddy and playful on the beach. Had she planned to kill Freddie at Healing Sands before the evening of the glowing sand? With Freddie's health declining because of nerves, his body perhaps even weakened from lead poisoning as Hornsby diagnosed, and Moss waiting in the wings, she must have been watching for the perfect time to get rid of one in order to snatch the other. And here was an ocean she mistakenly believed was filled with glowing phosphorus. She must have seen that nobody feared touching the glowing water, must have heard Doctor Hornsby and David and Moss mention they'd seen the phenomenon before. So she deduced it was not enough for Freddie to get wet: it had to appear he'd swallowed some glowing sea water. So she'd pushed him, dunked him, to get her alibi.

After rigging the electrotherapy machine, she'd spied the colorful jars of ethereal oils and tinctures in Hornsby's office. She'd likely seen them before. She grabbed the bottle of gentian, knowing Freddie had been given doses of it. And then what? She searched for matches, finding a box in the library. She broke off the tips, slipped them in her pocket or handkerchief, and tossed the sticks into the hearth.

What had she done next? Convinced her husband to take a dose of gentian? It would have been so very easy. What had she done with the evidence? The tincture and soaked match tips? Freddie had been sick in the night, but as she said, he hadn't glowed. She must have thought he hadn't swallowed enough poison to glow or die. Did she think she hadn't soaked the match tips long enough? If she'd prepared the tainted gentian that evening, she couldn't have let the tips soak long.

But her electric trick had worked. In the chaos of David's death, had she removed the cheese foil, balled it up, and shoved it under Loomis' mattress to frame him? Bradshaw's thoughts stalled. Something felt wrong about that part of his scenario. If she'd wanted to frame Loomis, she only had to leave the cheese wrapper in the machine. So why place it under Loomis' mattress?

Had she removed it from the machine after David's death so that his death would appear to be an accident? And then when she learned there was to be an investigation, did she fear someone would figure out the machine had been tampered with and hide the foil in Loomis' room in case a scapegoat was needed?

Or was he forcing David's death onto Ingrid Thompson?

Had it been Loomis after all who killed David? But why would Loomis put the wrapper under his own mattress? Bell hadn't thought it hard to believe, and considering the stupid things he'd witnessed criminals doing over the years, it was no wonder. But Bradshaw found it hard to believe Loomis had either intentionally or unintentionally killed David and then kept the foil in his possession. There was an entire ocean in which to lose it.

With David Hollister, Freddie Thompson, and Arnold Loomis dead, would the full truth ever be known?

Bradshaw found himself standing before the cellar door but couldn't make himself go down. He turned away and attempted a deep breath, but the oppressive air of the house was claustrophobic. He went outside, pried a few boards off the windows in the parlor and kitchen to let in sunlight, then returned indoors to open a few windows to let in the fresh air. In the brighter kitchen, he studied the water pump at the sink. The water he'd brought wouldn't last long. He lifted the pump handle, but pumping produced only the hiss of air. He headed outside and found running beside the field a small, swiftly flowing creek. He could well imagine what Henry would say about the creek. *Ha! Water for horses, Ben. Told you so.* He scooped up a bucketful of water and carried it back to the house, pouring it carefully into the pump to prime it. When he pumped, he now felt resistance and heard gurgling. He kept pumping until the water flowed cold and clear, then held his palm under the stream to drink.

A movement outside the window caught his attention. It was far too soon for Henry to be back. He opened the kitchen door expecting it was perhaps the deer wandering into the yard, but it was a man stumbling out of the tangled garden.

The man was covered in briars and twigs and scratches, wearing a backpack and cursing up a storm. A bee buzzed around his face, and he swatted at it with a crumpled piece of paper. When he saw Bradshaw, he stopped in his tracks and gave a final cuss.

Bradshaw said, "Good afternoon, Mr. Moss."

Chapter Thirty-seven

Moss stared at him. "You gonna tell me where the hell I am and what in tarnation you're doing here?"

"This is Mrs. Thompson's house."

Moss' scowl deepened as he ran his eye over the decrepit house and then down at the crumpled paper in his hand.

He gave a snort of acceptance. "Any water in the place?"

"Inside."

Moss marched in and accepted a glass of cool water, drinking it down in one breath. He presented the glass for a refill, then refused a third.

"You look confused, Mr. Moss."

"I don't know what the hell's going on."

"If you tell me how you came to be here, I might be able to sort it out."

"I was told to come. Told not tell anyone and not be followed. She didn't say you'd be here."

"She? Mrs. Thompson sent you?"

Moss scrunched up his face, aware he'd given away too much by his choice of pronoun.

"You didn't come by the main road."

"Followed the new rail line, didn't I? Just like she said. Just like the map shows." He waved the crumpled paper.

Bradshaw held out his hand. "May I?" Moss handed it over. It was a map of the coast torn from a newspaper showing the future railroad line from Hoquiam to Moclips. It had been marked with a bold black pen showing a route that followed the railroad for a few miles before heading west into an area depicted as forest.

"Easy trek, she said. Like hell. Pert near killed myself." He pulled a chair out from the table and sat heavily. "Not a solid, level piece of ground between here and the railroad. Trees growing outa trees like a crazy jumble. Worse than Alaska."

"What are you to do now that you're here?"

"Wait for her. She'll be along soon."

"How soon?"

"No idea."

"And then what? When she gets here, what do you expect to happen?"

"I dunno! She just wants to get away from all the commotion."

"Why didn't you travel together?"

"Her place is surrounded, ain't it? She's got to sneak out. I still don't know why you're here. She send you here, too? By gum, you better not have any ideas about her."

"No, she didn't send me, and my ideas about her are not what you imagine. Come with me."

He led Moss to the parlor and showed him the old photos of Ingrid. She was much younger in them, but they were unmistakably her with that square jaw and sultry eyes. He would have shown Moss the Bible, but Moss couldn't read.

"So her pictures are here, so she lived here as a girl, so what?"

"Have you ever heard the name Vogler?"

Moss narrowed his eyes.

"Marion Vogler?"

"Yeah, so?"

"This is the Vogler farm. Mrs. Thompson grew up here. She lived here as Marion Vogler, but her legal name was Marion Ingrid Colby."

Moss said again, "Yeah, so?"

"Did you know she was orphaned? Then sent here to live with her aunt, uncle, and cousin?"

"She don't talk about her childhood."

"I don't blame her. It wasn't very pleasant. Come on, I have more to show you."

As they walked through the house and upstairs, Bradshaw told Moss all he'd learned about Marion Ingrid's life. He need tell no lies or add embellishments. The simple truth painted the portrait of an unwanted and unloved child, raised by undemonstrative relatives, brutalized at a young age, who had turned to wealth in search of happiness, and who had learned from her experience with her cousin that she could attract a man, and that she could kill one.

In Ingrid's chaotic bedroom, with its memorabilia that displayed her worship of wealth and possessions, Bradshaw read aloud from the letters from the men she'd lured to the farm.

Moss flushed, showing he recognized elements of his own relationship with Mrs. Thompson. He said, "Men give women stuff all the time. It's what we do, ain't it? Don't mean nothing."

"Doesn't it? Don't men give in hopes of winning a woman's heart?"

"Ain't no guarantee. You takes your chances."

"How much have you given Ingrid?"

Moss locked his jaw.

"Wealth won't make her happy. You know that. Better than anybody. She'll never be happy. She's chasing an empty dream."

"Maybe she can learn from me."

"How to be happy?"

Moss looked away and mumbled, "How to love."

"Mr. Moss, I wish that were possible."

"How you know it ain't?"

"I'm no expert on the human mind or soul, but I do know that the ability to love and care for others is nurtured in childhood, as is the ability to know right from wrong, good from evil. Marion Colby was either born without a conscience or something went wrong within her as a child that turned her into the monster she is today. She is incapable of loving."

"You ain't got no right to call her a monster!"

"I wish that were true. Come with me."

"What, again?"

"One last time." Bradshaw brought him down to the cellar, but he wouldn't budge near the open door to the handmade morgue.

"I can smell it, can't I! There's dead in there, now get me outa here!"

He clambered up the stairs, out the kitchen door, and into the yard, just as Bradshaw and Henry had done. He paced the yard, face between his hands.

"Was that the men? The ones she sent for?"

"I believe so, yes."

"But you don't know for sure?"

"What I know for sure is that there are four bodies buried in the cellar and this house belongs to Ingrid Thompson, who was raised as Marion Vogler, moved to Seattle as Ingrid Colby, and married Freddie Thompson, who is now dead. She was recognized by David Hollister, who is now dead. She flirted with Arnold Loomis, who is now dead.

"She didn't shoot Loomis, that deputy did that."

"That's true, but I'm fairly certain he was running because of his relationship with Mrs. Thompson."

Moss continued pacing, his fingers dug into his hair, mumbling, occasionally gagging. He spit a few times, then sat down in the dry grass.

Bradshaw brought him more water.

"She gave you no clue about what you were to do here?"

"Women are fickle. I don't ask questions."

"Mr. Moss, the Secret Service knows you were one of the miners Freddie Thompson cheated at the assay office. You are being investigated in connection with the theft."

"Me? What fer?"

"You didn't file a complaint. Instead, you befriended the Thompsons, or at least Mrs. Thompson. It appears now that you were either Mr. Thompson's accomplice, or you are acting in that capacity for Mrs. Thompson."

"I don't know what in tarnation you mean by ca-pass-a-tea, Professor, but I wasn't helping either one of them with stealing gold. I wasn't hiding it for them either, if that's your next question."

"I know that now, Mr. Moss, and that's what frightens me."

"Why should it?"

"Because you're her next victim."

"Like hell, you say!"

"Mr. Moss, Ingrid Thompson does not keep men in her life for long. You were never to be a part of her future. You were to provide her with more wealth than she's ever known before, once she got rid of Freddie. Then you would be cast aside. Or buried in the cellar."

"Never!"

"It's no accident she chose you. Who better to disguise her illicit wealth? Who would question a deposit of gold dust from the wife or *widow* of a known gold-millionaire?"

Zeb Moss cupped his hand over his mouth. His ruddy complexion had drained to paste.

Bradshaw asked, "You have something to tell me?"

Moss paced for a few minutes, tugging his hair. He finally sat on a stump, his hands on his knees, shaking his head.

Bradshaw waited.

"On the way home," Moss began. He coughed and cleared his throat. "On the way home from the sanitarium, she said she couldn't live in Seattle no more, not with everyone knowing her husband had been a thief. She asked would I take her away. I said it wouldn't be proper, us not being wed, so she said for me to get a license quick as I could."

"A marriage license? Did you?"

Moss was quiet so long, Bradshaw had to ask again.

"The train had a layover in Tacoma. I got off and went to the courthouse."

"Weren't you being escorted by one of Bell's men?"

Moss looked smug. "Not me, just her. He didn't look none too happy when I got up, but what could he do? He had orders to stick with her."

"How did you acquire a license for Mrs. Thompson to marry? You couldn't have had Mr. Thompson's death certificate."

Moss shifted his eyes away. "Didn't need it. She told me to use her maiden name, Vogler, said it was legal and that nobody would ask questions."

"She said to use the name Ingrid Vogler?"

He shook his head. "Marion. Like you said."

"And did you get the license?"

"I got it. And got back on the train."

"And now you're meeting her here to run off together to get married?"

"Too late for that. We got married on the train."

"You didn't."

"Thought that'd surprise you."

"How did you manage it?"

"You won't believe what money can buy, Professor. A special license and a J.P. willing to play along. Bought him a ticket and he boarded with me."

J.P. Justice of the Peace.

"With Bell's man as witness?"

"Nah, we waited until he was using the facilities three cars down. Got another passenger to witness. By the time Bell's man got back, it was done, and we weren't even sitting together. He was none the wiser."

"So what's the plan now?"

"She just wants out from that hotel where everyone's watching her. We're going off to start a new life somewhere. She ain't under arrest or nothing. We can go."

Moss' tone had flipped from frightened to defensive. He seemed unable to grasp that the woman he'd fallen for, had married, was a murderess. He still thought of her as the woman he loved.

"Did she ask you to change your will?"

"Didn't have one to change." He crossed his arms and glared at Bradshaw. Then his eyes shifted away. "She wrote one out for me. When she sent Bell's man for something from the dining car."

"Don't tell me you signed it."

"I can sign my name. I'm stupid with books, but I can sign my name!"

"I'll write you a new will. Now."

Bradshaw marched Moss into the house and through to the parlor where they found writing paper, pen and ink, in a dusty roll top desk. He wrote out a simple will and handed the pen to Moss.

"I won't do it, I tell ya!"

Bradshaw grabbed Moss' arm and pulled him to the cellar door, flinging it open.

"Confound you, I ain't dying today, what's your rush? I got no intention of ever going near that woman again! I'll get the marriage annulled. I'll leave town. By God, she ain't killing me."

"All the same, you need a new will. Now." He dragged Moss back into the parlor, and Moss frowned in concentration as he carefully signed his name. Then he threw down the pen, splattering ink on the will.

"Mr. Moss, I'm going to help you, but I need you to help me, too."

"That don't sound good."

"My associate Henry Pratt will be here later today or tomorrow with Captain Bell. If Mrs. Thompson—Ingrid—what do you call her?"

"Dunno, ain't called her nothing since Tacoma. Mrs. Thompson, I suppose. It's what I'm used to. Don't seem right to call her Mrs. Moss. That's my mother's name."

"If Mrs. Thompson gets here before Bell, we'll have to detain her."

"What, tie her up?"

"If we have to, yes."

Moss' face reflected his repugnance at the idea. He shook his head.

"She's clever, and she knows these woods. If she runs, she won't be easy to find."

"Well, mebbe them men all had it coming? The cousin attacked her, didn't you say? And Freddie used to beat her, she told me that herself. Mebbe them others were cruel, too."

"All of them? She hired four managers who just happened to be so cruel and abusive her only option was to kill them?"

"It could happen."

"I know it's hard for you to believe, Mr. Moss, but surely you understand that the need to kill six men is beyond bad luck."

Chapter Thirty-eight

They waited upstairs in the house, watching out the windows for anyone approaching. It was a coin toss who would arrive first, Henry and Captain Bell, or Mrs. Thompson. If he left Seattle as soon as he received Henry's wire, it would take Bell a minimum of nine hours to reach this house. Bradshaw checked his pocket watch. It was nearly five. Henry would have sent the wire about an hour ago.

When had Ingrid left the Lincoln Hotel? Yesterday? This morning? Or had she not yet escaped her watchers? It was likely to be a very long, sleepless night.

She wouldn't find it easy to get out of the hotel and all the way to Hoquiam without being seen. As far as he knew, her picture hadn't yet been published in the local newspapers with any of the articles about the theft and the gold hunt, but her description had—petite, square-jawed, sultry-eyed—and the hotel was surrounded by opportunists. The slightest hint of her leaving would have every train station, steamer dock, and livery stable swarmed.

Still, Bradshaw insisted they watch from upstairs in case Mrs. Thompson was as resourceful as she was evil.

Moss paced from room to room, window to window, his temperament vacillating between horror and disbelief. Bradshaw kept up a steady stream of conversation with the aim of getting Moss angry rather than afraid.

As they passed in the hall, he asked Moss, "Why did you tell me Arnold Loomis wore his slippers on the beach?"

Moss stood in the doorway of Ingrid's bedroom. "Cause he did."

"You saw him wearing slippers on the beach?"

"No, but he did. She told me he made a mess of them slippers and wore them into the house leaving sand everywhere."

"Did you observe that yourself?"

"I slept in a cabin, didn't I? What do I know about what they wear in the main house?"

They returned to their pacing and when they next met in the hall, Bradshaw asked, "Do you understand what happened with the electrotherapy machine? How it was altered and killed David Hollister?"

"What, you ain't figured that out yet? I thought Captain Bell said it was Loomis who did something to it."

"What did Loomis do to it?"

"I ain't got a clue. I told you, I don't know nothing about electricity."

"Why do you think I was asking about the cheese wrapper?"

"Now, I'm glad you brought that up, Professor, because that's had me stumped. Seemed petty to accuse a man of cheese stealing when you were 'sposed to be figuring out how someone died." A smile lifted the corner of his mouth. "Hey, but Loomis was sure fired up when you found it under his mattress."

"How do you know it was under his mattress?"

"You said so."

"When?"

"I dunno. Just now."

"No, I didn't."

"Well, that night in the library when you picked it apart and asked us if we knew what it was."

"No, I intentionally did not say where in Loomis' room I found it. I only said I found it in his room. How did you know it was under his mattress?"

"Dang nabbit, I put it there. And before you go blaming me for cheese stealing, I got a witness."

"A witness to what? Not stealing cheese?"

"That's right. Mrs. Thompson gimmee that wrapper, said it proved Loomis did something he ought not to have done."

Bradshaw shook his head. Zebediah Moss truly was a decent, stupid man. Denser than dirt, as Henry had said. It was a wonder he'd managed to keep possession of his gold when he accidentally found it after falling off a cliff. The man needed protecting. Even after he was saved from Ingrid Thompson, there would be others lining up to take advantage of him to get his money. When this was all over, he would introduce Moss to his lawyer.

"I want you to think very carefully, Mr. Moss. Whose idea was it to put that cheese wrapper in Loomis' room? Was it your idea, or Mrs. Thompson's?"

"Mine. All mine. She said that what with the handyman dying, it didn't seem nice to worry the Hornsby's about what Loomis done, but she felt bad he was gonna get away with it. So I told her it ought to go in his room. Then later it'd get found. And it did, you found it. He was sure mad, wasn't he? Teach him to go round stealing cheese and flirting with other men's wives."

"Weren't you flirting with another man's wife?"

"No, I weren't. I behaved the perfect gentleman with her. She needed a friend and I didn't offer her no more than that until she was a widow." Moss marched off, cocky and proud, and it took another half hour of reminding him about the bodies in the cellar, the deceitful letters luring men here, and the deaths at Healing Sands, before Moss again declared he would not be Ingrid's next victim.

Moss' vacillation didn't bode well. If they had to detain Ingrid for very long, Moss would become more of a hindrance than a help. Bradshaw hoped with each glance out the window that Henry and Captain Bell would arrive before Ingrid Thompson.

They did not.

Moss spotted her first. His involuntary gasp alerted Bradshaw, who hurried to Moss' side in Ingrid's room, peering through the sheers. She'd come by the road, riding a donkey and leading a second animal, unconcerned that she might be recognized.

She slid off the donkey and stared at the house, her expression unreadable but hard, her square jaw thrust unattractively forward. Was she looking for Moss? Wondering why boards had been removed from the windows? She'd abandoned mourning black and high fashion. In a practical brown summer suit and sturdy ankle boots, she was dressed to travel by train, donkey, or foot.

The donkeys moved away a few feet to nibble on grass. She followed to untie the pack from the saddle.

Bradshaw's pulse raced. He had a length of sturdy twine in his pocket, but to face her he needed a weapon. She was small but strong, and she could be armed with a knife. He grabbed the heaviest thing he spotted, a brass candlestick, one of a pair, and stuffed it into his jacket's inner pocket.

Moss looked sick.

"Be strong," Bradshaw whispered. "I won't let her harm you.

Moss' eyes widened and he grabbed the other candlestick.

Bradshaw shook his head.

"You got one!" Moss hissed, refusing to relinquish the candlestick.

"It's hidden. I don't want her to feel outnumbered or physically threatened the minute she walks in." Bradshaw pried the candlestick from Moss' grip and pressed him toward the stairs. "Down you go."

With Bradshaw pushing him, Moss stepped down the stairs. They paused in the dim parlor, listening. Footsteps outside paced around to the back of the house and crossed the porch, then the kitchen door squeaked open.

A sweet, feminine, sane voice called, "Zebediah Moss, are you here?"

Moss froze. Bradshaw nudged him forward, whispering, "Answer her."

Moss croaked, "Here." Bradshaw prodded him until they entered the kitchen.

Ingrid Thompson stood just inside the open door, sunshine flooding in behind her, illuminating the filth. She registered no surprise at seeing Bradshaw. She registered no emotion at all. With anyone else, he would say that revealed remarkable self-control. But Ingrid Thompson had no genuine emotion save self-preservation.

Her expression remained blank, her eyes like dark, lifeless marbles under their sultry lids, shifting from Bradshaw to Moss, where they lingered. And then, quickly, she transformed herself. Her eyes lit with life as she tilted her head quizzically, and a smile hovered around her mouth, softening the masculine line of her jaw.

"What's going on?" She tossed her hat on the table, giving her head a feminine toss, her fingers fluffing her hair. "I believe the warm weather is returning."

She moved toward the sink. "I could use a drink. Have either of you primed the pump?"

"I did," said Bradshaw.

"Thank you, Professor." She pumped the handle to get the water flowing then sipped from the stream, running her tongue along her lips. She cupped her palm to capture a pool and took several long swallows. "The water is so cold and refreshing here. I appreciate that now, but as a child, I hated how long it took to heat for a bath. We'd put the old tin tub right there next to the table. I dreaded Sundays." She loosened her collar, stroked her neck with her damp hand, and lifted her hair. "Funny isn't it, how things we hated in childhood we love as adults? I take a long hot bath everyday now. Just turn on the tap and out comes hot water. I do love the modern life at the Lincoln."

Moss had said nothing, nor had he moved.

"The pair of you certainly know how to make a lady uncomfortable." She smiled at Bradshaw, and he felt every muscle in his body tense. He now knew what prey felt when confronted by a predator. Her smiled slipped to a pout. "You're not here to put me under some sort of citizen's arrest, are you, Professor?"

"You were on the same train as Mr. Moss?"

"Why, yes. You are a good detective."

Bradshaw calculated her timing. If she'd traveled on the same train as Moss from Seattle to Hoquiam, she would have barely managed to hire the donkeys and make the journey to the house by the road. She must have mailed Moss directions to follow the newly laid, unused railway and the shortcut through the forest so they wouldn't be spotted together and he wouldn't be seen heading here.

As clear as it was to Bradshaw, it was like mud to Moss. His face contorted as he looked at Ingrid, trying to work it out.

Bradshaw said, "I hear congratulations are in order."

"Not really." She waved off Moss with a tender frown. "Mr. Moss agreed to rescue me in my time of need. He is a very dear friend."

Moss looked more confused than ever, but Bradshaw knew it wasn't the right time to explain. Ingrid's arrival now meant they must detain her for several hours, or overnight, and he refused to play prison guard that long, especially with Zeb Moss as his deputy.

"Mrs. Thompson," Bradshaw deliberately choose the name he felt would elicit the least reaction, "Captain Bell requested you remain in Seattle until the end of his investigation. I will now escort you and Mr. Moss back to Hoquiam."

"Must we go so soon? I'm exhausted." She pulled out a chair and sat, stretching her arms overhead with a yawn. "You were very clever to find my old family home, Professor. How did you do it?"

"I had a drawing of your likeness. You were recognized."

"Well…you can't blame a girl for trying. Freddie simply ruined my life with his thieving ways, and I thought I could get a fresh start here. He never knew about the place. I was a bit ashamed of it. He couldn't have put his stolen gold here, so there's no use looking. Or have you discovered that already?"

Her gaze slid from the cellar door to Bradshaw.

He'd looked into the eyes of many who'd killed. He'd seen anger, fear, regret, defiance. Always some powerful emotion protecting or masking the soul within that still held the potential for redemption. In Ingrid Thompson's eyes he saw nothing redeemable. Nothing human. What had gone wrong with her? How had she become a monster?

While she was without conscience, she wasn't without strength, and she was healthy and cunning. She knew her freedom hung in the balance as she stared into his eyes, and he knew she was plotting the most efficient way to kill him.

He said, "We must go now."

She shifted to her new, stupefied husband. "Mr. Moss, you're being awfully quiet. Won't you take my side and tell the good Professor I need time to rest?"

Moss swallowed hard and cleared his throat. "Course I will." He rubbed his neck, turning his head in Bradshaw's direction without meeting his eye. "Lady needs rest, Professor."

Bradshaw couldn't spare Ingrid time to scheme or Moss time to fall apart. He had to get them both outside immediately, and tie her hands before she mounted one of the donkeys. He would ride the other animal to stay apace of her, and Moss would have to take the bicycle.

"On your feet, Mrs. Thompson."

Mrs. Thompson yawned and stretched again, reaching a hand out to Moss. She gave a playful laugh when he hesitated. "It's all right, Mr. Moss, we are married. You can take my hand."

Moss shuffled toward her, but Bradshaw stepped between them blocking Moss from her, fearing her touch would crumple the man.

She lifted her glowing eyes to Bradshaw and smiled, slowly trailing the fingertips of her outstretched hand down his jacket. When he felt the pressure of her fingers on his thigh, he grabbed her wrist, pressing her arm away.

Her eyes flashed at him under those sultry lids. "I heard I resemble your late wife, Professor. Is that true?" She tugged her arm, and he gripped harder.

In less time than it took to blink, expression vanished from her features and she was once again blank, a porcelain doll staring up at him.

She struggled to be free of his grasp, but he held fast as he dug into his pocket for the twine to tie her hands. He opened his mouth to tell Moss to go ready the donkeys, and the words had not yet formed when he heard a grating sound, and something heavy and solid slammed against his skull and bounced down to crack against his shoulder. He thought, *cast iron pan*, before crumpling, and the world went black.

Chapter Thirty-nine

His sense of smell came around first. The ripe, metallic scent of decay hit his nostrils like some kind of horrific smelling salts. His eyes flashed open to utter darkness, pain throbbed in his head and down his neck to his shoulder blade, and he felt damp, gritty earth beneath him.

Oh, God. The cellar. The morgue.

Panic flashed through him and he thrust his arm over his mouth and nose both to filter the smell through the cloth of his jacket and to prevent himself from hyperventilating. Something tickled his cheek, something small but multi-legged, and he swiped at his face, choking down panic.

Only his right arm had obeyed his command. The other remained motionless, lifeless but for the pain that shot down to his wrist.

He allowed himself a piercing, mental scream before taking charge and thrusting his mind out of the cellar. He visualized the university, Mount Rainier, his home, Justin. But his son's image, and the idea the boy might grow up without him brought back the panic, so he pictured Missouri standing before him with the ocean wind blowing her hair and her eyes looking directly into his. *I love you. I love you. I love you.* He heard her words to him, and he echoed them back to her as he should have done that day on the beach. Why hadn't he? What was wrong with him? What could be more important than loving her?

He was consumed with anger at himself for letting a single day go by without her in it. What was it all worth if she was not in his life? What the hell was he afraid of? If he got out of this alive…by God…he flung out his good arm, scrunching his face and uselessly closing his eyes against what his hand might meet. His fingertips felt something hard, solid, cool, damp. Wood. The door.

He moved himself around until he could place his feet on the door with his knees bent, and he kicked as hard as he could. The jar sent a stab of pain through his pain. He hadn't known until then that pain could have such dimension. He kicked again and again, heedless of the noise he was making, until the door gave way, and he saw a wedge of grayness. He crawled out, up the cellar steps, and into the kitchen on all fours, collapsing by the table. He lay praying for the wave of pain and nausea to pass. The light in the kitchen was dim, he realized, before he shut his eyes to focus on not vomiting.

He didn't know how long he lay there before he could open his eyes. He saw a man's boot, caked with dust, a feathery weed tangled in the lace.

"Moss?" Bradshaw's voice emerged gravelly and weak.

He heard no reply. He thumped the boot with his fist and was rewarded with a grunt.

"What the hell." Moss' voice was weak, too. "You're supposed to be dead."

"Where is she?"

"She didn't do it, Professor. You lied to me. She didn't do none of it. It was that Loomis who killed at Healing Sands, and she don't know about the bodies in the cellar, she ain't lived here in years, someone else put them there."

"Where is she?"

"She's gone, ain't she? Gone! She don't want nothing more to do with me after I told her the horrible things you said."

Bradshaw crawled to the wall and slowly eased himself into a sitting position.

He guessed it to be about an hour from sunset, judging from the angle of filtered golden sunlight through the windows.

He looked at Moss. Around the man's head was a cloud of green. His mouth oozed phosphorus vapors.

Oh, no. "What did you eat?"

Chapter Forty

Trying to catch a donkey was more difficult than Bradshaw imagined. It didn't help that only his right hand had full strength because something in his left arm, or maybe his shoulder, was broken.

The trick, he learned, was to give up, to lean against a splintered fence post gasping and wincing, and then the donkey will take pity on you, after laughing at you with a mocking heehaw bray, and step up to see if you really are holding an ear of corn. Mrs. Thompson must not have tried it, or she wouldn't have left this beast behind.

With the donkey happily munching the corn he'd found growing in the wild garden, Bradshaw took hold of the dangling reins and lead the beast to Moss, who lay sprawled on the ground where he'd crawled to get away from his puddle of vomit. It wasn't food but whiskey that had contained the poison. Moss' new bride had insisted he drink it, and he had, even though it tasted foul, even though it burned his throat worse than moonshine. He drank to show her he trusted her. Bradshaw had administered the only remedy he knew, turpentine.

After finding no turpentine in the house, Bradshaw recalled that sometimes farmers used it to keep their fowl free of worms. He'd staggered to the dilapidated shed and found a rusted gallon can of Brown's Worm Killer. The smell told him it was turpentine, and its age gave him hope it had absorbed enough oxygen to become resinified and effective, as Dr. Hornsby said, as an antidote. He'd gotten Moss to drink a couple doses of the oil floating in water he'd heated quickly over a crude fire on the kitchen stove, in fifteen minute intervals, before he vomited. Had it been in him long enough to bond with the phosphorus? Surely vomiting at this stage was good. Better the poison out, than in.

"Up, Moss." Using his good arm, Bradshaw hauled Moss up to his feet and draped him over the saddle. It took a few minutes of wrangling to get Moss securely seated, bent over, hugging the donkey's neck and moaning.

Bradshaw studied Moss' crumpled map and took another few minutes to walk the perimeter of the yard with his compass. When he entered the forest, it wasn't where Moss had staggered out of the garden, but where he found a worn deer trail. Fresh droppings revealed the other donkey had passed this way, too. Carrying Ingrid Thompson? Possibly, but he wasn't following her.

It would have been hours by bicycle and donkey to the doctor's house by the way he and Henry had come. He doubted Moss could last that long. Moss told him it was about a half-hour hike through the woods to the railroad line, and the poles were set and strung with telegraph wire. He didn't know if the donkey could make it all the way through the difficult terrain carrying Moss' nearly dead weight, but it was his best hope.

Moss needed medical care, now.

He'd sacrificed five minutes to finding rope, two leather belts, a hammer and nails, which he stuffed in his tool bag and secured to the donkey, along with a lantern. And now they were ready. The forest rose before them like live ramparts of a giant castle. The deer trail allowed them to slip between the battlements of bark.

Bradshaw moved slowly at first into the darkness, letting his eyes adjust. The beauty engrossed him. Even in pain, concerned for Moss, and dismayed at Ingrid Thompson's escape, Bradshaw felt the power of the virgin forest. For a thousand years these trees had stood peacefully as human civilizations rose and fell, untouched by greed or insanity. Content merely to be. At this moment it seemed the perfect existence. He knew it was an illusion. Battles waged continually in the forest. Creatures ate creatures, older trees blocked life-giving sun from saplings. But as Missouri often said, nature understood cycles. One form died, giving up its nutrients so another might live. And when hunger was satiated, when the young were safe, the most vicious creatures left the weaker alone.

Bradshaw sighed as he trudged ahead, knowing he shouldn't let his thoughts turn philosophical or melancholy. But he was in Missouri's favorite cathedral, and he felt a powerful presence. Evergreen needles carpeted the trail, and ferns formed leafy walls as high as his head. Rising behind the ferns, two hundred-foot cedar trees and Douglas firs towered, their canopies stealing most of the meager light. Bradshaw held the compass very close to see the direction of the needle.

With each intake of breath, clean, cool, oxygen-rich air spiced heavily with cedar bolstered his strength. The trail dipped, then rose, following the contours of the land, skirting long-ago fallen trees with new giants growing up out of their decaying remains.

He checked his pocket watch to keep track of the time, knowing if he traveled much longer than a half hour, he risked missing the new rail line. He was fairly sure he was having an easier time hiking the forest than Moss had. Moss hadn't looked for a trail, he'd simply followed the map exactly, turning away from the railway bed and plowing through underbrush and over fallen logs, determined to veer not a foot from the direction of his compass. How had Moss survived Alaska? How had he not perished over that cliff, or tumbled into a river, or frozen in his tent? Against all odds, Moss had survived and struck gold. The only time in his life the man had luck, and it had brought him to this. Moss wasn't smart, but he was kind-hearted and devoted, and he deserved a woman who'd appreciate him. If he lived.

A tinkling sound startled Bradshaw. He halted the donkey and stood listening beneath a big leaf maple, a hand on Moss' back to gently hush his moaning. He heard the crash of breaking glass and turned his head toward the sound, but the forest was too dense and the light too dim to see anything.

He remained still for a full minute, listening to the forest. A squirrel scampered overhead, sending a maple leaf larger than Bradshaw's hand floating to the path. A flicker somewhere distant drilled on a hollow log, and the rat-a-tat echoed intermittently. The longer he listened, the more he heard. Birds singing, leaves rustling. The enormous tree trunks creaking. The day creatures were saying good-night, and the night creatures were beginning to stir. Loudest of all was the sound of his own breathing, shallow and quick.

Another tinkling crash was followed by the braying of a donkey, which set Bradshaw's beast heehawing. He tried to shush the donkey, but it only brayed louder, so he tugged on the harness and got it moving again. The donkey quieted, but Bradshaw feared Mrs. Thompson was now intently listening for footsteps.

She was breaking open the jars to get the gold. An assumption he trusted. In soft, heavy pockets, the gold would be easier to stuff into saddlebags. What had she thought when she heard his donkey? Did she think it had simply wandered into the woods on its own? Would she wonder if the men she'd left for dead had found the strength to flee, to follow? He tried to step quietly, tried to match the gait of the donkey, aware each time he snapped a twig or brushed the thick ferns where they reached into the trail. He gently halted the donkey again and listened. The absence of breaking glass worried him.

He was in no shape to fight if she came after them. If he stayed still, she might return to her work and move on. But Moss couldn't spare the time.

Bradshaw tugged on the reins, looked down the dim path, and a small gasp escaped him.

Ingrid Thompson stood on the path a few yards away, a dark but distinct figure. Her arrival had been silent and stealthy, but now she raced toward him, arm raised, a hatchet in her hand, issuing an animal growl.

Bradshaw reacted instinctively. In one movement, he dropped the reins, bent at the waist, and charged at Ingrid Thompson leading with his good shoulder.

He crashed into her with such force she dropped the hatchet and fell backwards onto the leafy trail. He landed on top of her, pinning her with his body, aware of searing pain in his head and shoulder beneath the pounding of his blood.

She spat in his face, and he jerked his head aside but resisted the urge to pull completely away. He sat hard on her abdomen, expelling the remaining wind from her lungs, and he leaned forward, pinning her arms down. She smelled sharp of sweat and sweet like roses. His left arm hadn't much strength, and he knew she must feel the difference, yet she didn't immediately take advantage. It was then he noticed that her right hand was bandaged, the white handkerchief wrapped around her palm reflected the meager light, a red spreading stain in the center. She was bleeding.

She struggled beneath him, staring up at him with dark eyes that held no hatred or fury or fear, only an intense animal determination. She lifted her bandaged hand, easily overcoming his weak arm, then swung at his head. He lifted his good arm to meet it.

He would never forget what happened next.

He swung with all his might at her wounded hand, repulsed at the instinct to attack where it would cause the most pain. The collision of their hands echoed through the forest and sent them both reeling, but it wasn't the pain that astonished him.

It was the fire.

Upon contact, her hand burst into flames. Blinding white flames tinged yellow, with a heat so intense, it knocked him over.

He fell back, rolling away from her, as she screamed and writhed. White smoke billowed from her hand. Scrambling to his feet, he ripped away an armful of giant ferns fronds, and threw them and himself on Ingrid's burning hand to douse the flames. She kicked at him, and struck him with her free hand, as if not understanding he was trying to help. She yanked her arm out from under him, tearing the scorched cloth away, then held up her hand, staring at it in shock. Even in the meager light,

Bradshaw could see it was blackened and raw. The smell of burnt cloth, and burnt flesh, blended with a pungent, garlic-like odor.

She began to scream again, a piercing cry, broken only by gasps for breath. Her screams became hysterical, possessed, and the donkey joined in, adding its brays to the cacophony. Bradshaw pulled the twine from his pocket, and she seemed not to notice him knot it tightly around her ankles, and she didn't resist as he tied her undamaged hand to a thick exposed tree root. She held her charred, bleeding hand before her face and screamed.

It took a great deal of coaxing, and eventually swatting, to motivate the donkey to move past the screaming woman, but at last the braying beast hurried forward, and quieted. Bradshaw moved as quickly as he could, Ingrid's screams following him, fading, then silencing. His watch told him ten minutes had passed when a soft glow ahead, a touch of golden red at the end of the fern and evergreen tunnel, revealed he was nearing the cut swath of the new railway line. When he spotted the black silhouette of the telegraph pole against the dimming sky, he almost wept.

He soon stepped into a wide corridor of destruction bisected by an elevated path of perfect geometric proportion. The gleaming new rails glided in both directions along the creosoted ties, with short telegraph poles aligned at regular intervals. Not a soul was in sight.

As gently as possible he lowered Moss, who was not fully conscious, to a patch of fresh sawdust and tied the donkey to a stump. With his tool bag, he climbed the right-of-way embankment. Although prepared, he was still dismayed to find that the telegraph poles were of a height that put the lines out of reach from the ground. He would have to climb. The faint light of sunset was quickly fading, and with the cloud cover, darkness would be profound. He put his ear to the rail but heard and felt no vibrations. This line didn't yet carry regular service, but it was used by the construction crews who lived and worked in these woods. The telegraph line would be set up for local communication only, and he hoped somebody was now listening.

After taking a moment to light the lantern, he sat and removed his boots, unlacing them fully and opening them wide. His left arm had regained a bit of strength, but it was still awkward hammering the nails through the solid heels. He put on the improvised cleats, lacing them tightly, filled his pockets with the tools he'd need, and secured the lantern to his waist using his suspenders. He then buckled together the two belts he'd brought, making a pole strap.

With a deep breath, he began to climb.

One foot at time, he jammed his nailed boot into the pole, pushed upward, then slid the connected belts up to help hold his weight. After every step and every adjustment of the improvised strap, he was forced to stop to recover from the shooting pain across his shoulder and down his arm. It wasn't a good sign, he knew, that he began to feel cold and clammy, and he feared the darkness pressing around him was not from the vanishing of the sun.

By the time he reached the wires he was in a cold sweat from both exertion and a violent nausea, breathing heavily through his mouth. He rested again before reaching into his pocket for his cutters. An intermittent static buzzed in the line. He tapped it with the back of his hand to test the voltage and found it bearable. After disconnecting the ground lightning wire from the pole in readiness, he secured the telegraph wire so it wouldn't fall away, he cut it through. Grasping the cut ends, he tapped them together. Dot-dot-dot-dash-dash-dash-dot-dot-dot. S.O.S. He paused, then sent the signal again.

It was all he could manage.

Sagging against the pole, trusting the nails in his boots and the leather of the belts to hold him, he took hold of the ground wire and touched the back of his hand to one of the cut wires. He felt nothing. With his last ounce of strength, he licked the back of his hand and tried again, pressing it against the cut wire. This time he felt a slight tingle.

Dot-dot-dot-dash-dot. Understood.

Chapter Forty-one

Help arrived within minutes. The message had been received and acknowledged a mile up the line at the construction camp. Two handcars pumped vigorously by able-bodied men came speeding down the line, an oil-burning searchlight focused on the telegraph line. Bradshaw was still on the pole when they braked. He hadn't the strength to climb down on his own.

For men who spent their days felling giant trees and moving small mountains, helping a professor from a pole was easy. With scrap lumber, and Bradshaw's hammer and extra nails, they pounded steps into the pole and climbed up to fetch him. Bradshaw was able to stagger to a stump to rest while Moss was carried to one of the handcars, unmoving and unconscious, but still breathing.

A young man, who looked like Bradshaw's son all grown up, fair-haired, gentle-faced, hunkered down before him and introduced himself as Hans.

"Thank you for coming so quickly, Hans." Bradshaw explained who he was, and that Moss had been poisoned with phosphorus and needed immediate care. Hans quickly passed on the information to the others and gave orders for the handcar to set off for Hoquiam.

"And you, Professor?" Hans returned to hunker before him.

"Not yet. There's a woman in the forest who's been injured. A mad woman. A murderess. She's tied but she'll give you a fight."

"If we leave her until morning, that should take the fight out of her."

"No, son," he said, for he suddenly felt ancient and Hans looked so young. "She is a monster. We are not. I'll show you where she is."

"Do you want to ride?" Hans gestured toward the donkey.

"No, thank you, but bring it along. It might easier to carry the woman than get her to walk."

Hans called to the remaining men and held the oil lamp to light their way. Bradshaw led them through the dark forest, using his watch and compass to be sure they stayed to the trail and didn't go too far.

Ingrid Thompson was where he'd left her, propped against the tangled thick roots. Silent. Unmoving.

Hans lifted the lantern to her face. Her eyes were open, staring vacantly, her mouth agape as if frozen mid-scream.

"She's dead, Professor."

Bradshaw had no words. He hadn't expected to find her dead, but it came as no shock. No relief. He felt…empty. Hell was made for the likes of her. And yet…if no soul had existed within this shell of a human, what was there to punish in the hereafter?

"We will take her into Hoquiam. We can't leave her for the coyotes."

"Yes, sir," Hans said, but he didn't move, nor did the others. In the meager lantern light, Bradshaw felt more than saw the young men's horror. They'd likely seen their share of hardship and accidents in these woods, but the silent scream upon Ingrid's face and the blackened claw of her hand, propped up by a gnarled root, was something out of a nightmare.

"Her name was Mrs. Ingrid Thompson. Her husband was the gold thief from the Federal Assay Office in Seattle." He spoke in a matter-of-fact manner, pushing through his exhaustion to give them knowledge and guidance to lessen their fear. They would never forget the sight of her, but perhaps if they understood they wouldn't be haunted.

"No foolin'?" asked one of the men from the darkness. Footsteps crunched closer.

"She poisoned Zeb Moss, the man your friends are now taking into town."

"With phosphorus, you said?" Hans stepped closer to Ingrid's body, peering at her charred hand. "How did she get burned?"

"She soaked match tips in solution to make her poison. My guess is that some of the solution spilled onto her handkerchief. And then she put the handkerchief into her pocket where it had dried, becoming, in essence, a giant match."

It had been a foolish mistake for someone so familiar with phosphorus. Had she been distracted? Agitated? So obsessed with the details of escape she'd been careless? The white hand-kerchief had reflected light, but it hadn't glowed a telltale green. He thought of her rose-scented youth lotion, which she used so liberally and which may well have been on her handkerchief. Was there some essential oil in her lotion that extinguished the glow? Masked the scent? Prevented her from feeling the sting of the phosphorus when she wrapped her hand with the cloth? Or had she attributed the sensation to the painful cut?

Had her obsession for youth and wealth blinded her to the instrument of her death?

"She looks to have bled an awful lot." Hans moved the lantern over Ingrid, revealing splashes of blood on her clothing and down her arm.

"She cut herself," Bradshaw explained, withholding the fact that jars of gold dust might be very nearby. Besides needing their help to get back to town, he didn't want to tempt them into a federal crime. The gold belonged to the assay office. "And she wrapped her hand in the poisoned cloth. It takes very little heat to ignite white phosphorus, that's why lucifer matches are made of it. The friction of pulling the kerchief from her pocket could have set it off, or the friction of pulling the bandage snug into a knot."

He didn't think they needed to know it wasn't either of those two actions that ignited the cloth, but his own hand as he fought with her.

"My cousin once burnt down a barn with a couple lucifers stuck in a cowpat," one of the young men began, and Bradshaw knew he'd said enough to mitigate the shock of what they'd seen.

"Took a couple weeks," the young man continued as they draped Mrs. Thompson's body over the donkey. "When that cowpat dried out and heated up, the lucifers caught fire, and down came the barn."

The walk back to the tracks passed for Bradshaw in a vague dark blur. With respectful care that revealed the humanity of his rescuers, Ingrid's body was secured to the remaining handcar. One of the men volunteered to ride the donkey to the logging camp, and they'd barely begun when the darkness echoed with heehaws, and the other donkey came charging out of the forest. The beast greeted its friend noisily, then happily followed behind.

"Ready?" called Hans, taking charge once more. Bradshaw climbed into the small space reserved for him on the handcar, sitting with his legs dangling. His head swam, and he was overwhelmed with gratitude for this group of strong and helpful men, thankful that Hans, a natural leader, had stepped forward to speed the rescue. "Let's roll!"

Bradshaw tended to be a leader himself, he knew, in some circumstances. Colin Ingersoll was a leader. Colin Ingersoll was leading Missouri away. The thought came as Bradshaw's brain clouded, and the young men began to run and push the handcar into motion. He braced himself, and a fresh wave of pain shot through his head, down his arm and back, blocking out all thought save hanging on and staying awake. Then the men leaped aboard to pump. They didn't let up until the car came to the end of the line in Hoquiam.

◇◇◇

Bradshaw recuperated in the Hoquiam hospital for one day, diagnosed with a moderate concussion, a cracked rib, and a bruised but thankfully not broken shoulder. Moss, apparently, had not put his all into swinging the cast iron pan or Bradshaw's skull would have been crushed.

Dr. Hornsby came to see him and insisted he return to Healing Sands. Once tucked snugly in bed in Camp Franklin Cabin, he was dosed with homeopathic remedies, anti-inflammatory herbs, and a diet of fermented foods for which he had inexplicably acquired a taste. He slept much, but even his waking hours were restful. For the first time in his life he was content to do nothing. He felt as peaceful as Old Cedar—who also stopped by to pay his respects and wish him well. He didn't read, or write, or sketch circuits. He listened to the waves crashing and the birds crying.

All the Hornsbys waited on him at intervals, and when news arrived they brought it to him. Zebediah Moss had been sent to a hospital in Tacoma and was expected to live, although he'd been told he should never again touch alcohol as his damaged liver could no longer tolerate it.

The coroner had plucked tiny shards of glass from Ingrid Thompson's cut palm and found phosphorus in the burned tissue and in her lungs and blood. She'd breathed the deadly vapors, and the flames had hastened the absorption through her flesh. Traumatic shock due to severe burn and blood loss, combined with poisoning, were determined to be the cause of her swift death.

Digging on the beaches ceased and was replaced with a forest hunt for gold. The donkey that had followed its friend to the logging camp was found to be carrying thirty pounds of gold dust in soft cloth packets. The Secret Service retraced Bradshaw's steps and discovered a cedar stump and several dozen broken mason jars, all of them empty.

The rest of the gold, about a hundred and seventy pounds of it, was still missing, and Bradshaw wondered if it would become the stuff of legend like pirates' treasure.

◇◇◇

After a week of rest and Dr. Hornsby's ministrations, Bradshaw's strength returned, and it was time to go home. But first, he removed the electrotherapy machine from Healing House for Doctor Hornsby and dismantled it. Together they burned the wooden case, smashed the glass components, and packed up the other pieces for Bradshaw to take away.

Chapter Forty-two

When he stepped from the Capitol Hill streetcar onto 15th Avenue, Bradshaw sighed. Clear weather had returned to Seattle, and the late afternoon air was pleasantly warm, laced with the best and worst scents of city life—tinges of smoke, cooking, cut lumber, tar. These smells meant home to Bradshaw, having lived with new construction and a changing landscape from the moment he arrived in Seattle with his infant son a decade ago.

It was a short walk to 1204 Gallagher, the address of Bradshaw's modest home. Two stories of white clapboard, leaded windows, a wide front porch, and a small patch of lawn shaded by a maple tree. It was there he found Justin and Paul, high up in the branches.

"Ahoy, father!" Justin called down.

"Ahoy, son! Ahoy, Paul!" Bradshaw returned. "Spot any enemy ships?"

"Aye, but we blasted her with our cannons."

"Well done. Is it safe to enter the castle?"

"If you've got armor. Mrs. Prouty's cooking again."

"And Missouri?"

Justin's voice returned to normal. "She's up at the university. She said she'll be back for dinner."

Bradshaw went around the house to enter through the kitchen and found Mrs. Prouty, as he'd been warned, cooking up a storm, but the smells were promising. Something savory simmered on the stove, and the smell of warm yeast told him bread was in the oven. Mrs. Prouty stood at the kitchen table, stirring a mixture of onions and celery in her electric skillet, the cord dangling from the fluted wall light.

Last year he'd turned his attention to small electrical kitchen appliances, tinkering with tea kettles, frying pans, hot plates, and toasters. Mrs. Prouty had at first resisted being his tester, being a woman rooted in her ways, but the convenience of electric power slowly won her over. During an unusually long stretch of hot weather, she'd not lit the cook stove for four solid days, preparing everything from the morning coffee to apple pie using the electric devices.

"Welcome home, Professor. Your luggage arrived a few minutes ago. I put it in your room, except for your electrical bits. I left that crate in the hall for you."

"Thank you. Has all been well?"

She met his eye and gave him a sincere nod. "Justin's been in heaven, what with Missouri staying overnight since we got back from the ocean. She's out now, but she'll be back. I reckon she'll be going to her own place tonight?"

The question threw him back to when Missouri first arrived in Seattle and stayed with them for several months. Henry had been in Alaska then, and Mrs. Prouty had been vocal about the impropriety of an unmarried woman staying in the home of a widowed man without a proper chaperone. That wasn't an issue now, Henry was here.

"I'll leave that to her. Where's she been sleeping? My room?"

"Most certainly not! I put Henry in your room and she took his."

"You know it's not improper for her to sleep in my bed if I'm not in it."

Mrs. Prouty held up her spoon. "You've had a rough time of it, Professor, so I'll forgive your cheekiness. I must say, you don't look as bad as I expected for a man who took a blow to the head, was thrown down a flight of stairs, and stuffed into a cellar. You'll be the death of me yet, with these investigations."

"Doctor Hornsby restored my health. Do I have time to run up to the university before dinner?"

"If you don't stay long. Missouri's there now."

"I know."

He felt her eyes watching him as he left the kitchen. He went upstairs to quickly change into a fresh suit and a few minutes later was pedaling toward the university. His muscles and injuries gave him small protests, but otherwise he found the ride invigorating.

Once on campus, he glided by the new red brick Science Building that had opened last year. He would be teaching one class there in the fall quarter, but since the engineering labs were still housed in the basement of the Administration Building, most of his classes and his office were still there, which pleased him. He'd grown fond of the place and always enjoyed his first glimpse of its castle-like edifice each day. Now, as he parked his bicycle beside the wide stone steps, he was hailed by President Kane and Joseph Taylor, a former professor of mathematics and astronomy, who had built the magnificent observatory. Both men had followed the newspaper accounts of Bradshaw's discovery of the Vogler farm and the search for the gold.

While he filled them in on details not included in the paper, he noticed a box kite hovering above the young trees between Lewis and Clark Halls. He ignored the kite as long as he could but finally excused himself to continue on his intended mission.

The kite led him to the sweeping new lawn between the dorms. Colin Ingersoll manned the string, and Missouri stood beside him, head tilted back, nodding at what he said. Bradshaw couldn't hear Colin's words, only the deepness of his voice. What was he saying to her? Explaining the physics that kept the kite in the air? Impressing her with his ideas for the future of flight? Charming her?

He stood watching them. They looked good together. Perfect, really. They matched the way salt and pepper shakers match, different but belonging together. A set. The same age, same youthful hope shining in their faces. He had a flash of vision of them together, getting married, having children, Colin becoming famous for daring feats of flight and Missouri curing the masses with her remedies. He could see clearly their disordered, chaotic, happy life.

No.

He would put a stop to that. If there was one thing he had over young Colin Ingersoll, it was his ability to plod over the potential for happiness wherever it existed.

With a smile, he headed down the path. Missouri looked toward him. A grin spread over her features, lighting her eyes, warming his heart. She moved away from Colin and stepped toward Bradshaw's outstretched arms.

Author's Note
and Acknowledgements

I find great pleasure in weaving Professor Bradshaw's fictional whodunits with the factual details of life in the Pacific Northwest in the early days of the twentieth century. For this book, I especially enjoyed my time in the North Beach area of Washington State where my fictional Healing Sands is located. From the bustling town of Ocean Shores to the cozy town of Pacific Beach, the idyllic community of Seabrook (with a great little bookstore, Blind Dog Books), and historic Moclips with its Museum of the North Beach, I found inspiration in the people and places.

I discovered two sanitariums once existed on the North Beach, and there may have been more. Sanitariums and health resorts were all the rage back then. At Iron Springs, where there is now a lovely resort with echoes of history, a doctor named Chase ran a modest sanitarium and even dabbled with electrotherapeutic devices. And a bit later further north, the Moclips Sanitarium once set up shop, but other than a fabulous old photograph of a small weathered shack, I found no details on that establishment. The first Moclips Hotel, which opened in 1905 when the railroad at last arrived, boasted that the location was ideal for restoring health and beckoned tourists to come rest and play. Thousands came. The hotel burned down that same year, was rebuilt on an even grander scale, and thousands more came. Sadly, this second hotel was destroyed in 1911 by a massive storm, and all that remains today is a small plaque honoring its proud past.

The Moclips Depot of the Northern Pacific Railway opened July 1, 1905. For several decades the train served the area, but with the rise in popularity of the automobile roads were built, and eventually train service was discontinued and the rail lines removed. Hopes and fears for development weren't fulfilled. More than a hundred years after Professor Bradshaw's visit, the area is quiet, minimally populated, and still provides a wonderful escape. I owe a huge thank you to Kelly Calhoun of The Museum of the North Beach for a fascinating couple of days, digging into the rich resources of the museum. They are working to build a replica of the Northern Pacific train depot, and when complete, it will be the museum's new home.

Electrotherapy has a long and interesting history. From the first harnessing of static electricity to present day physiotherapy, electricity has been explored as a method of healing and observing medical conditions. In those early years when there were few regulations regarding treatments, legitimate men of medicine experimented with therapies we today know to be either ineffective or harmful, but their pioneering work led to important discoveries. Of course, quack electrotherapy medicine has always thrived. Open just about any popular magazine or newspaper from the mid-1850's until today, and you will likely find within the pages an advertisement for some revolutionary electric or magnetic device guaranteed to melt away pounds, eliminate pain, or restore virility. Then, as now, the legitimate electrotherapeutic devices are more likely to be found in medical facilities or used by trained alternative healers.

For the historical details of electrotherapy in this book, I am especially grateful to Jeff Behary and his Turn of the Century Electrotherapy Museum. I spent many hours exploring and mining his website and scheming with him on the phone, and he provided the photograph of the 1915 Mcintosh autocondensation chair featured on the cover of this book. Bill Beaty, friend and electrical engineer at the University of Washington, was once again a valuable resource as the plot developed, and he applied his keen eye to the electrical and electrotherapeutic portions of the manuscript, giving great advice. Throughout the writing year, John Jenkins and all the folks at the SPARK Museum of Electrical Invention in Bellingham, Washington, continue to be a constant source of information and inspiration.

I named my sheriff after the real Sheriff Graham, who arrived in Gray's Harbor in 1884. A respected and beloved pioneer, over the years he did it all, from logging the rich forests to building a volunteer fire brigade, and serving as town marshal, sheriff, prison guard, and finally serving with the Aberdeen police force. He died at age eighty in 1942. I don't know if the real Sheriff Graham would have worn his boots in the main house of Doctor Hornsby's Sanitarium, but I intended no disrespect by having my fictional one do so. My thanks to Dann Sears and Byron Eager of the Aberdeen Museum of History for their help researching this remarkable man.

Captain Bell, too, has a real-life counterpart who headed up the Northwest division of the Secret Service. In the days before the founding of the F.B.I., the Secret Service was in charge of investigating federal crimes. In 1906, Bell quit the service to start his own private investigation company, but sadly, a brain hemorrhage took his life just two years later. His obituary in the November 16, 1908, edition of the *Seattle Post-Intelligencer* said he "gained the reputation among his associates of being a fearless man, and for unusual bravery and success in bringing to justice a number of important federal criminals."

Several threads of the plot of *Capacity for Murder* are based on real events that occurred during this era, but if I elaborated here I would give away too much. If you would like to know more send me an email (contact@bernadettepajer.com) with the words "CAPACITY scoop," and I'll be happy to fill you in.

For the scenes in this book referring to phosphorus and gentian, I gave my characters the information that would have been available to them in their time and relied upon several historical scientific publications including the *Pharmaceutical Journal* by the Pharmaceutical Society of Great Britain (1878), the *Manual of Qualitative Chemical Analysis* by C. Remigius Fresenius (1897), and *A Manual of Legal Medicine* by Justin Herold (1898). Turpentine is no longer a recommended antidote.

Every writer should be so lucky to be treated with such respect and guided so expertly as I am by my editors, Annette Rogers and Barbara Peters. I'm equally grateful for my publisher, Jessica Tribble, everyone at Poisoned Pen Press, and my friend and agent, Jill Grosjean. And to my early readers Barbara Ankrum, Jesikah Sundin, Torie Stratton, Jeannie Dunlap, Wendy Wartes, Mari Bonomi, and Aurika Hays—I am so very grateful for your taking the time to test-drive this novel and find the bumps in the road. A huge thank you to my heroes, Kelly and Larry (Mom and Pop) for spreading bookmarks across the greater Puget Sound area, selling books where no books have sold before. For emotional support, I am blessed with great writing friends and groups, and I'm especially grateful, honored, and humbled to belong to the Seattle7Writers.org. You all inspire me! And Larry at Barnes & Noble in Woodinville, Washington—so pleased to count you as a fan of Professor Bradshaw. Thanks for your support!

And my love and thanks to my husband and son for putting up with an often-distracted wife and mom. You make everything in life worthwhile.

The Washington Academy of Sciences
Seal of Approval

The Washington Academy of Sciences offers its members who have written a science-heavy book the opportunity to submit the book to the Academy editors for review of the science therein. The manuscript receives the same rigorous scientific review that is accorded articles published in the Journal of the Washington Academy of Sciences. If the science is determined to be accurate, the book may display the seal of The Washington Academy of Sciences.

To receive a free catalog of Poisoned Pen Press titles, please contact us in one of the following ways:

Phone: 1-800-421-3976
Facsimile: 1-480-949-1707
Email: info@poisonedpenpress.com
Website: www.poisonedpenpress.com

Poisoned Pen Press
6962 E. First Ave. Ste 103
Scottsdale, AZ 85251